To Jean Swa
Enjoy!

10 Minutes Past Too Late

by

Anika Malone

A. Malone

Jan 19, 2002

Cover Design by Deloris B. Mickle

ISBN: 0-75961-252-8

This book is printed on acid free paper.

1stBooks – rev. 4/2/01

ADAVANCE PRAISE FOR
ANIKA MALONE'S DEBUT NOVEL,

10 MINUTES PAST TOO LATE

"Fans of Lolita Files will fall in love with this impressive first novel by Anika Malone. Set in 90's California, it has enough plot twists, humor, and "in your face" characters to make readers want to read it to the finish in just one sitting".

--Mary Monroe
Best-selling author of ***God Don't Like Ugly***

"Anika Malone is a fresh new voice in contemporary fiction whose spicy words sizzle on the page and leave you hungry for more".

--Tracy Price-Thompson
Best-selling author of ***Black Coffee***

"*10 Minutes Past Too Late* is a page-turner from the onset with sassy, seductive characters that you just love to hate".

--Magdalene Breaux
Author of ***The Family Curse***

"An engaging first novel ... brilliantly represents many women in today's society struggling to make sense of their lives. Anika Malone grabs the reader's attention immediately and never lets go".

--Timmothy McCann
Best-selling author of ***Until, Always*** and ***Forever***

For Asya
Here's to opening doors and walking through

This book is dedicated to the loving memory of:

My Grandfather – James Getter Sr.
My Grandmother – Gardenia Getter
My Uncle – James Getter Jr.

Not a day goes by . . .

Acknowledgements

I would like to give a very special thanks to my sister Aisha Malone. When I first told her I wanted to write a novel, she told me to go for it. From day one she has been supportive, and encouraging. She's worked just as hard as I have to bring this book to fruition. I love you.

To my aunt Kenya Brown, you have always been there for me. Thank you for your open door policy, your shoulder to cry on, and for being nonjudgemental. I love you.

To my editor, Ava Delorenzo who answered every question and went above and beyond to assist me. And for your kind and encouraging words.

Above all, I would like to thank God for his unconditional love.

Prologue

It was a late Friday afternoon. Barely able to stand, Lisa struggled to make it out of the office. As she walked towards her car she noticed a white BMW parked alongside of her car. No one in the office owned such an expensive vehicle. "The nerve of some people; the fact that this is a restricted parking area doesn't seem to matter," she muttered to herself.

Lisa opened the passenger-side door and placed her briefcase on the floor. Walking to the back of her car, she couldn't help notice the New York plates. The car was magnificent, she thought. Lisa had to step back and take it all in.

A shadow approached over her shoulder. She quickly turned around and confronted a tall, lightskinned brother with curly hair and green eyes. A pair of Calvin Klein's and a white Calvin T-shirt clung to his well-toned body. She thought it would be a sin to look that good and not have to work for it.

"You know, if you wanna ride, I'll take you for a spin," he said with a New York accent.

"I'm sure you would," Lisa replied. "By the way, this is a restricted parking area. I know where you're from you tend to overlook things like that. Around here we take this a bit more seriously. You're lucky I didn't get on my car phone and have your car towed immediately."

"Look I was just trying ..."

"Save your excuses. You probably think just because that car is so expensive you can park it anywhere. I bet you're one of those people that take up two spaces at a mall."

"You sure have a lot to say, Ms. Munroe."

She raised her left eyebrow, "How do you know my name?"

"If you had given me a chance to properly introduce myself, all of this could have been avoided." Lisa stepped back ever so slightly, her stance begging an explanation. "I'm Mike Wilson the new Assistant District Attorney. I'll be starting on Monday."

"I didn't hear anything about any new ADAs," she said, as he was getting into his car. As he handed her a business card, she caught a flash from his gold Rolex. He started his car and leaned out the window.

"You know, Ms. Munroe, things would have been a lot easier if you'd just accepted the ride." Then he sped off.

Is this what she had to look forward to on Monday morning? He was so full of himself. Then again, he didn't know who he was dealing with.

PART ONE

1

"Lisa, what are you doing?" Natasha asked, walking into her apartment. She stood over her sister who was sitting on the floor Indian style going through some old letters she had hid in a shoebox.

"I'm going through some letters from my exs."

"Why are you here in my apartment?" Lisa continued looking through boxes as she tried to avoid Natasha's glare. "You and Darnel had a fight didn't you? What did you do now?" Natasha said shaking her head.

"What makes you think it was me?" Lisa asked, offended.

"It's always you."

"I resent that."

"Come on and tell me what you did." Natasha waited. "You can tell me now while you're sober and able to edit it along the way. Or I can pour some drinks into you and get the X-rated, explicit, uncut version." Throwing up her hands, she said, "It's up to you."

"Okay, you win. But it was just a little bitty one."

"Everything's little to you. It's only big when someone else does it."

Lisa resumed what she was doing until she came across a very special letter.

Listen to this Tasha. This is the letter that poetry guy from college wrote me. It's one of my favorites."

Lisa,

When you first walked into my life my heart was ripped out right before my eyes. No longer belonging to me, but a part of your being forever.

> *Your lightskinned caramel complexion. Your hazel eyes wide and big enough to see into one's soul. Your blond shoulder-length locks begging for my attention. The way your bosom filled up your blouse. Full and ripe and ready for tasting. The way your nipples stood out firm and hard. Oh how I longed for them to brush up against my body. You have legs as long as the Nile. How I wanted them wrapped around my body.*

"Okay, enough I get the point. If it wasn't so corny, I'd swear I'd need a cigarette."

"I don't know; it's just something about this letter that makes me feel good."

Natasha rolls her eyes. "It's about you. That's what makes you feel good. It feeds your oversized ego."

"Do me a favor call my house and ask for me?"

"Oh no, not this again."

"Just do it." Natasha walked over to the phone and dialed Lisa's number. Darnel said she wasn't there, and then they hung up.

"Did he sound worried?"

Natasha replied in an exasperated tone, "Yes, Lisa."

"Serves him right. He had no business in my business."

"You're amazing," Natasha said as she strolled over to the kitchen. "You want a beer?"

"You know I don't drink that stuff."

"Well, I don't have any cosmopolitans in here for your uppity ass. Take it or leave it. Going once, going."

"Okay, bring me one, but I'm not going to enjoy it."

Natasha laughed at her. "I couldn't care less. While you're still on my floor, will you please clean up that mess you made."

After a few beers and a couple of hours of going down memory lane, Lisa begged Tasha to call Darnel again. As Natasha staggered over to the kitchen to make the call, Lisa waited with baited breath. Natasha repeated the routine, but not with much clarity this time. She staggered back into the living room.

"You blew it girl. You didn't sound too convincing."

"Lisa, leave that man alone he ain't bothering you. Besides, finish telling me what happened to poetry man."

"After he got kicked out of school, he spent some time in and out of jail."

"Jail, jail. Did he make the bail?" Natasha started laughing hysterically.

"That's not funny Tasha. He had problems."

"Problems, problems. Did he solve them?"

Lisa grabbed her crotch and made a mad dash for the bathroom. "I have to pee!" she yelled as she ran down the hallway. When she returned to the living room, she glanced at the time on the VCR. "Natasha I have to get out of here."

"You're not going anywhere. You're drunk. Call that man and tell him where you are." Lisa stumbled over to the kitchen and proceeded to dial her number.

"Hello," she waited for a reply. "Hello," she repeated. Turning to Tasha, she said, "Tasha I can't hear him."

Tasha peered over the chair. "Turn the phone the other way, fool."

"Oh, okay." She turned the phone around. "Hi Darnel, it's me Lisa. I'm at Tasha's house. I just walked in."

"When did you get there?" he asked.

"About eight hours ago. I'm a little under the weather so I'm spending the night here."

"You mean drunk," he said.

"Yeah that too. Bye. I love you." She hung up the phone and headed for the couch.

"We should go to bed Tasha."

"I'll sleep on the couch. You get the bed Lisa."

"No, I'll sleep on the couch. You go get in your own bed."

"Okay, fine." Neither one of them moved. Lisa fell asleep on the sofa and Natasha slept in the chair.

***

"Did you have a good time last night?" Darnel asked.

"Good enough."

"I guess you tried to prove a point. What it was is beyond me. You really make me laugh Lisa. Every time you do something wrong you punish people for finding you out."

She batted her eyelashes at him. "Aw, look at you over there acting like my husband. It's so cute."

"If it's so cute, how come every time I propose to you—you say no?"

"Not this again."

"No, tell me Lisa."

"Because there's no piece of paper that could make me love you any more than I already do." She bent down and kissed him gently on the lips.

"Lisa, you can't fix everything with sex."

"You know Darnel you better stop talking before I lose interest." She kissed him again. She might not have been capable of fixing anything, but she sure was going to have a hell of a time trying. She looked in his eyes as she unbuttoned his shirt.

"You know I love it when you look at me like that," Darnel said.

"It's because I love looking at you." She smiled seductively then she pulled his shirt up and gently kissed his chest. He reached underneath her shirt and unbuttoned her bra from behind. Pulling her shirt up over her head, he took it off. "Ow, your watch is caught in my hair."

"Ooh, I'm sorry baby let me get it out."

"You know you probably did it on purpose."

Darnel laughed. "Lisa hold still." Trying not to pull out any of her hair, he got his watch out as quickly as he could.

"You sure know how to ruin a mood Darnel." But by this time he was too preoccupied doing what he was doing to even notice her comments. He pulled off her bra like the skin off of a ripe mango and leaned towards her breast. Quickly covering her breast, Lisa pulled away.

"Don't start teasing me Lisa. You always do this baby." She let down her hands slowly and pulled him closer to her, licking his face like a lollipop when you get to the good part. His fingers ran gently down her back. Unbuckling his belt, then his button, she pulled down his zipper. He motioned as if he was going to pick her up and carry her to the bedroom. Lisa put her arms over his shoulders and held on to the chair. Darnel looked puzzled. She pulled her skirt up to her waist. Darnel, stuttering, said, "You don't want to do it in the chair?"

Lisa smiled. "What's wrong Darnel?" She shook her head letting him know that he wouldn't be going anywhere soon. Kissing him, she let her hands glide into his pants. His breathing elevated just enough for her to notice the difference. Meanwhile, with her hands still in his pants, as she moved closer to him, Darnel cringed. "Sorry baby," Lisa said.

"Lisa, move a little to the right."

"Here?"

"No over more."

"Here?"

"Yeah that's good." Their bodies connected like two pieces of a puzzle. Sweat trickled down Darnel's forehead, as heat emanated from their bodies. His firm hands against her buttocks, he pulled her closer and closer so powerful and in control. She wanted—to match him in every way. The deeper he went the more she wanted to take him in. His body started to quiver, and he clinched his teeth because he didn't want to cry out. Exhausted, she leaned towards him and collapsed. When the chair started to tilt, she panicked. "Just lean up some Lisa. No, not that way. Up Lisaaa!" They fell backwards and laid there laughing.

Later on that night Natasha dropped by. Earlier that day she had called to let Lisa know their father was coming to town. Lisa hadn't seen him in nearly five years. She always made it a point to be unavailable when he came to town. Night and day is what she called them, but her mother called Lisa his twin.

Yes, she did have the same European features. Their complexions were the same and she had his hair, except hers was a shade lighter. According to Lisa that's where all their similarities ended.

"So Lisa, the lady continues to yell at me. Now, you know, everybody is watching me to see what I'm going to do. I'm standing there calm, rolling my eyes, then she throws the dress at me."

"No, she didn't! I don't even want to know what you did," Lisa exclaimed.

"Lisa, I went over to her and I said, 'Mom, stop blowing this out of proportion." They both burst out laughing.

"You're kidding; it wasn't Ma was it?"

"Hell yes. Otherwise, I would have knocked someone else down."

"I believe you. Why was Mama down there?"

"Well, you know Sister Andrews at Mama's church. I told her daughter-in-law that her husband was sleeping with Sister Mitchell's daughter."

"What did you do that for?" Lisa asked.

"Like I care. Rhonda asked me if he was cheating, and I said yes. What do I look like covering for a man? Well anyway, Mama got mad. Now there's this big thing at the church. Everybody is blaming Mama because I opened my mouth. I told her if they had a problem to come see me. She got mad and threw the dress at me. Sometimes I don't know about her Lisa. That's all she lives for you know—that church. She has no one to spend time with. You don't ever visit her; Daddy's gone; and I can't be with her all the time."

There was rattling at the door, indicating Darnel's arrival. He walked in and after taking off his jacket, he said, "Hi baby."

"Hey sweetie, how was work?"

"Fine, how was your day?"

"It was an earful; we'll talk about it tonight."

"Excuse me—hello? You're not going to speak to me? I know you see me sitting here Darnel," Natasha gibed, angry at being ignored.

"When are you going home Tasha?" Tasha stuck her middle finger up at him. "I wouldn't do that if I were you," Darnel said with a smile on his face. "We all know how long it's been for you."

"Go to hell!" she yelled as she turned her back to him.

"Must you two do this all the time? It gets tiring," Lisa complained. Natasha and Darnel were like a match and gasoline, combustible.

"What's for dinner?" Darnel asked.

"Dinner? I didn't cook; I'll order something." Darnel leaned over and kissed Lisa. "Are you joining us for dinner, Natasha?" he asked.

"No, I have a date."

"Yeah right," Darnel muttered. Lisa laughed at his remark, but quickly covered her mouth because Natasha was cutting her eyes at her.

"I suppose you think you're funny, huh Darnel," Natasha said angrily, thinking he always had some smart-ass remark. He was so smug.

"Never mind, Natasha. See you later," he said as he went upstairs.

"You know I can't stand him don't you? It's true, I can't stand him."

"Whatever." After a few minutes, Lisa and Natasha began to settle down and continued to talk about less divisive matters. "You didn't tell me you have a date."

"Yeah, it's this guy that works at the mall as a security guard."

"Only you," Lisa said under her breath, rolling her eyes.

"What's that supposed to mean?"

"A security guard Tasha. Come on, I could fix you up with someone at work, or I can get Darnel to introduce you to some people."

"What? Are the security guards that work at your job a better breed than the ones that work at the mall?"

"You know I'm not talking about them."

"Lisa, I just want to be with someone who treats me good. And I'm open to the idea that he may come in a different package. Anyway, Darnel has a big nose."

Lisa's mouth opened wide, "He does not!"

"Oh yes he does."

"You're just starting that same stuff you use to do when we were kids. Like when I used to like someone and there was something different about him."

"Different? That's a good one?" Natasha laughed.

"Yes, different. Anyway, you would make fun of him so I wouldn't go out with him. That's because you would tease me until I was ashamed to be seen with him. Am I right?"

"Of course you're right. The only reason it worked is because you're so vain."

"I am not," Lisa replied.

"Yes you are and you're in *dee—nile.* In fact, you're extremely vain. That's where you and Daddy are alike."

"Don't even mention him and me in the same sentence."

"Truth hurts doesn't it."

They settled down and continued to talk. Lisa was happy to avoid any conversation that included her father.

"Lisa!" Darnel called down from upstairs.

Lisa turned to Tasha. "I'll be right back." She got up and went upstairs to the bedroom. She opened the bedroom door, calling, "Darnel ? Where are you?" Darnel came strutting out of the bathroom—naked. Her face turned pink. "Oh god, Darnel, put some clothes on!"

"Why do you always get so embarrassed?" he teased her.

"I don't know, I just do." She walked over to him, then tried to find a towel to cover him. "Put the towel around you please."

"It's like you have a split personality. You can't be good girl/bad girl. It's one or the other. How many times have we made love?" She opened her mouth to answer him. "Don't even try to answer, because it's been too many times for you to remember."

"But that's different Darnel."

"How?"

"I don't know it just is."

Natasha yelled from downstairs, "Hey Lisa, I'm getting ready to go!"

"I'll be right back I'm going to walk her to the door."

Natasha was waiting by the door and said, "Okay Lisa, I'll see you." She kissed her sister goodbye.

"Okay, call me when you get back from your date."

"Okay, bye."

"Bye. Remember no glove no love." Natasha laughed, waving goodbye and then walked away.

Returning to the bedroom, Lisa found Darnel lying on the bed. As she entered the room, he leaned up into a sitting position. Walking towards him, Lisa asked, "So what were we talking about Darnel?"

"You have to ask? Take your clothes off."

"You're not serious."

"Go ahead."

She unbuttoned her pants and let them fall to her ankles. Stepping out of her pants, she eased her blouse over her head. Next she took off her bra and panties. "I'm naked, are you happy?" As she looked him up and down, she said, "Now you stand up!"

Darnel stood up so they were facing each other. "Look down," he told her.

"What?"

"Look down."

She lowered her head, then lifted it quickly. "What is the point?"

"Have you ever looked at him before?"

She glanced at it one more time. "No, not long and hard."

"Well, go ahead then."

"Is this some ego thing or something? Am I suppose to gasp and say, 'Oh my God it's so huge?'"

"Hey, the truth never hurts."

Lisa playfully punched him, and then looked down again. She was amazed that this awkward looking thing could provide such pleasure. Darnel pulled her closer, lowering his head as if to kiss her, but he purposely misses her lips and kisses her neck. Leaning his head forward as if he's going to kiss her, he misses again. Grabbing the back of his neck, Lisa said, "Kiss me now!" She grabbed his tongue with hers as if to swallow it whole sucking it as if it were the sweetest thing she'd ever tasted. He placed his hands on her behind and gently squeezed. Although she liked the way it felt, she pushed his hands away. He tried again and she again pushed his hands away. Darnel opened his mouth to speak, but Lisa placed her finger on his lips. "Sssh," she whispered. Slowly she walked around him, facing him she raised his arms, motioning to let him know to keep them up. She took both of her index fingers and ran them down his side. When she reached his foot, she sat down on the floor. She made him spread his legs open and then rubbed them up and down. Placing her index finger in her mouth, she sucked it seductively. Lisa took her finger and rubbed her nipple in a circular motion, while looking up at him. When she motioned for him to come down, Darnel knelt down. He pushed her hand away, replacing it with his tongue. Lisa leaned back, then he kissed his way up her neck. Gently, he pushed her down on the floor, and began kissing his way down, down and down.

2

Monday morning at work everything was still the same. The copier didn't work; the air conditioner was on the blink. And the security guard smelt like rotten onion dip.

Lisa headed to the break room. Pouring a cup of coffee, she took a seat near Andre. He was already on his second cup. "Hi Lisa, how are you doing today?"

"I'm all right." She gestured for him to move closer.

"What's going on?" he whispered in her ear.

"I don't know, but I would sure like to find out. Friday afternoon I met this guy named Mike Wilson who claims he's going to be working here. I've been trying to get some information on him, but Hank's secretary is being so secretive. Did you hear anything about this?"

"No, I didn't. You know if I heard anything, you would be the first person to know. If you want, I can go and work on Mildred later to see what I can find out."

Smiling she said, "I was hoping you were going to say that. I knew I could count on you. If you could get to her as soon as possible it would be helpful." Lisa took another sip of her coffee, waiting.

"All right Lisa, I'm on it—don't worry." They heard a commotion coming from the break room doorway. Hank's head towered above the crowd. He came towards them, but stopped in the middle of the floor. Lisa was trying to figure out what was going on. Hank gestured for everyone to be quiet. Then Lisa saw Mike standing next to him. "Is that him, Lisa?" Andre whispered.

"Yes, that's him."

"You didn't tell me he was so good-looking," Andre said smiling.

"Does that matter?" Lisa asked scrunching her nose. "Be quiet. I want to hear what Hank is getting ready to say."

Clearing his throat, Hank began, "I have an announcement to make. You are all fully aware of the vacancy created by Harvey Feldman's untimely death. He was a great attorney ..."

Andre leaned over and whispered in Lisa's ear, "I think Hank's drunk; we all knew Harvey couldn't win a case with the murder weapon and a confession." Lisa laughed and turned her attention back to what Hank was saying.

"There were many qualified applicants, but no one stood out like Mr. Wilson." Looking over at Andre, she could see the lust in his eyes. Poor Andre—he was always attracted to straight men.

As Hank was nearing the end of his little speech, Lisa stood up and said, "On behalf of all of us, I welcome you to the office. I hope that you grow to love it just as much as we have. Despite the fact that you'll have to be working for Hank." Mike laughed along with the others. "If you need any help, please don't hesitate to ask. Welcome to the family." Everyone gave him a round of applause. Hank left the break room. Some people were introducing themselves to Mr. Wilson. Lisa whispered into Andre's ear, "Andre get me his file and bring it to me right away." As Lisa stood up to leave, she noticed Mike looking at her from the corner of his eye. She held his stare for a second, then slipped out the back door.

Lisa was sitting behind her desk when Andre entered without knocking. He squeezed himself in through the door, trying not to open it too wide. She noticed that behind his back was a file folder. Looking like he had just run a marathon, he crept over to her desk and sat in the chair in front of her. "Andre, I like your vest it's very colorful. I don't know if I would have chosen those pants, but I can see where you might have went wrong. People sometimes lump all the darker shades of green in one category, but if you're one shade off it just ruins the outfit," she said, giving him the once over.

"That's all you have to say to me. I'm going to jail for you and that's all you can say."

"Andre calm down—no one's going to jail. Where is your backbone? I see you have what I've been waiting for. Are you going to keep complaining or are you just going to hand it to me?"

"Here," he said as he threw it at the desk. "I have to get that back as soon as possible. I don't have time to make you feel guilty." She grabbed the file and opened it immediately, scanning over the unimportant information.

"So Andre, how did you get Mildred to let go of this file?"

"I already knew Mildred wasn't departing with the file. So I had to get her out of the office."

"How did you do that?"

"I offered to cover for her while she took a cigarette break. Hank wasn't in the office, but he was due back at any minute. Lisa, I almost peed my pants."

"But you got it—didn't you. You know you're the best."

"Stop trying to suck up to me. What you need to do is get me an ambulance. I'm over here having a heart attack."

"Stop whining and let me finish reading this." Andre sucked his teeth, slouched in the chair and waited. She went over the file as fast as she could, trying to soak in all the information. "Hmm, interesting."

"What? What's interesting?" He jumped up, came around the desk and stood behind her. "I can't believe it, Lisa, he's really a part of that family. No wonder he got this job."

"Andre, look, don't you mention this to anyone. Promise?"

"I promise, Lisa."

"Good, now go and put this back." Andre grabbed the file and walked to the door as if he was preparing for battle. Before he walked out, he turned around one last time. "Andre don't get caught. If you do—I don't know you," Lisa said.

He looked at her and rolled his eyes. "Bitch," he mumbled as he closed the door behind him.

At work the next day, someone knocked on her office door. Lisa yelled, “It’s open.” Hank walked in. “Hank, what brings you my way?”

“A number of things, but none of them social.”

“Stop! You’re too much,” Lisa joked as she rolled her eyes at him.

“I’ve been meaning to sit down and talk to you. What it boils down to is I’ve been thinking about making some changes around here. Well hell, Lisa, they’re already going into effect. You have a partner now.”

“Partner?”

“Yes, his name is Mike Wilson. My secretary has arranged for you two to get acquainted. I believe it’s over dinner.”

“Over dinner?”

“Yes, my treat.”

“Forget dinner. What do you mean partner?” Lisa asked staring straight into Hank’s eyes.

“Well, I’ll have it arranged so that you will be handling all the major cases together.”

“Together?”

“Well, just collaborating. You will work together. Decisions will be made by both of you, but approved by me.”

“This wouldn’t by any chance have to do with you running again?” This was so typical of Hank, Lisa thought.

Smirking, he said, “Of course it doesn’t. I’m just experimenting on how to make this office run more efficiently. The people want convictions; they want murderers off the streets. I can’t think of a better way than to have my two best attorneys working together.”

“Bullshit!” she yelled as she slammed her fist on the desk. “Hank, you know I hate asking you about my own cases. Now, I have some new partner that I have to collaborate with.” Hank made his way to the door.

“I think you’ve got it all in a nutshell dear,” he replied.

"No, not quite." Lisa muttered mulling it over in her head. "There's more to it isn't there? How silly of me. You're pitting us against one another for the job of head prosecutor. Right?"

"I never said that," Hank replied, getting ready for a quick exit.

"You didn't have to. If you want to play your little game then fine. You know Hank, this reminds me of a bible story we all know so well. David and Goliath. You do remember that one don't you? Wilson's only Goliath in your eyes because he's a man—pure and simple. I'll be your underdog, Hank, because we all know who kicked Goliath's ass. Now, if you'll excuse me, I have work to do."

***

Darnel was late getting home that evening. Lisa was getting ready to dine with her new partner, when he walked into the bedroom. She gave him a kiss on her way to the bathroom. "Where are you going?"

"I have a business dinner."

"With who?"

"Mike Wilson."

"Who's that?"

"The new guy at the office that I was telling you about."

"Well, that should be interesting."

"You're telling me."

"Did you by any chance cook a little something for me?"

"You're so pitiful. There's a plate for you in the microwave."

"Thank you, I'm so hungry."

"You're welcome, dear. I should be home early; I know I'm not going to enjoy myself."

"Well at least try. Don't go in there with a chip on your shoulder, Lisa. You just might like him."

"It doesn't matter whether I like him. He's after my job. So all I can do is hate him. Give me a kiss. I'll see you later, try not to miss me too much."

***

Lisa arrived at the restaurant fifteen minutes late. She checked out everyone to see if she could spot Mike. Most of the tables were filled; there was a band in the corner playing jazz. Glancing in the direction of the bar, she saw Mike sitting on a corner stool. She walked towards him. He hadn't noticed her yet. Sitting down beside him, Lisa ordered a cosmopolitan. Looking over at her with his drink in his hand, Mike said, "I didn't think you were going to show up."

"I'm only a few minutes late. I don't just fall out of bed looking this good."

"Aw come on, I don't believe that."

She smiled, picked up her drink and took a sip. They sat there for a few minutes in awkward silence. "Well, why don't we take these drinks to our tables and get this over with," she said as she glanced at her watch. He walked over to the maitre'd, whispered something into his ear and returned to the bar; he said the table was ready. She grabbed her drink and followed him to their table. The waiter sat them in a secluded booth, just far enough away so they could have privacy, but not too far that they couldn't hear the band.

Mike finished his drink and pushed it aside. Lisa continued to work on her cosmopolitan.

"Ms. Munroe, I didn't know you were so quiet."

"'Lisa' is fine, and no, I wouldn't use quiet to describe me."

"What's the problem? Are you scared? I don't bite you know."

"I'm sure you don't. I'm just sitting here trying to figure out what Hank thought this dinner was going to accomplish."

"You're paranoid aren't you? This is a get-to-know-you dinner. Nothing more, nothing less." He waved at the waiter.

"Let's order." The waiter came over, took their orders and then he disappeared. "Hank tells me you're one of his best attorneys."

"The best."

"So modesty isn't one of your strong suits."

"I guess not." She picked up a piece of bread and buttered it.

"It's nice to dine with a woman who likes to eat."

"What makes you think that?"

"Your order. You ordered more than I did." She started laughing. "What's so funny?"

"Nothing, it's just that Darnel says the same thing all the time."

"Darnel's your husband?"

"I'm not married."

"Your boyfriend?"

"I guess you can say that."

"How long have you been together?

"A little over two years. So are *you* married, Mr. Wilson?"

"Widowed, and call me Mike."

"I'm sorry. Why don't we change the subject?" Luckily, their food arrived as she was running out of things to say to him. His file reported that he was single. All of a sudden she felt sorry for him. Finding that out about his wife made him seem a little bit more human.

"She died of cancer," he blurted out.

"Who?"

"My wife. I saw the face you were making while you were eating. Either you wanted to ask me or the food isn't so great."

"When did she die?"

"It's been three years now. It's part of the reason I moved here. It was time to move on."

"Good for you. Why California?"

"I've always loved it here. I vacationed here often, and I told myself one day I had to be here permanently. So here I am." She half smiled at him and finished eating. He was after her job. She knew with his family connections that the job was as good as his. Spoiled brat. She had had enough; it was time to get out of there.

"Look, I'm not really up to being phony tonight. I'm going home, I'll see you at work." She grabbed her purse and headed out the door to the parking lot.

She heard footsteps from behind, and turned around. It was Mike rushing towards her. "Lisa!" he yelled. "Wait up!" She stopped next to her car.

"What is your problem now? I thought we were having a decent conversation. You jump up and storm out of the restaurant in a huff. And what's all this phony stuff? I was being myself so the only phony at the table had to be you. You haven't liked me from day one. At first I thought I was overreacting, but it seems like you are just what they say you are behind your back."

"Is that supposed to shock me? You think I don't know what they say about me. Hell, I made some of it up myself. Look Mike, you might be the sweetest person in the world. It doesn't mean we have to be friends or even like each other. You stay away from me and I'll stay away from you. Okay?"

"Fine, I can take a hint. I never go where I'm not wanted."

"Then we shouldn't have any problems. Good night Mike."

"Oh, by the way, I wouldn't use sweet to describe myself. You're really quite amusing. It seems like you're used to getting your way. But now you're playing with the big boys. Watch yourself." He turned around and headed for the restaurant.

She opened her car door and sat there for a second. What was he doing? Threatening her? She wasn't scared of him. The nerve of him. Yes, he might be one of the big boys. But this was her territory. Come on Mike, give me your best shot. I'm ready.

***

Lisa climbed into bed. After tossing and turning for a bit, she finally got comfortable and laid her head on the pillow. "So Lisa, how was it?" She turned around towards Darnel.

"I didn't know you were awake?"

"I'm so used to falling asleep beside you."

"Oh, it was fine. I wasn't with you so it couldn't have been all that great."

"Good." She reached out and softly touched his nose. He smiled. "I'm glad you had a nice time."

"So am I. Come here." He moved closer to her. "Are you jealous?"

"No!"

"Yes you are."

"No I'm not."

"Okay, then we're having dinner again tomorrow night." Darnel's eyes widen. He slowly opened his mouth. "What Darnel? It's okay isn't it?" Lisa asked with a straight face.

Darnel cleared his throat, "You're kidding right?"

Mimicking a man's tone, she said, "No, no I am not." Then she started to laugh. Darnel looked a little embarrassed. "No, we aren't having dinner Mr. Jealous. Give me your hand."

"What?"

"Come on give it to me." She took his hand and placed it on her heart. "You feel it? Well it belongs to you and no one else." He leaned over and gave her a long passionate kiss. "Get away from me. I let you put your hand on my breast and you lose your mind. I have to get up early tomorrow." She turned around and he grabbed her shoulders, turning her back around. He kissed her hard, as she lay there motionless.

Leaning up, he said, "Okay good night." Just as he was about to turn back around, Lisa grabbed the back of his head and kissed him long and hard, then ripped off his nightshirt. "Hey Lisa, let's not get crazy."

"You started this. Now finish it," she said as she bit him on the ear.

"You're damn right I will." Darnel's face was serious now. He took hold of her and flipped her over until she was underneath him. Then he pulled off her nightgown. They grabbed at each other like wild animals—pressing her nails deep into his skin; pulling her hair. Lisa bit him on his neck and on his back. Darnel bit her breasts, sucking them hard, then he bit her nipples. Then they began to kiss and slow down a bit. Up on his knees now, Darnel opened her legs and penetrated. Pulling her up to him, they locked eyes for a brief moment. As Darnel pulled her closer, they start moving rhythmically. Moaning and jumping a little bit, Lisa leaned all the way back with her head moving around on the pillow, while she bit on her fist. Darnel pushed in harder and faster now. Her moaning grew louder and louder. She leaned up and put her arms underneath his and up over his shoulders. He slowed down. One thrust then a few seconds then another thrust. Lisa scratched his back and he let out a little cry of pain. Breathing hard, they fell down on the bed, their bodies covered in sweat. Slowing their breathing down, they finally rolled over and fell asleep.

3

The weekend ended late Sunday afternoon. Darnel and Lisa were tired and wanted to prepare for the next week. Lisa was in the kitchen cooking dinner. As the rice boiled, she heard Darnel put on some music. It was her favorite song, “Baby I’m Scared of You.” When she heard it, she went into the living room to dance. They both danced and laughed, and were having such a good time, then the doorbell rang. “Will you get that, honey?” Lisa asked. “I’m going to check on the rice.” Lisa ran into the kitchen while Darnel headed for the front door. He looked out the peephole then slowly opened the door.

“Hello Sandra, come in,” he said a little surprised at seeing her. How have you been?”

“I’m fine, and yourself?”

“This is a surprise. I didn’t know Lisa was expecting you. She’s—”

“Who’s that?” Lisa yelled. Walking into the room she saw her mother standing there but said nothing. Darnel finally broke the silence.

“Lisa, it’s your mother.”

“I can see that. Hello Mother.”

“Hello Lisa, how are you?”

Darnel started to inch away, “I’m going to go and turn the music down.” They both watched him leave.

“I’m fine, Mother. I was just in the kitchen cooking. You’re welcome to join me.”

“That’s fine.” They both walked towards the kitchen. Darnel looked at them suspiciously. Lisa rolled her eyes and gave him that look letting him know he’s in trouble later. Lisa returned to the stove to stir something in the pot. Her mother pulled out a chair and took a seat. “How’s work, Lisa?”

“It’s fine,” Lisa replied shuffling her feet, while drying her hands off on the dishtowel. “Ma, what do you want?”

Raising her voice slightly her mother answered, "What do you mean what do I want? I just came over to see how you were doing."

"Well, I said I was fine. Why are you still here?"

"You invited me in."

"Well, I didn't think you would accept."

Sandra is taken aback. "You know, you'll never change Lisa. No matter how old you get or how much time goes by. No matter how much I try."

Lisa grumbled, "I wonder whose fault that is?"

"What did you say?"

"Nothing. Look Mother, you just have to face the fact that we'll never be friends. It doesn't matter how you feel about it."

"You have made that perfectly clear time and time again. I just wanted to see you face to face. I don't care what you think about me. All I know is that you are my firstborn. I will always love you." Sandra got up and left Lisa in the kitchen. As she walked by the living room she said, "Good-bye Darnel."

Darnel jumped up to get the door. "You know, Sandra, I think Lisa will eventually come around."

"I know that stubborn girl and I don't think so. You know Darnel, you are a good man, and I'm glad you're able to see past all her ugliness."

"Lisa's a good person and I love her."

"Don't get me wrong Darnel, Lisa has good qualities. But she also has her ways."

After Lisa's mother left, Darnel walked into the kitchen. Lisa straddled over the chair, biting her nails. "You know you're awfully hard on her. She tries," Darnel argued.

"And?"

"And what? You know what I mean."

"I don't want to get into this with you, Darnel."

"We have to talk about it sometime. You know family is important to me." He paused then continued, "Lisa, I want to have a family of my own someday."

"Look, Darnel, not all of us lived with Cliff and Claire Huxtable. I don't have strong family ties. Natasha and you are my only family. I like it like that just fine."

"You know, sometimes I don't know about you. At times you can be so loving, caring, and gentle. But right now you're acting like a spoiled brat."

She rose out of the chair knocking it to the ground. "Why the hell would you call me that?"

"Because it's how I feel. I can't understand how anyone could disrespect his or her mother like you do. If you don't like her that's fine, but at least give her some respect."

"That's so damn easy for you to say. I hate people who judge me and have never walked in my shoes. I'm so happy that you love your mother. It's great that you call her every weekend and that you spend time with her. I can't be you and you can't be me. So don't try."

4

It was hard for Lisa to keep up with her cases and keep an eye on Mike at the same time. Every time she turned around she saw him laughing with Hank in the hallway. When she approached them, they would lower their voices and say a polite "hello" and "how are you doing?" She knew that they were up to something. But, maybe it was just her imagination. It's probably just a man thing, she thought. Why was she surprised, she did grow up in America right? This has been happening for years. This is the nineties, but unfortunately, it doesn't mean a damn thing.

It was about ninety-three degrees and the heat index was even higher. "I feel like I'm about to burst into a flame," Lisa said aloud. Her blouse clung to her body from the sweat and her hair had started to curl at the roots. Unfortunately, the air conditioner was being repaired again. She couldn't take it any longer so she went outside. Lisa walked to the bench in the far corner, the one under the shade. Sitting down, she leaned her head back. The heat was unbearable. Lisa unbuttoned the top two buttons on her blouse. Her hair was sticking to the back of her neck so she gathered it up and pulled it on top of her head to let a cool breeze hit the back of her neck. Lisa leaned back and closed her eyes and lost herself in another world. Looking up she suddenly saw Andre standing over her.

"Hello, Miss Thang. The heat's got you hasn't it? Here you are showing all your business to whoever wants to see it." He sat down beside her. "I haven't really seen you around lately. Been busy?" She nods in the affirmative. "So you're not talking today?"

"Andre, it's too hot to even talk. I wish I could get naked and run through some water."

"That could be arranged."

She smiled at him. "What are you doing out here?"

"I had to run across the street and pick up some files. Well, let me go. I have to deliver these. After that I have to stop by Mr. Wilson's office and let him know that his meeting with Hank has been moved up."

"Andre, what time was the other meeting?"

"It was scheduled for this afternoon at four, but Hank has to leave early so he pushed it up to one o'clock."

She was attentive now; she started to perk up. Opportunity was knocking. "You know, Andre, I'm headed that way—I'll let him know."

"Fine, it'll give me a chance to do some other things that have been piling up on my desk. You're being awfully sweet today. Thanks." He turned around and sashayed up the courtroom steps.

Lisa headed straight for Mike's office; it was twelve thirty now so she needed to get there as soon as possible. She gently rapped on the door. "Come in!" he yelled.

She opened the door slowly. "Hello."

"Hi Lisa, come in. This is a surprise. Is there something I can do for you?"

"As a matter of fact you can. How about lunch?"

Surprised by the invitation, he asked, "Lunch?"

"Yes, lunch, you know that little meal between breakfast and dinner. Come on what's the big deal? I guess I ought to show you some of this beautiful city. How about it?"

"Sure, that sounds good. What time is good for you?"

"One o'clock will be fine. Let me run to my office and I'll meet you by your car in fifteen minutes." She turned around and got out of his office as quickly as she could. She stole down the hall to her office, trying not to be noticed and hoping she wouldn't run into Andre. She had to get Mike out of the building and soon. Running into her office and almost tripping over the chair, she grabbed her purse out of her desk and pulled out her hairbrush. She went over to her closet door and opened it to the mirror. Her hair was a mess. Brushing it back, she leaned over and shook it to give it some body. After a little lip gloss, she stuck a piece of gum in her mouth and headed out the door.

Mike was unexpectedly waiting by the stairs. "Come on let's go," she said as she bounded down the stairs.

"Sure, we'll take my car; you'll finally get that ride." At his car he opened the door for her. He climbed in, started it up, shifted down and sped away. "So, where are we headed, Lisa?"

"This restaurant called "La Rubia." It's on the corner of Elm and Sunrise." Mike made a left at the next light and they were on their way.

The restaurant was packed, as she expected it to be. Lisa walked up to the hostess and asked for a table for two. The hostess said it would be a fifteen-minute wait. Lisa said fine and asked her if Luis was around? The hostess disappeared for a few seconds and came back with Luis trailing behind her. "Lisa, is that you? La Rubia!" he yelled. He walked up to her and hugged her. "You look so beautiful. How are you?"

"I'm fine. How are you doing?"

"I can't complain. Look at you. That hair, I love it. Are you here alone?"

"No, I'm with someone." She pointed at Mike, and Luis said hello. Then he pulled her to one side.

"Where's Darnel? Who is this?"

"He's just a friend. We work together."

"Good, good, because I really liked the other one. How's Andre?"

"He's fine. Aren't you two talking yet?"

Rolling his eyes, "No, you know how he is. He's such a baby. I refuse to cater to him this time."

"I'll tell him you asked about him."

"If that's what you want to do." He winked at her. "Let me get you a table." He grabbed two menus and seated them directly. He planted a kiss on her cheek and told them to enjoy their meal.

"It must be nice to have connections?"

"Oh, he's an old acquaintance. It's funny that you should mention connections. It would seem to me that you would know all about that."

"What do you mean by that?"

"Oh, don't try to act naive. Wilson as in Bernard Wilson the third. Stock market genius born in Virginia to a farmer. Worked all his spare time in the fields with his father. Begged his father to let him stay in school to continue his education, promising to work twice as hard after school and on weekends. Worked his way through college, with barely anything to eat. Often borrowed textbooks from fellow classmates. Graduated magna cum laude then went on to graduate school to receive a Masters in Business Administration. Made a bundle in the stock market. Also known as a real estate mogul." Lisa took a deep breath and continued on, "Now, how many successful children did he have? You have judges in your family, councilmen, and doctors, not to mention that your family is one of the richest African American families in the United States. Now, I wouldn't compare my little connection to a restaurant manager to yours." She sat back and waited for his reaction.

"First of all, I never made a secret of who my family is. It's not something that comes up in casual conversation. I'm very proud of my family and I would never try to deny them. If you wanted to know, all you had to do was ask instead of snooping around."

"Snooping?"

"Excuse me, let me finish. From day one you have been hostile towards me. I sincerely hope it's not because of who my family is." He sat back and looked at her and shook his head. "You think I got this job through a connection right?"

"I didn't say that."

"You don't have to. Look at your face."

"Well, let me put it this way, I'm sure who your family is didn't hurt your chances."

"I'm not going to sit here and deny that it did. However, I think you would be intelligent enough to know that Hank only hires competent people. Hank runs the office. If I do well, he looks good. While you were busy investigating me, you should have taken the time to find out if I was a good attorney. I have an impeccable record. Instead of making up things in your head about me, maybe you should sit in on one of my cases and see for yourself."

"Maybe I will," Lisa retorted. He burned her up. Sitting across from her looking so cocky. He continued to eat his lunch as if nothing bothered him. She tried to smile and act the same but for some reason she didn't think it was working. She decided to go ahead and finish her meal. A devilish grin came over her face. She thought, wait until you get back to the office. We'll see how cocky you are then, Mr. Wilson.

***

At seven thirty Lisa was finally getting out of the office. Her arms were full of files as she headed for the parking lot. The building was deserted now; she heard some rustling of papers and a few voices in the corridor. It was nothing like it was during the day. Hurrying along she tripped and fell, dropping the files all over the floor. "Shit!" she yelled. Papers were everywhere. She couldn't leave until she picked up every single one. Biting her lip she proceeded to pick up the papers practically on her knees with her hair hanging in her face. She was in her own world and didn't notice that someone else was in the hallway. Suddenly, a hand appeared. She looked up and it was Mike. "Thank you," she said. He continued to help her pick up the papers without saying a word. She put them into the neatest pile she could make. He grabbed her arm and helped her up. Picking up her briefcase, she headed for the door.

"What's your hurry, Ms. Munroe?"

"I'm tired. I just want to get home and into a cold shower."

"That doesn't sound too bad." He held the door open for her and let her pass. She brushed up against his chest. They heard the guard yell good night as they walked to the parking lot.

"Excuse me," he said. "Where are my manners; let me carry that file for you. I wouldn't want you to drop it again." She handed it to him with no argument. "You know, Lisa, I missed a very important meeting this afternoon. It was moved to one o'clock. Exactly the same time you took me out to lunch."

"Really? What happened?" she asked about to put her fingers in her mouth to bite her nails.

"I'm sure you know how Hank can get. Let's just say he wasn't pleased."

"He'll get over it he always does. I wouldn't worry about it."

"It's a good thing it wasn't crucial, because then I would definitely have to get to the bottom of this. That poor assistant's job would be in jeopardy." He looked directly at her and smiled. She knew he knew. He was warning her, threatening Andre's job. He had already gotten to the bottom of it. He knew Andre was responsible and he also knew how close Andre and Lisa were. When they arrived at her car, he handed her the file. "Good night, Lisa."

"Good night," she said. Mike walked over to his car. Lisa got into her car, backed up and pulled off. She could see him coming up in her rear view mirror. Once they got on the freeway, he pulled alongside her and then sped away. "Show off!" She yelled. She popped in a CD and thought about him for a moment. He was on his toes; he didn't let anything get past him.

His eyes were sea green; if you stared long enough, you could get lost in them. He had this cute thing he did with his lips when he spoke. He would be talking and when you responded he'd lick his lips in slow motion. It was mesmerizing. It could make you lose your train of thought. For some odd reason she was looking forward to seeing him tomorrow.

5

"Unfortunately, it can go either way. I presented a good case but the defense tore her up with her sexual history. I mean, Jim bore into her. I wanted to punch him in his face. I made a wisecrack and got reprimanded."

"Who's the judge?" Mike asked.

"Judge Wallace with his fat bald head." There was a knock at the door and Lisa yelled, "Come in!"

Andre walked in, fidgeting as he announced, "The girl in your rape case tried to commit suicide. She's at Cedars Hospital now."

Lisa jumped up, "Oh my God! I need you to cover for me. I'm going to the hospital. If you need me, you can reach me at the hospital. I'm going." She ran out of the office. Suddenly she heard footsteps behind her.

"Lisa, I'll drive you," Mike said.

"Okay, let's go."

***

Lisa hurried up to the front desk. "Ma'am, I need to know what room Allison White is in?"

"Um… let me see… She's in the psychiatric ward. Only family members are allowed. Are you a family member?"

She pulled out her ID, "Ma'am, I'm with the District Attorney's office."

"Okay, she's in room 404. Just follow the yellow line to the elevator; you should find your way from there."

"Thank you."

When Lisa and Mike arrived on the fourth floor, Lisa headed straight for Allison's room. Taking a deep breath, she opened the door. Lisa wound up spending a couple of hours with

Allison. When she came out of the room, Mike walked up to her and asked, "Is she okay?"

"Yes, she's going to be fine," Lisa answered, pulling her hair back with two fingers and breathing a sigh of relief.

Mike placed his hand on her arm and gently squeezed. "How about you?"

"I'll be fine."

"You want to go and get a cup of coffee?"

"Coffee?" She shook her head. "No, I think I need a drink."

"Fine." He put his hand on her back and guided her outside.

***

"So what happened in the room, Lisa?"

"We talked. We didn't talk about anything specific. Most of the time I spent in there I was just sitting. I could tell she didn't want me to leave."

"I didn't know you had it in you."

Puzzled, she asked, "Had what, Mike?"

"Compassion. You know when you let your emotions get in the way it affects you in the courtroom."

"I like to show the jury members that I'm just as appalled as they are. I sympathize with the victim. When we show we care, then they care."

"Lisa, they aren't supposed to care. They're supposed to listen to the facts and the facts only."

"That's what they're supposed to do, but it seldom happens. They're human; they can't help it. It's visual; sometimes it overrides the thought process. Right?"

"Yes, I see your point. I also hear you're like Dr. Jekyl and Ms. Hyde in court. You're gentle and kind to your witnesses. On the other hand, you tear apart the defense's witnesses on cross."

She smiled at him and said, "I'm good."

After a few more drinks Mike, digging into his wallet, asked, "So Lisa where do you want to go?"

"Go?"

"Yes, go."

"I better call it a night. I know Darnel's probably wondering where I am. Thanks for the invitation. You better just drive me to the office so I can pick up my car."

"Okay, if that's what you want."

"Yes, that's what I want. This is on me. Thanks for the company."

"Put your money away," he told her as he waved at the bartender.

"That's very kind, Mike, but I'm the one who wanted a drink."

"Lisa, put your money away. I've got it." He put the money on the bar. "There, let's go."

He pulled up alongside her car. She got out and so did he. "Look Lisa, I really had a nice time. I would like to do it again."

"As in a date?"

"No, as in friends. I like talking to you. I know you're determined not to like me, but you do."

"You're full of yourself aren't you. What makes you think that I can spend extended periods of time with you?" she asked, raising her eyebrow at him.

"Let's just say, it's a feeling I get."

"I wouldn't agree with you entirely, but I don't want you thinking I'm not hospitable. In fact, how about you come over to my house for dinner Saturday night."

"You're sure Darnel won't mind."

"Of course not, he'll be so glad that I'm cooking a meal."

"Okay, I'll come."

"Saturday at seven."

***

"Hello."

"Hello. Yes, Mr. Thompson this is Mike Wilson."

"How are you doing young man? I hear you're practicing law in California now?"

"Yes sir, I am. Working for the State of California. It's a hard job, but somebody has to do it."

Laughing he said, "Yes, yes son, I know how it is. So how's your mother?"

"Oh, she's doing quite well, sir. I believe she told me last week that she had lunch with your wife."

"Oh yes, I do believe Juanita did mention that. In fact, I played golf with the congressman the other day. He's a killer."

"Yes, my cousin does have a mean stroke."

Laughing he continued, "Oh, what it would be to be young again. Your father and I use to go at it day in and day out. The next time you're in town maybe I could teach you a little something."

"I'd be honored. I will definitely take you up on that."

"So what's going on son? Is there anything that I could do for you?

"As a matter of fact there is ...

***

When Lisa arrived home that night, Darnel was up in the bedroom sitting on the bed with his back against the headboard reading a book. He looked up at her. "Hello."

"Hello." She took her shoes off and placed them in the closet. "I'm sorry I'm late. Did you eat?"

"I had a little something," he said and returned to his book.

"You could have been more creative sweetheart."

"Yeah, whatever," he grumbled.

"Is something wrong?"

"I was just worried that's all."

"I said I was sorry." He continued to stare at her. "Darnel do you want to know where I was at?" He just looked at her. "Well, I'm going to tell you anyway. Today, one of my witnesses tried to commit suicide. I was at Cedar's tonight.

Mike drove me, and afterwards we went for drinks. I was really shaken up. I had a few drinks then he drove me back to the office so I could pick up my car. Are you satisfied?"

"I wasn't worried about who you were with. I trust you. It's just that today is my mother's birthday and we were supposed to go over there for dinner."

"Oh baby, I'm so sorry. I forgot. Did you go?"

"Yes, I did."

"Did you tell Estelle I was sorry?"

"Of course."

"Baby, I swear to you it just slipped my mind. With Allison in the hospital and all."

"I understand. How is she?"

"She's going to be fine. Didn't you call my job?"

"Yes, they just told me you were out with Mr. Wilson."

"You should have spoken with Andre."

"You know I hate talking to him."

"You do know that you don't turn gay if you speak to a gay man? Right?" She grinned. Darnel didn't find it amusing. "I know, I should have called. Come here." She said sitting next to him on the bed. She kissed him and gave him a hug. "I'm sorry for jumping down your throat. I promise I'll call when I'm going to be late. I'll call Estelle and explain." She walked over to the phone and he patted her on her butt.

6

Friday afternoon at work, Mike stopped by Lisa's office for a visit. "Are we still on for dinner Saturday night, Lisa?"

"It's a good thing you reminded me, I need to give Darnel and Natasha a call."

"Natasha?"

"Oh yes, Natasha's my sister. I promise you it's not a fix up. I just don't want you to feel like a third wheel."

"Whatever you say, Lisa. I've heard that one before."

"I'm serious, just be there."

"Okay, I'll be there. I'm leaving town today, but I'll be back tomorrow evening."

"You're leaving now?"

"Yes Ma'am, I am."

"Lucky you, have a safe trip."

"I didn't know you cared."

"I don't, I just don't want to be left with all your paperwork. Now get out of here."

"Okay, see you tomorrow."

"Okay, bye."

Later on the phone rang while Lisa was busy at her desk trying to tie up some loose ends before the weekend. "Hello," she said as she grabbed the receiver, dropping it twice.

"Hi, it's me."

She leaned back in her chair as a smile began to form on her face.

"What's going on Darnel?"

"I have to leave town tonight," he said.

"What?" she bolted up.

"One of our investors is threatening to pull out of the Thompson project. We are going to New York tonight. They specifically asked that I join them. This is a very important project. It's one of my biggest, Lisa. I have to go."

"I know baby. Don't worry about me. You do what you have to do. When are you leaving?"

"I'm at the airport now."

"Okay, so you're at the airport. You sure don't waste anytime. When will you be back?"

"I'm not sure. I'll call you from New York. Look baby, my plane is boarding now."

"Okay, I'll miss you and be careful. They don't call it a jungle for nothing."

"I'm a big boy, Lisa. I'll be fine."

"And don't forget ..."

"I know, I know, bring you something back."

"You better. I love you. Bye."

"Bye Lisa."

***

On Saturday morning, Lisa phoned Natasha. "Tasha, I can't get a hold of Mike; he's out of town."

"Well?"

"Well what?"

"I don't know. Help maybe."

"Well, I'll be there."

"Okay, that's good. I just feel funny about having him over while Darnel isn't here."

"Didn't you tell Darnel?"

"I forgot."

"What do you mean you forgot?"

"Please girl, it's not how it sounds. Darnel left before I had a chance to tell him."

"You know it's a little weird that Darnel had to leave town the same weekend Mike's coming for dinner."

"Natasha, it's only a coincidence; it couldn't be helped."

"You did say that they asked for him specifically?"

"Yes, they did. He's one of the key people."

"Well, I'll be there early so you won't feel awkward."

"You are a lifesaver."

"Yep, whatever. Good-bye."

"Bye."

***

Around six fifty Lisa began to wonder where Natasha was. She stuck her finger in the sauce one last time. As she brought it to her lips she smiled because she knew it was good. At six fifty eight, the door bell finally rang. Lisa rushed to the door, ready to grab Tasha by her throat. "I thought you would never get here!" she shouted then blinked twice. "Oh shit, I'm sorry. I thought it was Tasha. Come on in, Mike." He slipped out of his jacket and she extended her arms to take it. In his arms were flowers and a bottle of wine.

"The wine is for dinner and the flowers are for Natasha."

"What about me?" she said twirling one of her locks and batting her eyelashes.

"You get the pleasure of my company." He looked around the house, nodding as if he approved. "So where is the man of the house? I've been dying to meet him."

"He's going to be late."

They walked into the living room. "How late?" he asked.

"Oh a day or two."

"Excuse me?"

"He's out of town on business. Have a seat." Mike sat down opposite her. "I tried to call this off, but of course, I couldn't get in contact with you."

"Would you still like to call it off?"

"Of course not. I just felt funny about having you here without Darnel. It's his home, well our home. But Natasha will be here soon so I'm okay with it. I'm going to put on some music."

"How's your collection?"

"I love music, but it's Darnel's collection. He has some great stuff. Come take a look at it." As Mike went over and checked out the collection, the telephone rang. "I'm going to get that in the kitchen," Lisa said. But Mike wasn't paying her any attention. Lisa sauntered over to the kitchen and grabbed the phone on the third ring. "Hello."

"It's Tasha. I have some bad news."

"Don't tell me."

"I have to close tonight," she said.

"I said don't tell me!"

"Mona got sick and she can't close. I have to stay. I'm sorry."

"What do you mean you have to stay?"

"Come on now, Lisa."

"Fine. But I will get you for this. Bye," she complained. Hanging up the phone, she leaned against the refrigerator. She knew she didn't want to spend the entire evening alone with Mike. "Get yourself together," she told herself. "You can handle this; he's only a man. They're flesh and blood with no brains and they pee standing up." She repeated it three times before she left the kitchen.

Walking into the living room, she saw Mike sitting on the couch and said, "I see you made yourself comfortable. Well, I have good news and some bad news. Which do you want first?"

"The bad news."

"The bad news is that my sister won't be able to make it. Don't ask me any questions. The good news is you're going to get a cooking lesson. Get up and follow me." They marched into the kitchen. He took a seat on the stool. "Now, this is how it usually works. The women gather in the kitchen and help me prepare the meal while we gossip and put down our men. You would have been in the living room playing music, talking sports, drinking beer, and doing other insignificant things. But you, yes you, have hit the jackpot. You will be allowed into this glamorous life for one night and one night only. Do you think you can handle it?"

"I'm going to try," he said beaming.

"The chicken is in the oven; the spaghetti is on the stove. We just need to make a salad." She grabbed the vegetables and laid them on the counter in front of Mike then handed him a knife. She had him cut up vegetables while she made the base for the salad.

After dinner they went into the living room to relax and talk. "Your glass is empty would you like some more?" Lisa asked.

"Yes, I would." She poured him some wine and refilled her glass, sitting down across from him in the loveseat. "So why aren't you married Lisa?"

"Probably the same reason you're not."

"I don't think so Lisa. I'm waiting for the right one; I don't take marriage lightly."

"Would you mind defining what the 'right one' is?"

"Well, a lot like you. Independent, ambitious, career orientated, intelligent, beautiful, sensitive, and a great cook. Just to name a few."

"Thanks for the compliment," she said, smiling brightly.

"You still haven't answered my question, Lisa."

"I'm not married, because I'm scared. My parents are divorced. I just don't equate marriage with happiness. Every time I think of it, I think about the pain and the hurt."

"You can't base it on one bad experience."

"True, but if and when something goes wrong I can walk away. No divorce, no settlement, no children and no…"

Mike interrupted, "and no reason to stay and work it out." She looked at him and rolled her eyes. "Would you like to change the subject, Lisa? You don't have to get angry."

"I'm not angry."

"So what's all the pouting about?"

"I don't pout," she argued as she glanced down at her lips and pulled them in.

"Excuse me."

"Anyway, I wish I could say yes to Darnel. He loves me so much. I know that he's the one for me."

"Do you love him?"

"More than anything." She could hear the melody in the background. Every time she heard that song it made the hairs stand up on the back of her neck. "Hey, I love that song." She yelled, "Turn it up and let's dance."

After a few dances and some dessert, things began to wind down. "I think I'm going to call it a night." Mike started walking towards the door. He stood in front of the door for a moment, then turning to Lisa, "I really enjoyed myself this evening. I haven't felt so relaxed in a long time."

"I'm glad. You're nothing like I imagined. I hate to admit it, but I always have a good time with you."

"Would you please tell Darnel and Natasha that we have to try dinner again soon and that I'm sorry I missed them."

"I will."

"It wasn't so bad, now was it?"

"No, not too awful."

"Good night Lisa." He kissed her on the cheek. She closed the door behind him and rested against the door, then she heard a knock. She opened it and he leaned in, "Put those flowers in water."

Laughing, she said, "Okay, get out of here."

"Bye."

Lisa was in her room getting ready for bed when the phone rang. "Hello?"

"Hi, it's me."

"Hey, how's everything going?"

"Well, we don't meet with our client officially until Monday. Roger has it arranged so that we'll 'accidentally' run into him all weekend. We ran into him this afternoon at the racquetball club. I think we've made some progress."

"That's good."

"So, what did you do today?"

"Oh, nothing."

"I would have figured you'd spend the day with your sister."

"Oh, she had to work, besides I'm perfectly capable of entertaining myself in other ways."

"Really?"

"Yes really, and what do you mean by that?"

"It's nothing, Lisa."

"No, tell me, I'm listening."

"All I'm saying is that you need to get out more often."

"I do get out."

"I mean go out without me or Natasha, and I don't mean out to eat."

"Fine, I will go out more often."

"You say that all the time."

"I don't complain about not going anywhere. I enjoy what I do with my spare time."

"I'm not saying you don't. Let's not even waste our time talking about it. I miss you."

"I miss you too."

"I'm really lonely in this hotel room."

"You better be."

"You know I am. I want you baby."

"Well Darnel, I guess you're going to have to satisfy yourself in some other way."

"And how do you suggest I go about doing that, Lisa?

"You have a hand don't you?"

"It's not the same."

"I would hope not. Lay down. Are you lying down?"

"Yes."

"Well, picture my face. Can you see it?"

"Yes, I can."

"I want you to focus on my lips. Do you see them Darnel? The way they curve, the roundness."

"Mmm, I see it."

"What color is the lipstick? Tell me what you see, baby?" Lisa could only imagine what Darnel was doing on the other end of the phone. Herself, she was feeling flush and hot.

"It's red and they're wet."

"They crave something Darnel. There's something they want to taste. Reach out and rub your fingers over my lips. Mmm, I feel it—it feels so good. I want you to put your finger in my mouth."

"It's in there."

"Do you want me to suck it or lick it?"

"It's up to you."

"I'm going to lick it first, them I'm going to suck it hard. Would you like that?"

"Yes."

"I can't hear you. I need to hear it baby."

"Yes, Lisa."

"I like the way you say my name. Say it again."

"Lisa."

"Mmm, I like that." Little beads of perspiration trickled down her forehead.

"Ow!" she yelled.

"What? Lisa? What happened?"

"You didn't feel that?"

"No, what happened?"

"I just bit your finger. Good night, Darnel." She grinned and thought to herself I'll bet he'll need a cold shower after his finger stops throbbing.

7

About two weeks later Mike, and Lisa had a conference with Hank. They were in there twenty minutes, butting heads and breathing each other's air. "I really think that Mike has a good point, Lisa," Hank said.

"I think it's a good one too, but it's not a solution. If we're going to have to move faster with our workload, I think we should continue as we are. Which is advising each other, not sharing our work. That's silly."

"I thought you said it was a good point."

"I didn't want to hurt Mike's feelings."

"My feelings?" Mike asked, with a raise of his eyebrow.

Having had enough, Lisa stood up and looked right at Mike. "Look Mike, let's cut the bull. The mayor wants us to rush through our cases because he's up for re-election next year. I mean Hank he's starting pretty early isn't he?" She said shifting her gaze onto Hank.

"The Democrats have let it leak out that Jerry Gold might be running. Mayor Phelps just wants to squash their hopes now," Hank explained.

"I really don't care what Mayor Phelps wants," Lisa sparked.

"He's your boss, Lisa," Hank said as he took a drag off of his cigarette.

"Lucky me. Hank, how many times do I have to ask you not to do that in front of me. There's a law against it. Don't make me report you, and you know that I will." Hank grunted, but put the cigarette out on the sole of his twenty-dollar Payless shoes. "Anyway," Lisa continued, "we need to hire a few more ADAs. There's no way things will move faster by giving us more cases. Things will just get worst. You tell Phelps that Ms. Munroe said if he wants things to move any faster to get his one-testicle-having-ass in the courtroom himself." Mike and Hank look at her, stunned. She turned around and stormed out of the office.

As she walked down the hallway, she heard someone yell, "Lisa, wait up!" She turned around to see who it was and then kept right on walking. Mike caught up with her not one bit out of breath, his clothes as crisp as the five dollar bill your grandmother puts in your birthday card year after year. "Lisa, what happened in there?"

"Nothing," she muttered.

"There's got to be something; you've never acted like that before."

"Oh grow up!" Mike looked at her strangely; he couldn't figure out where all her anger was coming from.

As they continued down the hall, one of the interns walked up to Lisa.

"Ms. Munroe, one of the Public Defenders sent this plea bargain over with a change in it. He's only ready to sign if you agree to it." After giving it the once over, Lisa agreed to the changes, and gave it her Hancock. While she was signing it, Mike stood by waiting for her. She looked at him and said nastily, "Is there something you want too?" The intern looked away in embarrassment. Handing the plea bargain to the intern, Lisa turned to Mike, and said, "Well?"

Looking directly at her, Mike said with a very steady voice, "If you ever embarrass me in front of an intern again, I'll knock you off your ass." Then he walked away.

Lisa stood there humiliated. I should have replied, she thought to herself. She should have told him off. How dare he speak to me that way! Then she wondered, Did I deserve that? Was he justified? In any event, she knew that first she needed to calm down and get a grip.

Later that afternoon, she found herself in front of Mike's office. She knocked on the door. "It's open," he yelled. She opened the door slowly, and stuck her head in the room.

When Mike saw her, the smile on his face disappeared.

"I know you're not expecting me, but I think we need to talk," Lisa said tentatively from the door.

"It's all right, have a seat."

Lisa sat down and began, "I would like to apologize for this morning. I was way out of line, and my behavior was not called for. I shouldn't have spoken to you like that period, regardless of who was around. I'm very sorry and it won't happen again."

"That's it?"

"What do you mean is that it? You better be glad I said that much." Mike stared at her waiting for her to say more. "Okay, I'm sorry. I apologize again," Lisa finished under his glare.

"That was the sorriest apology I've ever heard. But I can see that it took a lot for you to say that much. You need to control your temper."

"Don't I know it; I thought I had it under control. There's only one person who brings out the worst in me, and unfortunately he's in town."

8

Somehow, Darnel and Mike ended up on the same basketball team. They were going to be playing together for a charity event on Saturday. Lisa felt nervous about their meeting one another. But Darnel and Mike were looking forward to the event and meeting each other. Lisa felt scared; she would just have to wait and see what happened on Saturday.

***

Darnel was up early on Saturday morning, in order to practice before the game and meet up with the other team members. Lisa stayed at the house doing little odds and ends, watering the plants, loading the dishwasher, and vacuuming.

Natasha and Lisa had decided to go to the game together. Actually, Lisa begged Natasha to go with her because she didn't want to go alone. She felt so nervous being with both Darnel and Mike. She would be stuck between them—a Lisa sandwich. Natasha was going as her support.

When they arrived, the game was already in progress. They stumbled through the bleachers almost falling, laughing all the way. Natasha spotted Darnel and yelled across the bleachers, "Hey Darnel!" He looked over in their direction then pretended not to know them. Sitting down, Natasha asked Lisa to point out Mike. Lisa looked over at the team and spotted him.

"Natasha, there he goes. He's number twenty-two."

"Mmm, not bad," Natasha said licking her lips.

Darnel and Mike seemed to be working well together. It was a close game. Darnel made a slam dunk and the crowd went wild. At half time, Lisa made her way over to Darnel. Giving him a kiss, "Good game, honey."

He smiled and asked, "Did you see that shot?"

"Yes, I saw that shot."

"Sweet wasn't it?" Lisa stood there wiping sweat off of Darnel's brow as he gulped down some Gatorade. Mike walked over and she made the introductions. She felt very uncomfortable but luckily a few seconds later the buzzer went off and Natasha and Lisa returned to their seats.

After the game, all four of them gathered in the parking lot. Natasha and Lisa waited by Darnel's truck, talking and fooling around like they did on the playground when they were young.

"Mike is cute, Lisa, but definitely not my type."

"What do you mean not your type? You can tell just by looking at him?"

"A girl knows these things. He looks bourgeois to me."

"Bourgeois?"

"Yes, bourgeois. He doesn't look down-to-earth. He looks so stiff, more like your type, Lisa. If I would have met him first, I would definitely have fixed ya'll up. I wouldn't have even thought about dating him myself."

Deeply engaged in their conversation, Natasha and Lisa don't see the guys approach them from behind. Natasha jumped almost losing her balance. "So, how are you guys doing?" Natasha said giggling like a school-girl.

"All right. My bones hurt," Mike said rubbing his shoulders. "I'm getting old." They all started laughing.

"Well, you sure don't look like it," Natasha teased. "It was a great game. I hope to see ya'll play together again. Maybe ya'll should do that hoop-it-up contest."

"That's not a bad idea," Mike said as he reached out and shook Darnel's hand. Mike left and walked over to his car.

Natasha turned to Lisa, saying, "Well, I'm going to get going. I'm having dinner with Ma and Daddy tonight. If you want to come, the invitation is still open. I'll talk to you later."

"Okay Tasha, I'll see you later. Bye."

When Lisa turned around Darnel was already in the truck on the driver's side. She opened her door and climbed in. Without a word, he pulled off immediately. Driving along the road, things are pretty quiet—unusually quiet. Lisa looked at Darnel and asked, "Baby, is something wrong?"

Darnel looked at her and said, "We'll talk about it when we get home."

"Great," she thought. She knew she must have done something really wrong for him not to want to discuss it with her right then. It meant he needed time to cool off before he said anything that he'd regret later. The first thing that came to her mind was that he'd found out that Mike had been at the house. She felt so stupid. She didn't know why she hadn't told him. But it never came up. And it was so long ago. She thought it would be better if he didn't know. Now, she knows it's not, because if he found out, the shit would hit the fan.

When they got home Darnel stormed into the house and went straight upstairs. Lisa let him past her, then closed the door behind herself. Sitting down on the couch, she knew she wasn't ready for this. Not for the questions or accusations. She jumped off the sofa and started up the stairs. Stopping at the foot of the stairs, she turned back around. She really didn't want to go up there. Maybe she should wait it out; let him come to her. Turning around, she sat back down on the sofa, wondering what was going to happen next. Lisa felt like a little kid who'd been caught stealing in a candy store.

She got up again. She had to go face him. So she slowly walked up the stairs; each step seemed to take ten minutes. It was an eternity walking up those stairs. One small flight sure felt like ninety-nine.

When she finally made it to the top, Lisa barged into the bedroom. Darnel was sitting on the bed with his back to her. Closing the door behind her, Lisa said, "Look Darnel, if you're going to start, I want you to get it over with now. I can't take this anymore. Go ahead and say what you have to say." There was silence. She went over and she sat down beside Darnel. As soon as she sat down, he jumped up. She was on a seesaw.

"Why didn't you tell me that Mike was in the house that week I was out of town?" Lisa opened her mouth to say something, but nothing would come out. He looked at her, he stared at her so hard it bore a hole right through her. He asked her again in a steady voice, "Why didn't you tell me he was at my house the week I was out of town?"

Looking him directly in the eye, Lisa said, "Darnel, I meant to tell you, but it never came up. I had planned for all four of us to get together and I didn't get a chance to tell you. You left, went out of town on that emergency business trip and I was stuck." She waited for him to say he understood. But he just stared at her, waiting for her to continue. "Darnel, Mike was out of town and I couldn't get in contact with him to cancel. But Natasha was supposed to come. So you see, it was supposed to be him, Natasha, and me. It was a fix up for Natasha. Unfortunately, Natasha had to work late. He arrived at the doorstep, and I couldn't cancel it. I felt since he had come all this way, I didn't want to turn him around and send him home. So, we ate dinner and listened to music, but that's all it was."

"If that's all it was, Lisa, why didn't you tell me about it? Why did I have to find out during basketball practice about my jazz collection? That's how I found out, Lisa. He mentioned how impressed he was by my collection. I asked him when he had seen it, and he told me it was when he had been over to the house for dinner. I knew it had to be the week that I was out of town. That's the only time that he could have come over. Do you know how embarrassed I felt? Do you know how disrespected I feel by you?"

"Look Darnel, don't get carried away; we just had dinner together. It wasn't even a planned dinner. It was by accident. I wasn't trying to hide anything from you; it just never came up. When you got back in town, there were so many other things going on. It never came up. I didn't think it was important enough to tell you."

"So, you didn't think it was important enough to tell me. But it was important enough for you to keep your mouth shut."

"I don't see why you have to put it that way, Darnel. You're making it sound like it was some kind of affair or something."

"No Lisa, you're making it seem like it was some kind of affair. You're the one keeping secrets. This is our house and I expect to know who's in it at all times. Furthermore, I don't want any men in my house with you while I'm not here. This is my house; I paid for it and expect to be treated with respect."

"Darnel, I'm sorry. I don't know why I didn't tell you. It was a small oversight. Now I know that I should have told you." Lisa lowered her eyes and continued, "It will never happen again."

"Damn right! It better not ever happen again, Lisa."

"I know, I'm real sorry Darnel." She walked over to him, reaching out to touch him, but he jerked away. Darnel left the room, slamming the door shut. Lisa stood there frozen. As she went to move, she caught a glimpse of her reflection in the mirror. She hissed at the snake and kept on moving.

Trust was very important to Darnel. Looking in that mirror once more, Lisa said to the reflection, "Lisa, you're just like your father. You look exactly like him. I bet this is the look he had on his face when Mama caught him." She turned away and closed her eyes.

***

A few days later, Darnel was still giving Lisa the silent treatment. She'd been tiptoeing around him. She knew he was still angry. Right now he couldn't stand the sight of her so he'd been staying at the office a little bit later and spending more time at his mother's house. Doing anything so that he didn't have to come home.

Lisa hated it when they fought and he would go to his mother's. It was bad enough he worshipped the ground Estelle walked on. But it only made things worse when he ran to her. As it was hers and Estelle's relationship wasn't strong. She could imagine Estelle saying, "What did that demon child do to you now?" Lisa cringed at the very thought of it. Why couldn't he just go to a bar with some of his friends, get drunk, and bitch about her. That's what she would have done. Who was the man in this relationship anyway?

***

Late one night Lisa stayed downstairs reading. When she woke up it must have been two o'clock in the morning. She decided to go to bed. When she went into the bedroom, she saw that Darnel was asleep. She sat down on her side of the bed, wanting to lie down. It felt like she didn't belong in her own bed. Darnel made her feel so unwelcome. "Darnel," she whispered. But he wouldn't say a word. He didn't want to turn around, so she placed her hand on his shoulder. He immediately pulled away. Lisa grabbed his shoulders hard and squeezed it tight. He relaxed some and let her touch him. Crawling into bed beside him, she whispered, "Darnel, I'm sorry about what happened. I'll never let it happen again. I lied to you and I was wrong. I can't stand it when you're not talking to me. It doesn't feel so great when you won't let me get next to you. I just want you to know that nothing happened with Mike. Nothing will ever happen with him. I love *you* Darnel. I just wish we could get past this. Let me make it up to you." She kissed him on his back and he just lay there. It had been awhile since they'd been together; she just wanted him to hold her. Pulling on his shoulder, she made him turn around. She looked into his eyes and could tell that she'd hurt him.

Darnel put a lot of faith in Lisa and expected a lot. Sometimes, she could be so stupid, letting little things get in the way and affect their relationship. She placed her hand on his face and rubbed his cheek gently. She kissed him softly on his lips and he let her. She kissed him again. The kisses were so sweet and gentle. Then he put his arm around her and held her close.

9

It had been three weeks since Lisa had seen Natasha. Natasha probably wasn't talking to her because Lisa hadn't shown up for the family dinner. Natasha had been avoiding her. Lisa had called her constantly. She really needed to talk to her about Darnel. Natasha just wasn't returning her calls. Finally, Lisa got a hold of her, and they agreed to meet for lunch at Lisa's office.

When Lisa came out of her office, she saw Natasha down the hall talking and laughing with Andre. It seemed as if they were having a good time. Lisa walked up to Natasha and they looked at each other without saying a word. Lisa could tell she was angry. But Lisa wasn't in the mood for it so she told Natasha that she had to be in court at one thirty and really couldn't have a long lunch.

They decided to grab a hot dog and catch up. They walked to the park and sat down on the bench. Natasha proceeded to bore Lisa with the usual small talk. She knew Lisa wanted to get to the nitty gritty. Natasha was going to make Lisa ask, make her beg for information instead of just telling her. Lisa hated her when she did that but swallowed hard and went for it anyway. "So Tasha, how was the dinner?"

"Fine."

"Just fine?"

"Well, the food was good."

"Now Tasha, you know I've been dying to find out what happened at that dinner. Why are you prolonging this? You know I don't have much time."

"Well, I feel like this, Lisa. If you would have showed up, I wouldn't have to be answering any questions. You would have seen everything for yourself."

"Look Tasha, we don't need to go through that again. I didn't want to go, so I didn't. Get over it."

"Oh, so now you want to get smart. It's not me who needs information. It's not me who wants information about Daddy. So, if I were you, I'd play nice."

Lisa bit her lip and clenched her fist, trying to play along. "Okay Natasha, I'll play nice how was your evening?"

"My evening was fine, Lisa."

"Oh Tasha, cut the shit. What happened?" Lisa asked as she leaned in closer to her sister.

"Nothing happened. Daddy looks good. He looks like he hasn't even aged."

"Must be those young women."

"Whatever."

"So how was Mama acting?"

"Oh, you know how Mama acts. She goes on and on if you let her. He pretended to be interested, but I could tell that he wasn't. But he played it off really well."

"So, did he ask about me?" Lisa sat there like a puppy panting for some affection.

"And why would he ask about you?"

"Look Tasha, you know that's what I want to know. Did he ask about me?"

"Of course he asked about you. He wanted to know how you were doing."

"What did you tell him."

"Well, I really didn't get much in, Mama did all the talking."

"What did Mama say?"

"She talked about how you took off of work last year because you had a nervous breakdown."

"I didn't have a nervous breakdown. I just took time off from work. Why does she continue to get that story wrong?" Lisa grunted.

"Well, if you were there, you could have corrected her," Tasha said smiling at her.

"Why didn't you correct her, Natasha?"

"Look, I was eating my dinner. They were talking. I was listening."

"What else did she say about me?"

"She reminded him that you were still living in sin. She even told him that Darnel wanted to make a decent woman out of you. But you keep refusing."

"Why did she have to go and tell him that?"

"Well, you know Ma, she could never think of the good things. It's the bad things she dwells on."

"So, you admit Mama dwells on the bad things."

"Well, I'm not saying all of that. Maybe she just tells him things that you need to straighten out in your life."

"What did he say?"

"He just listened and nodded his head. He asked why you weren't there."

"So, what did Mama say?"

"Mama told him to ask me."

"Did he ask you?"

"Yeah, he asked me. He asked me why you weren't there? I told him you had a prior engagement, but that you sent your love."

"Oh. What did he say then?"

"He told me to tell you to take it easy and that he'd see you the next time he's in town. Is that what you wanted to hear, Lisa?"

"No, not really. I don't know what I expected to hear. I know what I wanted to hear. Each time they get together it always surprises me what comes out about me."

"You know Dad doesn't really talk too much in front of Ma."

"Does that mean he called you afterwards?"

"Yes he called me from the hotel."

"What did he say?"

"He told me he was seeing this other woman. And that she's thirty-three."

"What?" Lisa scooted over to her.

"Yes, and he said that they have been thinking about getting married."

"Married? That's a joke. How is Ma going to take that one?"

"I don't know. I guess that's why he didn't tell her. I think he told me first to see what I thought about it."

"I can't believe he's getting married," Lisa shaking her head back and forth. "What makes him think he can make it work this time?"

"He's older and wiser, I guess."

"That's a good one."

"I don't know how Ma is going to take it. I think that somewhere in the back of her head she thinks they have a chance at a reconciliation?"

"Are you going to tell her, Tasha?"

"No. It's not my business I'm staying out of it."

"Humph," Lisa muttered.

"I know that look, Lisa. Stay out of it."

"I'll try," Lisa answered as she stood up. "I will talk to you later. I have to hurry back. Bye."

***

After her argument with Darnel, Lisa avoided Mike whenever she could. She thought it would just be better to stay away from him. Besides, she was kind of angry. She felt that he had let out information that he should have just kept his mouth shut about.

Lisa was working at the office late one evening, when Mike knocked on the door. She yelled, "Come in!"

Sticking his head through the doorway, he said, "Hi, haven't seen you in awhile." Lisa looked at him and smiled. "How are things going?" he said, casually.

"Fine. And yourself."

"Pretty well. So Lisa, is there any particular reason I haven't seen you around lately?"

"No, I've just been busy trying to catch up on some work. I've been doing a little overtime. I was in the law library doing some research and haven't had much time for socializing."

"Oh. It seemed like you were avoiding me."

"Me avoiding you, I don't think so. Why would I avoid you?"

"No reason."

"Yes, there has to be a reason. Why would you ask a question like that?"

"I haven't seen you in awhile. And usually, I see you quite often for your input. Lately it's been strictly business. I wanted to know was there a change in the way things were being done around here."

"There's no change. I told you I've been busy. I would like to ask you a question?"

"Go ahead."

"Why did you feel it was necessary to tell Darnel about the dinner at my house?"

"It came up in casual conversation. Why is there trouble in paradise?"

Lisa thought she detected a bit of enjoyment in his voice. "No, there's no trouble."

"You shouldn't keep secrets from your mate. Eventually he'll find out."

"What makes you think I keep secrets?"

"It's in your nature. I know your kind. You like to play with fire. Watching you fascinates me. I'm pretty sure you keep Darnel on his toes." He walked over to her desk and whispered in her ear, "I'll give you a secret worth keeping." She knew her face must have turned red. Her face felt flush and hot and a shiver went through her body. She had to collect herself and act as if she wasn't affected. Mike walked back around to the front of her desk.

"I'm not going to keep you. Actually, I'm going out this evening. I thought I'd try that new club Neon; it's opening on the boulevard. Someone told me it's a lot of fun and that it's usually jumping."

"You have a nice time."

"Why don't you and Darnel check it out? The drinks are on me."

He wasn't going to get her in the same room with the both of them. "Thanks for the invitation, but I think I'll pass."

"What about your sister Natasha? She seems like the type of person that would fit right in." Lisa's eyes opened wide. Oh, she thought, so now he wants to hang out with my sister. "I can tell her and see what she says. Or I'll just have her give you a call."

"Do that, have her give me a call. I'll probably be there around eleven, but I sure would like to have some company."

"I'll tell her."

"Okay. You take it easy, Lisa."

"All right, Mike. You have a good night." After he left her office, Lisa couldn't shake what he'd whispered in her ear and how it had made her feel.

She gave Natasha a call and let her know about the invitation. Natasha was more than eager to go although she had no romantic interest in Mike whatsoever. It was free drinks and she loved clubbing. Natasha thought it would be the perfect thing to do. She could get in free, mingle, and have fun. If she didn't want to be bothered, she could always pretend she was with someone. This was the perfect situation for Natasha so she thanked Lisa and told her she would tell her all about it in the morning.

10

When Lisa got home that evening Darnel was outside on the back porch, sitting in the lounge chair. She joined him saying, "Hi honey." He smiled and looked up at her. Smiling back, she went back inside of the house. She went upstairs to take a shower. It had been a long week and she was tired. Her muscles ached and she wanted to get in that shower and let all her troubles melt away.

When Lisa got out of the shower, she laid down on the bed in her robe, thinking about her father. She felt that her mother should know what was going on. Lisa had thought about it and decided if it were her, she would want to be warned, would want to have some kind of clue as to what was going on. Her mother was in the dark while her father had the upper hand. Lisa wanted to help her out, but knew helping her mother out meant that she would have to talk to her. For a good fifteen minutes, Lisa tried to dial that phone. Picking it up, dialing the numbers, then hanging up. Finally, she dialed all the numbers and let it ring. It rang twice. Just as Lisa was about to hang up, her mother picked up and said, "Hello."

"Hi Ma, this is Lisa. How are you?"

"Fine, I just came home from church not too long ago. It was a good service this evening. You know you and Darnel are always welcome to come."

"Yeah I know Ma, but that's not what I called for. I called because I wanted to talk to you about something else."

"Okay, what is it you need to talk about?"

"I talked to Tasha a few weeks ago after your dinner with Daddy. She told me something that Daddy told her that I think you should know."

"What is it, Lisa?"

"Ma, Daddy's seeing this other woman. Which I'm sure you probably already know. He told Tasha that he's thinking about remarrying." All of a sudden there was silence over the phone. "Ma, Ma, are you there? Ma?" Sandra got back on the phone with a whispery voice. Lisa knew she must have knocked the wind out of her. "Ma, are you all right?"

"Yes, I'm fine."

"Are you sure?"

"Yes I'm fine Lisa."

"So, you heard what I said Ma, right?"

"Yes, I heard what you said. Who is this woman?"

"I don't have all the details. Tasha probably has more, but I just felt that you ought to know. I didn't want you to fall apart in front of Daddy. I just wanted you to be prepared."

"Is that really why you called Lisa?"

"Yes, that's really why I called."

"You sure it wasn't for any other reason?"

"Ma, what other reason could there be?"

"You sure you didn't want to call and gloat?"

"Gloat? Ma, I'm just giving you information I thought was pertinent."

"I don't think so, Lisa. You can't pick up a telephone to call me and see how I'm doing. You can't pick up the telephone to say hello. You can't pick up a telephone to tell me what's going on in your life. But as soon as you hear something that can hurt me, you're the first one to call me. Why is that Lisa?"

"Ma, what are you talking about? I called you because I was concerned. I called you because I care, that's why I called. I just wanted you to know. I didn't want you to be caught off guard. I didn't want you to be surprised."

"I find that very hard to believe."

"You know Ma, you're unbelievable. I'm trying to help you."

"No Lisa, this is probably what you've always been waiting for. You have always been waiting for your father and I to fail. You have always wanted us to get a divorce."

"What do you mean I'm waiting? You've already failed. In case you've forgotten, you are divorced."

"You are a miserable person, and you want everybody else to be miserable too."

"Every time you hear something you don't want to hear you resort to name calling. If Tasha called, you wouldn't attack her. Tell me, why do you think *I'm* a miserable person?"

"Lisa, you've always been that way. It's just something about you. I try to love you, but you make it very hard for me to do that sometimes."

"What does love have to do with this? You know, I really shouldn't have even bothered. Believe me I will not call you again with any information."

"I think that will be just fine. I don't believe that he's with somebody else or that he wants to get married. I'll believe that when I see it."

"Well Ma, if that's what you want to do then do that."

"That's exactly what I want to do. Maybe you've got your information wrong. Your father isn't marrying anyone else."

"How can you be sure Ma?"

"I just know that."

"Ma, I'm sorry I wasted your time. I've got to go now. Bye."

Lisa couldn't believe the same old shit had happened. Instead of her mother accepting the truth, she looks for someone else to blame. It had always been Lisa and it still was. How about this? Sometimes it's hard to love her, Lisa thought to herself.

When Lisa went downstairs, Darnel was still out on the porch. She sat down on one of the beach chairs next to him. She told him what had happened and how her mother had reacted. She asked him if he could believe it? He turned to her and shook his head. She could tell he didn't want to get involved. "Well Lisa, it doesn't surprise me."

"Why doesn't it surprise you, Darnel?"

"I don't understand why it surprises you. Why did you think she was going to react any differently? To her he's still her husband. He has to tell her that he's going to marry someone else. She's not going to go by what she hears from other people. She has to see it face to face, and maybe even then she won't believe it. Maybe, when she sees the piece of paper that's when she'll finally believe it."

"Darnel that's ridiculous. I don't know why she didn't believe it when he walked out the door. What about signing the divorce papers? That should have made it real for her. I don't think he's coming back."

"You don't know that Lisa. She's still holding onto the past and she hasn't learned to let go. I think she didn't want to hear it, least of all from you. You never call her for anything else. The one time you call, you deliver her bad news. How would you have felt, Lisa?"

"I guess I would have been angry also, but I would have been thankful that she'd informed me. I hate surprises. I don't think I would have ever been in her situation. If anything was to ever go down and there was a family member who knew, I would want them to tell me. I did what I would want somebody to do for me."

"Lisa, next time before you open your mouth." She went to open it again and Darnel placed his finger on her lips. "You should think about not what you would want, but what that person would want."

"So, you're saying I'm wrong Darnel."

"I'm not saying that. I'm just saying you know her track record. You know her history. Did you really think she wanted to hear that from you."

"I guess she didn't. Next time I'll just look the other way. Forgive me for trying to be helpful. I really thought I was doing the right thing."

"Lisa, I'm sure you meant well, but…"

"But what?"

"But next time I think you should just stay out of it."

"You're absolutely right. Next time I will."

11

The next morning Tasha called Lisa. She sounded excited. She told her she'd met this wonderful guy. Lisa wasn't really interested this was just another guy she will forget about next week; Lord knows Natasha goes through men like an elephant goes through peanuts.

"Who's the new guy? How does he look?"

"Well, he's light skinned, kind of stocky, but well built. You know it's all solid, and he has hazel eyes and a Caesar hair cut."

"Well that sounds just like your type, Tasha. Light guys with light eyes."

"Sure does sound like my type. Mmm, he was fine."

"What did you think about Mike?"

"Mike was annoying?"

"Annoying? What do you mean?"

"Would you believe he talked about you constantly all night." Lisa had to stop what she was doing and give Natasha all her attention.

"Me? What did he talk about me for?" she pretended indifference.

"Yeah, that was my question. What was he talking about you for?"

"You didn't have to put it like that, Tasha."

"All right, he was drilling me for information."

"What kind of information?"

"Like how long you and Darnel have been together. Are ya'll serious? Is this permanent?"

"I know he didn't ask you those things about me, Tasha."

"Yes he did. He tried to be real sly about it. You know with that lawyer technique, but ya'll lawyers can't put that pass me."

"Oh really?"

"Yes really."

"So what did you tell him?"

"Well, you know I was really vague about it. I was trying not to get an attitude. I just didn't understand why he was asking about you. He knows you have a man. He met your man and that should have been the end of it."

"Girl, I'm shocked, I can't believe that."

"Well, it's the truth. He asked about you all night long."

"Um... I wonder what that's about."

"What do you mean you wonder what that's about. Lisa, you know what it's about."

"No, Tasha I can't be sure about that. He doesn't show any kind of interest towards me. Everything is strictly professional," She said lying through her teeth.

"Well, he doesn't want it to be professional anymore," Tasha said.

"I don't know. I'm just not sure."

"Oh Lisa, wake up and smell the coffee. That man is interested in you. I'm telling you—you better watch out. He's smooth. He wasn't asking those things because he's writing your biography. He wants to know for himself. I could tell by the way he was looking at me."

"Tasha, you're exaggerating."

"I have this feeling, Lisa. I mean the vibes just weren't good."

"You and your vibes."

"Look, my vibes are never wrong. I'm telling you he's no good and he's up to something."

"Tasha, your vibes have been wrong plenty of times. Look at all the men you've been out with. Losers! And you're going to tell me to trust your vibes."

"My vibes don't work for me, but they work for other people. Listen to me, I'm not going to tell you nothing wrong. That man is up to something, and he doesn't want to be your friend anymore. So you better cut all that late night stuff out. You better keep your eyes open. Just watch yourself. You know you're weak sometimes."

"Weak how?"

"Lisa, now you know you've been in relationships before and you weren't too straight with those men."

"Yes, I've been in other relationships, but those men weren't too straight with me. Why did I have to devote myself to them when that's not what they were doing to me. They tried to play me so I played them. I'm a big girl and I knew how to play the game better than they thought I did. I learned from a pro, Tasha. They can't teach me what Daddy taught me years ago."

"Yeah you say that, but you know you—you can always slip back into that."

"I can't believe you're even going there. You know how I feel about Darnel. I wouldn't do that to him. I love him and I have too much respect for him."

"I believe you love Darnel and I believe you wouldn't want to disrespect him. But I'm just saying you need to watch Mike and you need to watch yourself. I know you Lisa; we've been tight all our lives and you have done some shady things. You know you have been low down and dirty. All I'm saying is don't mess up this good thing with Darnel for no self-centered brother like Mike."

"Tasha that was years ago. I was younger then. I was in college, but I'm grown now. There is no way I will let anything interfere with something as good as I have with Darnel."

"I hear you, Lisa, and I know you. All I'm saying is to be careful. If you need to talk let me know."

"All right."

"If he tries something you let me know. Because I've got a little sumthin' sumthin' for him."

What Natasha had to say was pretty interesting, but Lisa still couldn't believe Mike might be interested in taking their friendship a little bit further. However, Lisa was flattered. Mike is a very attractive man and they have a lot in common. If she were single, she wouldn't even hesitate or think twice about dating him. However, she's with somebody now, and she doesn't want to do anything to jeopardize that. She'll have to leave it alone. Lisa had to admit she couldn't help but to blush when Tasha told her about it. Now Mike looked a little bit sexier.

12

The weekend of Darnel's mother's party arrived. She'd been planning it for months Darnel had been reminding Lisa every night. All Lisa really wanted to do was relax on the weekend. She tried to think of every excuse to get out of going. There was bound to be a big argument because Darnel had given her plenty of notice. Whenever his family throws these big parties, he always has to be right smack dab in the middle. He feels that it is very important that Lisa be at his side at all times. He wouldn't feel complete if she didn't show up.

Darnel had been in a wonderful mood all week and it was so annoying to Lisa. She felt like stabbing him in his head. She knew she should be happy because he was happy, but she also felt like there was going to be a lot of pressure like Estelle's always asking them when they're going to get married. And then, Darnel's brothers and sisters were always asking when they're going to have kids. It stressed her out because Darnel was ready for those things. Every time Darnel comes home he nags her about getting married and how he wants to be a father. Lisa doesn't think she's ready now; she doesn't want the responsibility of raising a child.

When Lisa and Darnel arrived at Estelle's house, they heard some Marvin Gaye playing in the background. The kids were running around. Lisa thought, "I swear if one of them steps on my toe today, I'll trip 'em then fade into the background." Darnel's sisters and sisters-in-law were in the kitchen preparing food. Lisa and Darnel had hardly gotten through the doorway before Darnel ditched her and headed straight for his brothers, who were in the living room. The table was already set up and dominoes had begun. Darnel's father was at the table with some other older gentlemen. His brothers were standing around and she heard the slamming. Lisa knew right then and there that it was on.

Lisa lingered around the doorway for a few minutes and then went in the kitchen to give Estelle a kiss. Estelle looked at Lisa and said, "Child, it looks like you lost some weight. I'm going to change all that today I have a little something for everybody. Don't be shy when it's ready fix as much as you want."

Lisa offered to help, but Estelle wouldn't let her. She wouldn't hear of it. So Lisa walked around to the back of the house where some of Darnel's sisters were sitting down. The men in one room, the women in another. She hated that she had to fall in line with their stupid tradition. She would have rather sat down for a mean game of dominoes, and left the chit chat to the other ladies. Some of the women were talking about their jobs, telling workplace horror stories. Meanwhile they were secretly checking out each others hair, nails, and clothing. New pieces of jewelry were prominently displayed for viewing. She really wanted to get out of there; Lisa just wasn't in the mood for the same old stories. How many times had she heard them? Instead, she sat back in the rocking chair and began to drift away.

Lisa rocked away until it was time for dinner. After awhile they said the prayer, then everybody started eating. The food was delicious. Lisa watched Darnel; she liked to see him enjoying himself. And that is exactly what he was doing. There were eight children in Darnel's family, he was next to the last. Their closeness seemed suffocating to Lisa. Whatever happened to leaving the nest? Lisa couldn't wait to leave her home. As soon as she turned eighteen she was off to school and hasn't turned back since. Darnel grounded Lisa, and Lisa brought excitement to his life. She hoped that their differences one day wouldn't tear them apart.

After dinner they are gathered in the family room. Uncle Isaac kept busy making drinks for everybody, keeping their glasses filled. From the corner of her eye, Lisa was checking out the game on TV. The Orlando Magic was playing the Bulls. She really got into the game. "Thank god, the game is on," she thought. Everybody else was busy talking and catching up.

All of a sudden Darnel said he had an important announcement to make and it got quiet. One of his cousins cut the TV off and called everyone into the room to come listen to Darnel. Standing in the middle of the floor, Darnel said, "I am the happiest man on this earth and I'm in love. I'm truly in love. I'm with the person I want to be with. The person I want to spend the rest of my life with. I'm getting down on one knee." In the background there were oohs and ahs. Lisa stared at him and thought, "He's not doing this." Darnel got down on one knee and solemnly looked into Lisa's eyes and said, "Lisa Munroe, I love you. You are the most important thing in my life. I want to spend the rest of my life with you. You are my woman and I want to be your man forever. What I'm trying to say is will you marry me?" Everybody started screaming and yelling as he pulled out a little black box and opened it. Stunned Lisa looked down at the ring he was holding. It was the most beautiful ring she'd ever seen. She looked at Darnel. His mother and sisters were looking directly at her. Everyone was watching her as she sat there with her mouth opened, totally surprised, not knowing how to react. Darnel held her hand and asked, "Will you, baby?"

Lisa's hand went to her throat. She felt flushed. Finally, she replied, "Yes." Getting up, Darnel lifted Lisa out of her chair and swung her around, kissing her. All his brothers congratulated him, while his sisters congratulated her. Darnel's mother came over and gave Lisa a kiss and told her that she was very happy for them then, all of a sudden out came a big cake. It read, "Congratulations Lisa and Darnel on your engagement." Someone cut the cake and they passed it out, everyone talking and laughing at once. All this time, Darnel couldn't take his eyes off of Lisa. He kept smiling, as he held her hand. He wouldn't let her go for the rest of the evening.

On the way home Darnel held Lisa's hand as she sat beside him. He turned to her and said, "Lisa, I love you and I really do want to spend the rest of my life with you. I'll never do anything to hurt you. I will do anything for you and you can count on me.

You will always be able to trust me. My love will be here for you." She looked at him and smiled. Kissing him on the cheek, she laid her head on his shoulder. He wrapped his arm around her. And they rode the rest of the way home.

13

Darnel's proposal had left Lisa dazed and confused. She didn't know if she truly meant yes, or did she react the way his gawking family wanted her to. She was down in the cafeteria having some lunch, sitting by herself and going over some paperwork when Mike walked up.

"Is that seat taken?"

"No, help yourself."

"So how is your day so far?"

"Fine," she said without looking up and continued to do what she was doing. When she did glance up, she caught him staring at her. She followed his eyes and saw he was staring at her engagement ring. Self-consciously, she pulled her hand off the table and put it under the table. "Is there something I should know?" he asked.

"No, not particularly. Why? Is there something I should be telling you Mike?"

"I noticed the ring. Is it what I think it is?"

"Yes, it is."

"Well, congratulations."

"Thank you, but I'm pretty sure you already knew that I was engaged."

"Why would I know that Lisa?"

"Well, I'm pretty sure it's already gotten around the office. Especially being that Andre knows."

"You could say that I did hear about it; however, I didn't believe it. But I guess it's true. I didn't believe it because I just don't see you as the marrying kind."

"Well, what type do you see me as?"

"An independent woman who wants a lot out of life. Who wants a career and has a long-term goal. I just figured that marriage would not be a part of your life until you reached that goal."

"That's presumptuous of you don't you think?"

"That's just the type of signal you give off."

"You're partially right. My career is very important to me. I do have a lot of things I want to do. I have set many goals. Damn!" she snapped as she slammed her hand down on the table. "There are so many things I haven't done yet."

"Calm down. It's not the end of the world."

"Don't get me wrong—Darnel wouldn't stop me, but with marriage come many responsibilities."

"So are you ready for this, Lisa?"

"Well to be quite honest—no I'm not. I'm a little scared."

"What's there to be scared about?"

"There's a lot to be scared about—marriage the big 'M' word. I just don't know. There's so much responsibility, so much commitment. Working things out, sticking together. Marriage is forever. It feels like a death sentence. That's wrong; let me take that back. I wouldn't say a death sentence, but it makes me feel claustrophobic."

"Lisa, you have plenty of time. You can make it a long engagement."

"Yes, I guess I could. But at this point, a long engagement seems kind of stupid since we've already been together for a couple of years."

"So, if you don't want to get married, why did you say yes?"

"I said yes for a number of reasons. I said yes because I love Darnel and he's been asking me for awhile. I said yes because I felt like I was on the spot and all his family was watching me. All eyes were on me. And then he wanted it badly and I didn't want to disappoint him. I love Darnel that much. I also said yes for fear of losing him. Maybe it would have been the last time he'd ask me. So, I just went ahead and said yes." An awkward silence followed. "I don't know why I'm telling you these things, Mike," Lisa said, confused by her confession.

Mike stretched out his hand and took her hand in his. "You know, if you need to talk you know where to find me. Sometimes an objective viewpoint helps. I have something I have to take care of. If you need me you can reach me on my cell phone." Reaching inside the pocket of his jacket, he scribbled a number on his card and handed it to her. "Call me," he said as he rushed off. Lisa held the card in her hand, looking it over carefully. She thought maybe she would call him.

***

Tasha had been acting more like it was she who was getting married not Lisa. She really gets into things like this. Everyday she called about some other idea she'd come up with. Lisa tried to sound enthusiastic, but sometimes it was hard. Of all people, she thought, Tasha should realize that I'm not that excited. Lisa felt like the only one who understood her was Mike. She couldn't really talk to Darnel because she knew his feelings would be hurt. She'd expressed to him before what her feelings were on marriage. Told him that a man would have to truly prove himself to her before she'd ever say I do. She knew Darnel felt like he had and that she should be ready now. But she wasn't or maybe she just didn't want to be.

One day Darnel was showing Lisa some baby pictures and hinting that he was ready for a family. The thought of it made her want to throw up. She was worried because he was ready to set a date for the wedding. His mother had begun to pressure them. Lisa tried to stay clear of Estelle. She wished she would stay out of their business. But with her luck Lisa figured she'd probably get just the opposite.

14

Darnel sidled up to Lisa, "Lisa my mother called. She had a few suggestions about the wedding. She told me to tell you to give her a call when you can."

"All right, Darnel." Lisa had no intention of calling her. She wasn't going to let his mother rush her into making any decisions.

"I know that she spoke to one of the young ladies in the choir at her church and she agreed to sing," Darnel said.

"What?"

"I said there's this young lady—Lisa are you paying attention to me?"

"Yes, of course."

"Then what did I just say."

"Okay, so I wasn't paying attention. Now, what were you saying?"

"Nothing. It seems like you've been in another world lately. Every time I bring up the wedding you act so distant. What's going on?"

"I'm just tired of there always being some message from your mother about the wedding when I get home. She's getting on my nerves."

Darnel's nose scrunched up and he rubbed his forehead. That's what he usually did when Lisa said or did something he didn't like. "Lisa, she's just excited about it. All she is doing is making suggestions. If you don't like them, you don't have to do them. It's your wedding not hers."

"Well then, why don't you tell her that?" she challenged Darnel. He turned away from her. "See what I mean. Why can't you tell her that Darnel? Every time I ask you to ask her to stay out of things you get quiet. I understand you have the utmost respect for her, but this is my life. I don't see how asking her to back off can be disrespectful." Lisa stood looking at him, but Darnel didn't say a thing. Finally, totally exasperated, she threw up her arms and headed for the bedroom.

"Lisa, this has nothing to do with my mother. You're creating excuses so that you don't have to get things done."

"Shit Darnel, this is about her. I'm not marrying her. I can't stand you comparing me to her. You think if I spend more time with her some of her qualities will rub off on me."

"Don't start that again. No one's comparing you to her. She offered her help and that's it."

"Oh? And I'm not capable of taking care of this myself."

"You know what, Lisa, I'll call her and tell her you don't need her help."

"I dare you!" She ran over to him getting real close as if she were a child egging him on. She stood right next to him. The look on her face said, "I'm waiting."

"I'll do it!" Darnel yelled.

"Do it!" she insisted. But Darnel didn't move. "Yeah, just what I thought," Lisa jibed, then started to go upstairs. Grabbing his keys, Darnel stormed out of the house. You would think that with all the drama he would get the hint.

***

"Andre, these are the wrong files. I asked for the Redman files. What is wrong with you?"

"Nothing is wrong with me. I'm human for one thing and I do make mistakes."

"Look Andre, I'm not in the mood for your smart remarks today. Just get me the right files and leave out the commentary."

"I wonder what bug is stuck up your ass?"

"Excuse me?"

"You heard me. I don't have to be treated like this every time you can't handle your problems at home."

"Look Andre, you don't know what the hell you are talking about. Stop acting like a little bitch and get the files."

"Oh no, you did not go there." He went over to the door and slammed it shut. "What the hell is wrong with you, Lisa? I know you did not call me a bitch. When everyone around here knows you are the queen bee. Bitch?" he said almost choking on the word. "I can't believe you. You're acting like those other assholes I have to deal with all day. I thought at least that when I was in your company that I was amongst friends. I'm hurt."

"Andre please, I'm having a bad day. I don't need your melodrama. Stop being such a crybaby. I don't have a shoulder for you today. All I want are the files. Understand?"

"Okay so now I'm stupid? Why are you talking to me like this?"

Lisa hated it when he whined. "Andre the files! Just the files! Now!" He turned around and walked out of her office, leaving the door wide open. Mike walked in right after him.

"What's going on in here? Everyone in the building can hear you."

"I don't know what the hell is going on with him? I just don't have the patience to deal with him right now."

"What's going on?"

"A hell of a lot, but I don't feel like discussing it right now."

"It must have to do with your wedding. I'm just guessing, but I think I'm pretty close. Am I?"

"You've got it, but I still don't feel like talking about it right now" she replied walking towards him, pushing him out of the door.

"Well, when you're ready you know where to find me."

While closing the door in his face she said, "Thanks, I'll do that."

When Lisa got home Darnel wasn't there. She looked around and found a note saying there was a family emergency and that he would call as soon as he could. Her heart dropped; she prayed it was just a false alarm and that everything was okay. She tried calling Estelle, but her line was busy. Her mind was working overtime, and every bad thought she could think of was running through it. After making herself a drink, she turned on the television to see if, possibly, this emergency was national news. Lisa knew she was being paranoid, but she'd been that way since she was a child. If she were calm, it just wouldn't be her. She watched television, making refills when necessary. After making herself a little something to eat, she went upstairs and took a shower. She phoned Estelle one more time, but the line was still busy. She took out some work from the office, determined to stay up until Darnel got home. She knew she'd had too many drinks because she couldn't read what was in front of her. Deciding to lie down and rest her head, Lisa turned on the TV to music videos to help her stay awake.

"Lisa, wake up honey." She felt someone nudge her in the back.

"Huh?"

"Lisa, I need to talk to you. Why is this TV up so loud?" Darnel reached over and turned it off. "Lisa wake up."

"Okay, okay, I'm awake," Lisa mumbled, rubbing her eyes and checking to see if she was drooling. "Oh, it's you. I've been waiting up for you. I must have dozed off for a little while. Where have you been? What happened? Is everything okay?"

"Slow down. Let me tell you what happened. But first, let me get some water out of the bathroom." Lisa sat up with her back against the headboard. When Darnel came back he sat down on the bed. "Okay, I'm going to make this short. I know you have to get up in the morning and that it's late now. We can talk about the rest tomorrow."

"Darnel, will you quit stalling and just spit it out."

"Last night Theresa was admitted to the hospital."

"Who is Theresa?" Lisa asked puzzled.

"David's ex-girlfriend."

"Your brother David? Oh, I remember her, now."

"Yes, apparently she was beaten up badly. They say that it's drug related."

"What? I thought you told me she was clean."

“Apparently not, social services came to the hospital to pick up her child.”

“She has a child?”

“When social services got to the hospital, the boy said he didn’t want to go back into foster care. The social worker told him he didn’t have any family and that he had no other alternative. The boy freaked out and started yelling that he wasn’t going back. He locked himself in a closet until one of the nurses on duty talked him out. She promised him that he could go anywhere he wanted. All he had to do was make a phone call and have someone pick him up. Anyway, when the boy came out of the closet, the nurse asked him who he was going to call. He said his grandmother. The social worker said the boy’s file said his grandmother was dead. The boy insisted he had another grandmother. When the social worker said her file didn’t indicate he had any other family, the nurse asked him where was the Grandmother’s number? He pulled it out of his jacket pocket and the nurse let him dial the number. It was my mother’s number. He asked to speak to Ms. Estelle? My mother replied, “Speaking,” and he started crying and saying that she was his grandmother and he didn’t want to go back to foster care and please don’t let them take him. He kept saying, “Help me, help me.” My mother didn’t know what to make of it so she asked him to put an adult on the phone. The social worker explained the situation and told my mother that the boy’s mother’s name was Theresa Graves. My mother nearly had a heart attack. She realized this boy must be David’s son. She called me and we went up to the hospital. After my mother spoke with the social worker, they agreed to let her take him home. From what the boy told us it’s very likely that David is his father.”

“This must have come as a complete shock to all of you. Especially your mother. How is she doing now?”

“Actually, she’s doing pretty well. When we got to the hospital she knew right away that the boy was David’s son. He looks just like him. She’s been staring at him all evening and she’s been on the phone calling everyone to let them know.”

"No wonder I couldn't get through. So how do you feel Darnel? What's been going through your head?"

"It's been a mixture of emotions. I'm just real tired and I have to think about a lot of things right now."

"Well go ahead and take a shower; we'll talk about it in the morning."

"Okay." Lisa watched him walk into the bathroom then she laid her head down on the pillow. Who would have thought this? Life sure is a funny thing.

In the morning when Lisa got up, Darnel was already in the kitchen cooking breakfast. She thought, he must be in a good mood. For some reason, the news last night made him feel good. When she got close to the kitchen, she could hear him humming. Darnel turned around a little startled when she came in. "I didn't know you were up yet? I was just on my way up with the breakfast tray."

"That's okay, I'll eat it at the table. I really appreciate it."

"It's a beautiful morning isn't it?"

She looked at him skeptically. "I don't know yet, Darnel, but I am sure waiting to find out. What's making this such a glorious morning for you?"

He walked over and gave her a kiss on her forehead. "I have something very important I want to talk to you about."

"Go ahead." She braced herself because her stomach dropped and that wasn't a good sign.

"Well, I'm not sure what's going to happen with Jason, but I want to take care of him."

"Take care of him? He has a mother Darnel. Are you planning to take him from his mother?"

"I'm not planning anything. The state has already stepped in. He needs a place to stay for now. My mother wouldn't have any problem doing it, but she's getting old, Lisa. They've raised eight kids. They're tired, they need time to be with each other. This is a hard time to be raising kids and they don't have the energy. My other brothers and sisters have families and are trying to make it with their own. I'm the only one who doesn't have any kids, and I have the means to support him."

"Okay Darnel, you're just running on. When did you have time to think about this?"

"I thought about it all last night. I couldn't even sleep, I was thinking about it so much."

"Darnel, I know you have thought about Theresa right? She's his mother and she might not want him to be here. I'm sure she doesn't want to give him up at all. Don't you think there is a reason your family didn't know about him? She could have had all the financial help she wanted. He could have been with a family that cared about him. It's obvious that she didn't want your family to know. If you'd found out about her lifestyle maybe you would have wanted to take him out of her home sooner. She's been hiding him from you. Can't you see that? It's not going to be as easy as you think." Darnel looked so hurt. "Look baby, I'm not telling you this to burst your bubble. But you have to be prepared for what might happen."

"I'm prepared, Lisa. This is David's boy and I can't walk away from him. I have to do everything to help him. My brother would have wanted me to look after him. He would have wanted all of us in his son's life. The saddest part is that David didn't even get to know him. He didn't even know about him." She could see his eyes gloss over. She knew the kind of bond he had with David. That look in his eye told her how much he was hurting. She wanted to cry for him.

"What I really want to do is choke Theresa. How could she have put that boy through what he's been through? He's been around drugs. He's been in foster homes. I have to do something, Lisa. He's my brother's son. All I want to know is if he can stay here. Is it all right with you? I want him to stay with us until his mother gets her life together."

"That's no problem. In fact, today I'll make a few calls to a friend of mine in family court to see what I can do to help."

"I knew I could count on you. I knew you would understand."

Lisa really had a lot to think about. All of this was happening pretty fast. She didn't have a chance to decide whether or not she could deal with this. She just had to react. She thought what Darnel was doing was great. But she knew he hadn't thought it through, which was typical of him. She wouldn't expect him to do anything differently. If he did then he wouldn't be the Darnel that she knew.

15

"Thank you very much. I owe you one, Ida."

"You're more than welcome, Lisa. I really appreciated what you did for my cousin last year. It really has made him change his life around. Any other prosecutor wouldn't have worked with me like you did. My mother's sister asks about you all the time."

"Ida, I was happy to help. It's rare that a case ends up with a happy ending. I'm glad he stuck to the program and received some help. You know we have to stick together. We don't need any more of our brothers in prison."

"Well, I'm glad I could return the favor. Tell Darnel I wish him luck. You know we need more men like him."

"So true. Thanks again. I'll be talking to you soon."

"All right take care."

Later in the day as things were winding down Lisa heard a knock at the door. "Come in!" she yelled.

Mike popped his head through the door and asked, "Are you busy?"

"Thank God I'm not. I'm just about finished. It's been a long week. What can I do for you?"

"It's more like what I can do for you." Lisa raised her eyebrows. "There's this fundraiser dinner they're having tonight. I know it's short notice, but my cousin was supposed to attend. Due to some unforeseen events he won't be able to. He asked me to fill in. The problem is it's such short notice. I can't get a date. So I need an escort."

"You can't get a date; that's hard to believe."

"Well, you know women need preparation."

Laughing Lisa asked, "So what am I?"

"You know what I mean. Free food, champagne and dancing. How could you resist?"

"That sounds good, but there's a lot going on at home right now. I think I need to be there."

"Is there anything wrong?"

"No, nothing like that, but it's important."

"I guess I have to go stag then." Mike lowered his head and tried to give her this pitiful look.

"That face isn't working."

Lifting his head, he flashed back that beautiful smile. "Well, I tried. If you change your mind give me call."

"I won't be changing my mind, but have a good time for the both of us."

"I'll do that; I guess I'll see you Monday morning."

"Okay, have a nice weekend.

"You too."

***

When Lisa walked through the front door of her home, she overheard Darnel on the phone. "Okay Ma, I'll be over in a little while." Putting down the receiver, he turned around, startled. "Lisa, I didn't hear you come in. How was your day?"

Lisa placed her briefcase in the crack between the sofa and the coffee table. "It was all right and yours?"

"Typical day at the office. Besides, other things had me preoccupied. My mother told me you called her from work. She really appreciates what you did." Darnel walked over and lifted her off the floor, planting kisses all over her face.

"Okay Darnel, put me down." Lowering her to the floor, he kissed her neck. "Not now Darnel, we need to talk." He began to nibble on her ear—her one weakness and he knows it. Losing herself for a minute, Lisa pulled away, saying, "No Darnel, I'm serious; we need to talk." She backed away and sat down on the couch.

Reluctantly, Darnel followed her and sat on the opposite couch. "What's this all about, Lisa?"

"It's about Jason coming to live with us." Leaning forward Darnel motioned for her to continue. "I think it needs to be discussed further."

"There must be something you want to add, because I thought we'd all ready decided."

"No, you decided. I understand what you want to do, Darnel. But we are a young couple. I don't know if I'm ready to be responsible for a ten-year-old. There's more to it than him just living with us. We both have hectic schedules. Sacrifices will have to be made."

"Lisa, we'll get all the help we need from the rest of my family. And if it's time your worried about, I'll have to bring some of my work home. Believe me he won't disrupt our lives."

"Darnel, it's not that simple. Being a parent is hard work. There's homework, taking care of him. He'll need some of our time. I don't want him to feel like a boarder."

"Lisa, stop worrying about it. Are you scared? I'm sure you will both get along great. You're just a big kid yourself."

"See, there you said it, I'm a kid myself. I can't take care of a child right now. I'm not ready. Why don't you let one of your brothers or sisters take him in? They have kids; he'll be with his cousins. They're already raising kids, so why couldn't they take another one."

"Lisa, my brothers and sisters would take him in a minute. This is something *I* want to do. David and I were close. It only seems natural that his son should be with me."

"Darnel, what do you know about raising kids?"

"I'll learn."

Lisa kept shifting in her seat. "Darnel, are you hearing anything I'm saying?"

"Yes, I hear you. I also hear fear in your voice. There's nothing to be scared of. We can handle this."

"No, Darnel, you can handle this. You can't speak for me. What do I know about raising kids? Absolutely nothing. I never babysat. Tasha is not that much younger than I am. It's not like an animal. We can't give it back if things don't work out. This is insane!"

"What are you getting so worked up about? Calm down."

"No, I'm not going to calm down. I won't be responsible for another human being. I see it in the courts every day. Parenting is a big responsibility. That's one thing I don't take lightly. There's a reason I don't have any kids now. You need two people who are willing to give it their all and stick to it no matter what. We only have one person who fits that description. I don't know if I can make that kind of commitment. And I'm not sure I want to."

Darnel leaned back on the sofa and stared up at the ceiling. They sat in silence. Finally, Darnel asked, "Lisa is that how you really feel?"

"I'm afraid it is."

"I don't know what to do or say to make it better for you." Lisa looked at him hoping he had come to his senses. "Jason is moving in here."

Her jaw dropped. She couldn't believe the words that were coming out of his mouth. Slowly getting off the couch, she walked around the coffee table and sat right in front of him. "Darnel, you mean to tell me you're going to do this no matter what I say?" Her eyes were pleading with him to tell her that her opinion mattered.

"Yes. I didn't want it to be this way. I wish it would have turned out differently. But this is something I feel strongly about. There's nothing that's going to change my mind."

Laughing, she said, "You're serious aren't you?"

"As serious as I've ever been." Darnel stood up in front of her. "Lisa my mother is expecting me. I promised her I would do a few things for her." Lisa didn't respond. Grabbing his keys from the key rack, he walked out the front door. Lisa remained still, unable to move, replaying what had occurred over and over. What she said didn't matter. She finally managed to compose herself and walked over to the bar. She poured some vodka straight up. Lifting the glass, she drank it in one shot. It burned all the way down. She shook it off and headed for her bedroom.

Lisa sat on the edge of the tub as the water ran out of the faucet. At the same time, the tears ran down her face. She poured in the lavender bubble bath. Turning the cold water off first, she let more hot in. She let her robe drop and put one foot in the water. The sting of the hot water made her jump. She didn't care, the quicker she got in the sooner it would be over. She lifted her other foot in and sat down immediately. The bubbles rose and tickled the tip of her nose. She held her knees to her chest for a few minutes, then slid back and down until only her head was above water.

Lisa spent twenty minutes in the bathtub, running more hot water every so often. She tried to empty her head of all thoughts of Darnel. But the more she thought about it, the angrier she felt. After all this time together, his talk of trust. What a bunch of bull. This was the first time her opinion was vital to the situation; but it didn't count. Letting the water run out of the tub, she proceeded to dry off with the towel marked his. The cool air from the bedroom felt so nice. She strolled over to the bed and sat on the edge. She wanted a piece of chocolate. Chocolate always seemed to soothe her. She reached over and grabbed her purse, looking for some chocolate, and in the process, a card fell out. It was the card Mike had given her. She remembered he'd told her she could call and talk to him anytime she wanted to. Maybe he didn't have a date yet and she could be his escort. There's no harm in that, she thought. She needed to get out of the house and get this off her mind. Darnel's evening wasn't going to be spoiled so why should hers. The more Lisa thought about it, the more determined she was to have fun no matter what. At any cost.

Lisa reached for the phone on her night table and dialed Mike's number. Letting it ring twice, she figured he must have already left. She was about to hang up.

"Hello," Mike said in a hurried voice.

"Hello, this is Lisa, may I speak to Mike?"

"Speaking. It's good to hear your voice. What mischief are you thinking of getting yourself into?"

"Mischief? Me, never. However, I wanted to know if that invitation was still open? I've had a sudden change of plans and would love to get out of the house," Lisa spat out rather quickly. She felt the faster she said it, he would give her the answer she wanted.

"As a matter of fact, Lisa, I wasn't able to get anyone to go with me. You are really doing me a huge favor. I sure didn't want to go stag. I was going to leave in about an hour. So I'll be at your house then."

"No!" she shouted. "Excuse me, I mean no. How about if we meet at the dinner? If you will just give me the address."

"No, problem. If that's what you want."

"It'll just be easier for me.

"Okay then."

When Lisa hung up, she scrambled to find something to wear. She knew she had to have something lying around that was new. Jumping off the bed, she ran to the closet. Standing there naked, she caught a glimpse of herself in the mirror. She had a beautiful body and wanted something that would show it off. "The black dress," she said out loud, "yes, that is it." It wasn't new, but it would accomplish what she wanted. Now she wondered what to do with her hair. Luckily, it was still in half-way decent shape. Her hair had already begun to curl from the steam of her bath, she knew her options were limited unless she decided to blow dry it. She decided she would sweep it up into a bun and let a strand cascade down the side of her face. "Find some jewelry and pantyhose," she thought, "and I'm good to go."

***

"Hi Erica, I'm glad I caught you."

"You're lucky Mike, I was on my way out the door."

"I have a little bit of bad news. I'm not going to be able to take you to the banquet tonight."

"Oh Mike, I was so looking forward to it. I've been running around all day like a chicken with its head cut off."

"I'm sorry to do this to you dear, but something's come up."

"I hope it's nothing with the family."

"No, no nothing like that, but it's urgent. I'm so upset that I can't put this on hold. I was looking forward to tonight. I will make this up to you I promise. Can you ever forgive me?"

"It depends on what's your idea of making this up to me," she pouted.

"Don't worry, you won't be disappointed. Again my apologies, I'll talk to you later."

"All right, I hope things work out."

"Thanks," he said, with a smile in his voice.

16

When Lisa pulled into the parking lot of the hotel, she could see Mike in front waiting for her. As she walked up the elegantly lit stairs toward the entrance, she saw his face light up in recognition. He was wearing a tuxedo, custom-tailored to enhance his physique. She noticed that he'd cut his hair into a close fade. With his goatee and diamond studded earring, he looked good. Walking up to her, he kissed her on the cheek and whispered in her ear, "You look beautiful."

"Thank you." Lisa replied. Mike put his hand around her waist and escorted her into the building. There were a few familiar faces and several actors and actresses, not to mention well-known politicians. The ballroom had at least a hundred chandeliers hanging from the ceiling. A long table with a podium in the middle reached across the top of the room. Above the table hung a banner saying, "Welcome Republicans." In the middle of the room was a huge dance floor, surrounded by oval-shaped tables. While Lisa was soaking all of it in, Mike mingled. She saw a whole new side to him; he had people eating out of his hands, hanging on his every word.

"I'm sorry I didn't involve you in the conversation more," he said when he returned to her side.

"No you're not. You know you want all of the attention." He smiled. With the next group of people they approached, Lisa took full charge of the conversation. She glanced at Mike from the corner of her eye. And he stood there in amazement. As she continued to speak, she thought to herself, anything you can do I can do better. They shook hands all around, and excused themselves, and moved on.

Mike moved closer to her and whispered, "I didn't know you were so charismatic."

"There's a lot of things you don't know about me. Don't judge a book by its cover."

"When does the competition end for you Lisa?"

"It doesn't." Taking her hand, Mike led her to the table. As they approached their table, a photographer stopped them. Mike assumed the position and pulled Lisa by his side. And the picture was snapped. As the photographer walked away, Lisa thought she didn't want anyone to know she was here with Mike. There was no telling where that picture could end up. Turning to Mike, she said, "Look I need you to get those negatives."

"Why?"

"I don't have time to explain. There he is going towards the elevator. Will you please do this for me?"

"All right, I'll be right back," hurrying after the photographer.

When she found the table with the card marked with his cousin's name, Lisa took a seat. After several minutes Mike returned. Showing her the negatives, he said, "I've got them."

"Thank you," she said, breathing a sigh of relief.

"Would you like some champagne?"

"I don't see why not?" Mike motioned for a server to come to the table and requested a bottle of champagne for the table. Sitting back, he put his arm around her chair. It made her uncomfortable at first, but she became engrossed in the stories he was telling. After a while their dinner was served. They both appeared to enjoy their dinner and each other's company.

After most people had finished eating, the speeches began. Lisa was restless and Mike could tell because he was restless too. He told her to go out to the courtyard and he would follow. Rising as quietly as she could, Lisa excused herself and headed straight for the courtyard. A few minutes later Mike entered with two glasses and a bottle of champagne. "Have I told you that you look exquisite?"

"Yes, you may have mentioned it once or twice."

"This suits you, Lisa. You look at home, approachable and desirable."

Batting her eyelashes, she said, "I don't know whether to take that as a compliment or a complaint. Aren't you going to be missed inside?"

"No, as long as the check reaches the right hands I'll be all right." He handed her one of the glasses and popped the cork. As the champagne spilled over the sides of his hand, he put the bottle up to his mouth and licked it. Then he put it up to hers and she did the same. The champagne bubbles tickled her nose. When she wiped her nose, Mike reached into his pocket and pulled out a handkerchief to wipe away the champagne that was on her chin. After he'd finished, his hands lingered there for a moment. Lisa pulled away and sat down on a nearby bench. Following her, Mike apologized, "I'm sorry I didn't mean to..."

"It's all right. You haven't done anything." Sitting down beside her, Mike asked, "There's something wrong I can tell. Did I offend you?"

"No, my mind is just somewhere else." Putting on her best smile, she continued, "Hey, don't worry about it. I'm okay." She drew in a deep breath and expelled it. Her eyes began to water. She tried her best to control them, but nothing she did worked. Not wanting Mike to see her like this, Lisa turned her head away. She felt his hand on her chin guiding her face towards him. He looked her into her eyes and she held his gaze. As a tear slowly rolled down her cheek, he took his index finger and wiped it away.

The band playing in the background grew louder. Mike took Lisa's hand and pulled her up. And they started dancing. When he pulled her close to him, she could feel his chiseled body through his suit. The aroma coming off his body was intoxicating. Laying her head on his shoulder, she let the music take her away. "Are you all right?" he asked.

Lisa nodded. Suddenly he spun her around, and when he pulled her back into him they were face to face. The heat generating from their bodies was so intense she thought she would faint. Her head was spinning. Was it the champagne? Or was it him? She was taking him in like he was a drug. He made her head whirl. She could have sworn she was having palpitations; her heart was about to explode and her breathing was elevated. She could smell the scent of sex all over him.

What was that toxin he was putting in the air? She couldn't think straight. Mike leaned closer, and his lips touched hers. She could taste the sweetness. His lips were soft and smooth. She hesitated at first, but gave in—she had no choice. His body called for hers, and her body answered. The music stopped, but their lips remained locked. Shivers went through her body. She hadn't felt like this with anyone except Darnel. "I've been wanting to do that for such a long time," he said between kisses.

Suddenly, Lisa pulled away, clutching her chest. She rubbed her lips and looked at him accusingly.

"Why? This can't happen." Mike walked over to her and started to speak. "No, I don't want to hear what you have to say," Lisa said as she started fidgeting and shaking.

"Are you all right Lisa?"

"No, I'm not all right. I have to go."

"Lisa, I didn't mean for any of this to happen."

She shot him a look that could bend metal. You liar, she thought. "I have to go." Holding up the bottom of her dress, she ran out as quickly as she could. She stared straight ahead and didn't look back once.

17

Early the next morning Darnel and Lisa went to Estelle's house to see Jason. Darnel seemed excited; Lisa was nervous. She was concerned about whether they would hit it off. She wasn't experienced with kids and to be quite honest, she didn't care for them. Lisa knew Estelle would be checking her out to see her reactions. She had to be real careful. Estelle was always watching Lisa very closely. And now, Lisa would have two of Estelle's family members with her.

When they arrived Estelle was in the living room drinking coffee and Jason was in the backyard playing with the dog. Darnel walked up to his mother and kissed her. Lisa said hello then took a seat. Estelle offered them some coffee but Lisa politely declined. Estelle began to tell Darnel how things were going. He asked her if the social worker had called and she said she hadn't. Darnel was appalled. He couldn't believe that they had placed him there without checking to see if things were going well. Estelle told him to calm down, that Darnel knew that Jason was all right.

Lisa really wasn't paying much attention to them. She got up and went to the back door to have a look at Jason. She thought he was a handsome little boy, with a dimple in the middle of his chin, just like his father. She walked outside and sat on the back porch steps. When she sat down the dog ran over and started sniffing her. She hid her annoyance while trying to shoo it away without anyone seeing her. Jason ran over to her and said, "He isn't going to hurt you."

"I'm sure he's not; I just didn't want his spit on my shoe." Jason looked at her with indifference.

She pretended not to notice and asked, "So what's your name honey?"

"Jason."

"Well, my name is Lisa. Nice to meet you." Jason stared off into space, refusing to make eye contact.

"Did you have, a dog at home?" Lisa asked Jason.

"No. Are you one of my aunts?"

"Well you could say that. I'm engaged to your Uncle Darnel. I'm his fiancée. So I guess that would make me your aunt. Yes, I guess that would? How does that sound to you?"

"Do you live with him?"

"As a matter of fact, I do live with him so you'll be seeing me quite often. Come here let me pull those pants up they're driving me crazy. Doesn't your butt get cold?"

He looked at her barely cracking a smile and said, "This is the style."

"Oh really, and wearing it over your butt is not?" Jason sat down beside her on the steps.

"Did you know my father?"

"Yep, I sure did. He was a real nice person. You look like him, you know? Darnel and David were real tight. They're the two youngest. They used to call them frick and frock from what I hear. They caused a lot of ruckus, but it was all in good fun. Your father was the comedian. Darnel is the more serious one. They made a good team though. I know David would have sure liked to have known you." Jason turned his head away. Lisa gently laid her hand on his back. "If David had known about you, he would have been a part of your life. I'm sure your grandmother has already told you this. Nobody knew about you. I'm certain your mother has been trying her best to take good care of you. It must have been real hard alone. I'm positive that she doesn't want anything bad to happen to you."

He looked at her intently, saying, "I just didn't want to go to another foster home. Last year, when my mother came out of the hospital, she told me that she knew where my father's family was. She showed me pictures of my father that I had never seen before. She told me if anything ever happened to her that I should call them. She gave me a picture of my father with a phone number on it. She said this is where my grandmother lived and that I should only call them if it was an emergency. So I called. I hope she won't be mad at me."

"She won't be mad. You did the right thing."

"Everybody has been so nice to me. But I really miss my mother. I want to go and see her."

"Well, let's see what we can do about that. Wait out here. I need to go talk to your grandmother and your uncle."

When Lisa walked into the living room, Darnel and his mother were still heavily engaged in their conversation. "Excuse me. With your permission Estelle, I would like to take Jason down to the hospital to see Theresa." Estelle looked at Lisa like she'd lost her mind. Then she looked at Darnel and asked him whether he thought it would be a good idea. Before he could answer, Lisa turned to Estelle and said, "I think it's a very good idea. He's worried about his mother and he needs to see how she's doing. We all realize that she is the only family he knows, and it might do her some good to see him. I'll be happy to take him. You can sit and finish talking. I know these last days have been hectic. Consider this a little break. Okay?"

Darnel looked at his mother and Estelle nodded her head. She said, "Go ahead. I'll have dinner ready when you get back."

So, Jason and Lisa left to go see his mother. He was quiet in the car and didn't talk too much which Lisa didn't mind at all. She needed some time to think, and this was the perfect opportunity. When they got to Theresa's room, Jason went straight to the bed. Theresa was hooked up to some IV's. She looked terrible and there was nothing Lisa could do to hide this from Jason. However, Jason looked like he was glad to see her.

Lisa sat in the chair while Jason sat on the bed next to his mother. Jason was smiling but he had a sad look in his eyes. As Lisa sat back and relaxed, he laid his head down by his mother. Lisa must have faded away for a few minutes because she hadn't heard him start talking to her. He said that he hoped that his mother would stay away from the drugs this time. He told Lisa all they needed to do was to move out of the projects. "She was doing really good for a long time, but her boyfriend keeps coming around and giving her that stuff. That's the only way he could get Mama to let him do whatever he wanted. I told her to stay away from him. I hate him. I wish he would just leave us alone." The anger in his face—it was enough to make Lisa think twice about ever doing anything wrong to him.

Lisa sat there patiently and listened. She knew he needed someone to talk to and it couldn't be his family. Lisa knew he felt like he had to protect his mother. He didn't want them to know everything. He was fully aware of the reasons she'd kept him away from them. Theresa was frightened they would take him away from her. And from what Lisa knew of the family that's exactly what they would have done. If Lisa had been in her shoes she would have done the same. She didn't know why she felt like she had to protect Theresa also. She just knew that Darnel's family was angry with Theresa for not telling them about Jason. Lisa didn't think they'd ever get over the fact that David never knew him. Jason wanted a different life now and Lisa knew he must feel guilty about it. The most important thing to him now was his mother's getting better and getting her life together. Lisa hoped that now Theresa had people in her corner she'd do better. Lisa had seen it a thousand times and sometimes getting better was not part of the plan.

They stayed at the hospital for hours. Jason made Lisa promise to bring him back. When they got to Estelle's dinner was ready. Estelle and Darnel couldn't keep their eyes off of Lisa; they were dying to know what had happened. After dinner Estelle pulled Lisa to the side in the kitchen and asked her how it went? "It went fine. She's still in pretty bad shape, but I think Jason will sleep a lot better tonight knowing that she's all right."

"So how is he doing?"

"As well as can be expected. Estelle, Jason is fine. Look at him eat. He's okay don't worry."

"I want to thank you for taking him, honey. I don't know if I'm ready to see her just yet. I have all this anger in me right now and yet I'm filled with all this joy." She paused. "He looks like David doesn't he?"

"Yes, just like him."

"I miss him, Lisa," she said. As she turned her head a tear rolled down her cheek.

When Darnel and Lisa got home, Lisa began to do the laundry. She was carrying clothes back and forth to the laundry room. The basket was overflowing so Darnel jumped up and grabbed some of the clothes, following her to the laundry room. She looked up and could see him looking at her. "So, Lisa you got in pretty late last night. Where did you go?" She started grabbing the wrong color clothes.

"Lisa, that's white please don't mess up my T-shirts. So where did you go?"

"I went out with a friend."

"Anyone I know?"

"Could you please pass me the detergent? And the bleach please?"

"Was it anyone I know?"

"I heard you the first time, Darnel. No, it wasn't anyone you know." She slammed down the washing machine top and brushed past him.

That night in bed Darnel wanted to talk. "Go ahead I'm listening," Lisa said.

"Well, I was thinking it would be a good idea if Jason moved in with us now so he can get adjusted."

"Aren't you rushing things?"

"No. I feel since I'm the one who's petitioning the courts for guardianship, it's only logical that he be here. There's a lot that needs to be done. I need to register him for school and it makes no sense for him to go anywhere else if this is where he will be staying."

"It's your house Darnel."

"It has nothing to do with it being my house. I want us to be in agreement."

"Darnel, you've already made your mind up. Don't pretend that what I have to say counts. There are a few things that I feel we should discuss besides his rearing. I feel you are jumping the gun. The judge hasn't said he can stay with you. He still has a mother, Darnel, and that is not going to change. I feel that he is family and you should take care of him, but he is David's son not yours. I know you love him and you want to do the right thing. This is not "your" long lost son. You know he's not moving in permanently. His mother will be given every chance to get her life together, then he will be gone."

"Lisa, I don't have any doubt in my mind that the judge will let him stay here. I just want to be prepared."

"Fine, I'll do all I can as far as the court proceedings go. I will do my best as far as parenting him. I just want you to know that when Theresa comes out of the hospital, I want to do everything to try to give her help if she wants it. I will not participate in any proceedings that will try to take her son away until I know all the facts. The best thing for Jason is that we all try to help each other instead of fighting. Hopefully, Theresa will see it that way too and let him be a permanent part of our lives."

"Lisa, I just want to do what is best for everybody."

"No Darnel, you have to do what's best for him."

18

Later in the week Lisa ran into Tasha. Lisa had a lot of filling in to do. Natasha was very shocked that Lisa had handled the situation with Jason so well. "Tasha, I'm not as mean and cruel as you think."

Tasha looked around twice and said, "Who are you and what have you done with my sister?"

"It's not that big of a deal, Tasha. He seems like a nice kid."

"That's all good, Lisa, but he's not visiting—he will be living with you. You do realize that?"

"I know. At first I thought I would go through the roof. I wasn't prepared for any kids, but he's ten so there's not that much I have to do. No potty training—nothing."

"There's more to being a parent than potty training, Lisa."

"I know that, Tasha. The decision is already made. This is a battle I can't win. So I give up. I'll try to make the best of it. Just leave it alone, and tell me what's been going on in your life? Are you still seeing the security guard?"

"Yes."

"Tell me something, did you give him some?"

"Yep, a few weeks ago."

"Well, was it good?"

"Let's just say that he thought he'd rocked my world when he didn't even rock my boat."

"You've got to be kidding? All that talk about how fine he was and he couldn't do nothing with it."

"Girl, if B. B. King was his father he sure didn't give him no rhythm, but he gave me the blues."

"So why are you still talking to him?"

"He won't leave me alone, plus I see him at work all the time. He sure is such a pretty thing to have on my arm." They both started laughing.

"Tasha, you're sick. You need to let that go and move on. I know how you are about sex, and that's not going to cut it in a few weeks."

"I know, but he sure knows how to eat the cootie cat."

19

"There you are! I've been looking for you all week. Are you avoiding me, Lisa?" Lisa opened her mouth to speak, but, Mike didn't give her a chance. "Lisa, we need to talk."

They decided to meet at a club called City Lights. It so happened it was jazz night so they decided to stay and listen to some music. They were really jamming and the crowd was hype. They were having a good time. When the band took a break, Mike said, "So how's things with you, Lisa?"

"They're all right; I can't complain."

"I heard that you needed some help with a family member."

"Oh that was nothing really; I was helping out Darnel's family."

"Is everything okay?"

"Yeah, it's nothing to worry about. Darnel's nephew is going to stay with us for awhile."

"That sounds interesting. Are you ready for that?"

"I guess I am. It's happening whether I'm ready or not. But I really don't mind; he seems like a sweet kid. I don't think we'll have any trouble," she lied.

"Well I'm glad, because I sure don't want to have to deal with your attitude at work."

"Oh really, and what attitude is that?"

"You know what I'm talking about. No one wants to mess with you when you're in a bad mood." She looked at him and shook her head because she knew he was right. Lisa really needed to work on her temper. Not just at the office, but at home. She didn't want Jason to think she was some kind of homicidal maniac.

"You know what Mike? You're full of advice. Do you have anything else you would like to offer?"

"So you have jokes, huh? Anyway, how's the wedding coming along?"

"We've been too busy to even think about wedding plans. Why, are you a coordinator?" He cracked a sly smile. She looked at him closely. She has this thing for skin. No matter what the color is, she just loves beautiful skin. His skin was just as smooth as a baby's bottom. He had beautiful white teeth. She knew he'd caught her staring because he gave her this funny look then he turned away. She had to catch herself—she didn't want to cause any trouble. Luckily the band's second set began and she didn't have to keep up the conversation. Drifting off, she let the music take a hold of her as if it were a lover.

After the set was over they decided to head back to the office. She had a lot of things she needed to do. Jason was moving in on the weekend, and she knew it would be real hectic. They walked to their cars and lingered for a few minutes. "The sky looks beautiful and so do you," Mike said.

Lisa raised her eyes slowly, looked up at him and saw he was smiling down on her. "Thank you, I think I really needed that."

"Any man would be a fool if he didn't let you know once in awhile." He put his hand on her face. His hand felt so soft, when he pulled it away he showed her it was an eyelash.

She smiled and said, "Oh, for a minute there I thought you were trying to cop a feel."

He smiled. "If I wanted to do something, I would be direct. There would be no mistaking it."

Lisa stepped back and said, "I'm scared of you. I guess I better call it a night—I'm exhausted." Mike leaned over and gave her a soft kiss on the lips. She knew she had to get out of there.

As she turned around to get in her car, Mike grabbed her arm and said, "Good night, Lisa."

"Good night," she answered and jumped into her car. She peeked in the rear view mirror twice and took a deep breath. Her heart pounding, she turned on the engine and pulled away.

When Lisa got home Darnel was in the kitchen. He jumped slightly when she walked in. Walking up behind him, she gave him a squeeze. "What are you doing, Darnel?"

"I had a taste for something sweet. I'm in here trying to figure out what to get. You're getting in pretty late, where've you been?"

"Oh, I went for a drink with Mike. When we got there they had some music so I stayed awhile."

"Oh, I see," he said in that tone like he really didn't want to hear that. Turning around, he said he was going back upstairs to watch some TV. Lisa just looked at him and rolled her eyes; she was not in the mood for this jealous shit. She stormed upstairs right after him. He must have not seen her because he started to close the door on her. She pushed the door hard, knocking him in his back. He turned around quickly, and she said, "What the fuck is your problem?"

He looked at her as if she were a lunatic. "Look Lisa, I don't know what *your* problem is, but there is no need to be vulgar. You can control that."

"Oh shut the hell up with your condescending tone."

"You want to start a fight Lisa, and I'm not going to play your game." First she looked at him then she looked around to see what the hell she could throw at him. Not finding anything, Lisa took off her shoe and threw it at his back. Darnel jumped and yelled, "Shit woman, what is wrong with you?"

"You, that's what's wrong with me. If you don't like me spending time with Mike then you should have said something. I don't need your fake, 'Oh I see;' I'm not your kid." Darnel looked at her like she'd lost her mind and maybe she had. Lisa felt like, "Damn it, show me you care sometime." If this had been her parents' house, things would have been lit up by now. Oh, but not at his parents' house. It would have been just as calm as it could be. Suddenly she heard, "Lisa! Lisa!" She must have been drifting.

Darnel was yelling at her, trying to get her attention. "I would have rather you been here with me. But what you did wasn't wrong. Although, I think it was inconsiderate."

"You are such a good human being," she said bowing as if he were an emperor. "Does that come naturally or do you take lessons?"

"Look Lisa, I'm trying to handle this the best way I can," he paused, "because if I really do what I want to do..."

"What Darnel, what do you really want to do?"

He said nothing, while he paced back and forth in front of their bed. Then he turned to her, and asked, "how the hell can you spend the evening with another man?"

"I'm not your property Darnel."

"Shut up damn it! I'm talking now. You disrespected me once again. I don't want you out with other men. I bet if I came in here late and said that I had spent the evening with another woman, you would have thrown both your shoes at me. Look at you feeling guilty now. You know what you did wasn't right. That's why you're in here acting like a baby trying to pick fights. I'm getting tired of this shit, Lisa. You're testing me and one day you're not going to like the results."

"Oh really? What are you going to do leave me? You're not going anywhere," she laughed.

"Woman don't test me! I may love the hell out of you, but if you got to go, you will."

Lisa looked at him. She couldn't believe what he'd just said. She was hurt. Flopping down on the bed, she said, "Darnel, I'm sorry. I don't know what has gotten into me. I'm just so scared everything is moving too fast for me. We're getting married. We have a kid moving in this weekend. I'm still a kid, I'm not ready to be a mommie." She started to cry. She must have had more to drink than she'd thought because it was sneaking up on her now. Through watery eyes Lisa looked over at Darnel. He seemed like he wanted to come over, but wouldn't move. Then Lisa reverted back to a two-year-old and had a tantrum. She started kicking the bed and whirling around like she didn't have any sense.

Finally, Darnel came over and straddled her, trying to hold her still. "Lisa, cut it out." Then she started to fight him. Looking down at her, he laughed and that only infuriated her more. "Lisa, you can't beat me so don't even try."

"Shut up!" she yelled. Then she bit him on his chest. He clenched his teeth in pain. Holding her down tighter, he told her if she bit him again he was going to bite her back and see how she liked it. Lisa started laughing hysterically, which soon turned to crying. She didn't know what the hell was wrong with her. Darnel let her go, then she crawled into a ball and just lay there. He lay down on the bed beside her. Crawling over to him, she laid her head on his chest and he held her. They lay there for a little while without speaking. "Darnel?"

"Yes, Lisa."

"I want to have a baby."

"I don't think this is the time to be talking about it."

"Darnel, I want to have baby."

"Lisa, I know. I want to have kids too; you know that."

"I want to have a baby now," she persisted and before he could answer she kissed him. She climbed on top of him and pulled down his boxers. Getting off the bed, she pulled off her slacks and panties. She climbed back on top and rode him like it was going to be the last time. When Darnel came she rolled over and lay there. Neither of them said anything. Lisa didn't know what Darnel was thinking, but she felt she had probably just made the biggest mistake of her life.

20

The next morning Lisa got up and called Tasha. She told her it was an emergency and needed to see her right away. They decided to meet at Natasha's apartment. Lisa rang the bell, and Natasha came to the door in her housecoat. "Hi baby, how you doing?"

"Girl, why are you still in your pajamas?"

"It's early that's why. You're the only person I know who has a crisis and wants to talk about it early in the morning. Normal people talk about it late over a few drinks. You scared the hell out of me you know. Come on in here. You don't want the neighbors to see all my business do you?"

"Girl, I just don't know what the hell is going through my head these days. I let Mike kiss me. I had a fight with Darnel then tried to get pregnant after it."

"Wait a minute. Hold up." Natasha pulled the belt around her robe a little tighter. "You what?"

"Girl, you heard me. Don't make me repeat myself."

"You let Mike kiss you, Lisa?"

"Yes, I did."

"Kiss you how?"

"There's no mistaking it; we kissed."

"And you're okay with this?"

"Of course, I'm not okay with this. Anyway, that's the least of my troubles now. I tried to get pregnant. You didn't hear that part?"

"Yes, I heard that part, but then I had to wonder who you tried to get pregnant by."

"Girl please, I'm not sleeping with Mike; he's just a friend."

"A friend that kisses you on the lips?"

"Stop harping on that Tasha. That's not the most important thing that I said."

"Why did you try to get pregnant after that? I thought you didn't want any kids."

"I don't, but I was drunk and it felt like the right thing to do at the time. I needed Darnel to stop being mad. I had to prove to him that I loved him. And that I wanted to be with him forever."

"You had to prove that to Darnel or did you have to prove it to yourself?"

Lisa looked at Tasha because what she was saying had some truth in it. Lisa felt like there was no other way to prove her love. "Tasha, I don't know what is wrong with me. I feel like I'm being pulled in all directions. I'm attracted to Mike and I don't know what to do about that."

"Lisa, you've been attracted to other men while you've been with Darnel. I think that this time you're looking for a way out of this engagement."

"No Tasha, I'm genuinely attracted to this man."

"Yeah right, you never spoke about this before you got engaged. I should have never told you about Mike. You knew exactly who to run to. If you're not ready to get married, then you need to tell Darnel."

"I don't know how to tell him. This is the last time he's going to ask me, Tasha. He's ready now and I can't put it off much longer."

"Do you think he's going to leave you if you postpone it?"

"I know that if I do, he'll know that I will never be ready. He wants a wife. He's traditional in some ways. That's why all this time we've both been very careful about getting pregnant. He feels that we should be married before we have any kids. Like a fool, I didn't use anything last night. Tasha help me; I messed up bad."

"Lisa, I can't help you. You need to get some professional help. Go talk to somebody. You're doing the same thing you always do. You're fucking it up on purpose. You're trying to make him decide. You're going to push him to where he can't take it anymore. Then he's finally going to leave you. Is that when your conscience will be clear, huh Lisa? You can't go on living like this; you're getting too old for this. You can't make any type of commitment that involves people. Darnel is a good man, Lisa. If you lose him you'll never be the same after this. I know you love him. I have never seen you look at a man the way you look at Darnel. You need some therapy. Wait here while I go get you the number of my therapist. Maybe you can talk to him." While Tasha was in the back looking for the number Lisa called home. She told Darnel that she hadn't forgotten about Jason and that she would meet him at his mother's house. When Tasha returned, she handed Lisa a number and told her to give him a call.

"By the way Lisa, I have some news of my own."

"What is it?"

"I've decided to go back to school and get my degree. I think I want to work with kids. Teenagers that is. I'm tired of that mall and this dead end life. I want a career and I feel I can do a world of good."

"That's great Tasha, I'm so proud of you. You know you're right. You would do a world of good. If you need anything like money for books, tuition, anything you call me."

"I know Lisa, thanks, but I think I want to do this by myself."

"Girl, there's nothing wrong with doing it by yourself. I just wish I'd had more help than I did. Believe me, it's a heck of a lot easier to study when you're not worrying about where that next dollar is coming from. In fact, I'm insisting. I want to pay some of your expenses for school. I have some money saved, and it would make me happy if you would let me do this for you."

"Okay Lisa, I'll think about it."

"I'll see you later I have to go meet Darnel."

"Good luck, and I'm waiting for you to invite me over to see him."

"Since when have you ever needed an invitation?"

"You're right; I'll be over there soon." Tasha grabbed Lisa's arm, as she was about to walk out the door. "Lisa, call him. Okay?"

"Yeah Tasha, as soon as I get a chance."

"Make the time Lisa—I don't want to see you lose everything."

Lisa arrived at Estelle's to find Darnel and Jason waiting for her outside. She stopped in and spoke to Estelle for a minute then they left. Jason rode in Darnel's truck, while Lisa rode alone in the car. When they got home, Jason and Darnel brought the bags in. Lisa noticed that Estelle had already begun to spoil him. Jason didn't have as many bags when he'd arrived. She noticed he had a new outfit on too. It was a basketball jersey from the Orlando Magic. The number he was wearing was from Penny Hardaway. Jason had this big Kool-Aid smile on his face. Lisa wondered what Darnel had done to the guest bedroom. In all the excitement she'd forgotten to even look. If there was anything feminine in there, Darnel probably just took it out. But knowing him, he probably didn't replace it with anything. When she went up to the room, it was just as she had suspected. However, Jason seemed to be very pleased with it. It was probably nicer than any room he'd ever had. Darnel was grinning. Little things like this made him happy. "Darnel, where did you put all my pillows and knickknacks?"

"I put them in the linen closest."

"Well, we're going to have to do something about this room. It just looks so empty now. Jason, what do you think?"

"I don't know," he said.

"Well, I think it needs some posters, some books, some paintings." The thought of all that stuff sounded good to Jason. Darnel just laughed. Looking at him, she said, "You won't think it's so funny when you see your credit card bill." He grabbed her, lifted her off the floor and kissed her.

"I'm glad you're coming around. I hope you have this much fun when you're decorating the baby's room."

She looked up at him and smiled. You can fool the people some of the time, she thought. But she guessed he was all right with what happened last night. Today was going to be busy enough. She decided that they should all go to the mall and do some shopping.

When they got there they split up. Jason went with Lisa. Smart kid, he knew who had the credit card. Darnel went to one of those hardware stores to find some wallpaper for the room. Jason and Lisa were supposed to be finding little knickknacks to go in his room, but for some reason they wound up buying CDs and playing in the arcade. She had to admit she was enjoying herself—Terminator 2 always made her feel good. They were getting along pretty well.

Later they met up with Darnel at the food court. Lisa was famished. She also noticed Darnel had bought half the mall. They sat down at a table and began to eat. While they were eating, Darnel said he'd bought something for Lisa. She was excited. She loved presents and Darnel always gave the best gifts. He took hints pretty well. Lisa couldn't figure out what she might have said to get this one, but she sure was ready for it. He pulled out a little bag and her eyes opened wide. Darnel and Jason were both staring at her, waiting for her reaction. When she opened the bag, she saw a little pair of booties. She had to look twice because she wasn't quite sure what she was seeing. Oh yes—they were definitely booties. She pretended to be pleased. Darnel made a comment that he had a feeling about last night.

Jason looked at the both of them and asked, "Are you going to have a baby?"

Lisa froze because she didn't know the answer. Darnel jumped in, "We hope to soon."

Jason looked at them and said, "Oh."

Lisa felt Darnel staring at her; she did everything in her power to avoid his stare. She felt guilty, sick, trapped and deceitful. It was all a lie; it wasn't her anymore. This was not what she wanted. Hell, she really didn't know what she wanted anymore. She just needed help. It felt like the walls were closing in on her. She felt her breath slipping away. Suddenly, Lisa jumped up. She felt like she couldn't breathe; everything seemed hazy. Lisa tried to grab for Darnel, but knocked over his soda instead. She started slipping to the floor. Darnel rushed around the table, mouthing "what's wrong," but she couldn't hear him. What the hell was happening? A lady came over to see if she was choking. Someone else handed Darnel a paper bag, and he put it over Lisa's mouth. "Breathe baby, breathe baby," Darnel said.

Lisa finally calmed down. Darnel insisted they go to the emergency room, but she talked him out of it. Instead they decided to go straight home. The last thing Lisa remembered that night was Jason asking what was wrong? That was the only voice she heard. That was the only voice she remembered.

***

The next day Darnel insisted that Lisa take it easy. She really had given him a scare. Jason was busy in his room. Darnel made Lisa breakfast in bed. She felt better, but she thought she might as well take advantage of it. He sat down on the bed and watched the Sunday game. She got out of the bed and took a shower. When she got out Darnel was still there. This was starting to annoy her. "Darnel, you know you usually watch the game downstairs. Why are you in here?"

"I just want to make sure you're all right. You scared the hell out of me yesterday. I felt so helpless. There was nothing I could do for you and that's a scary feeling."

"Don't worry. I think I just had an anxiety attack. It wasn't your fault."

"I understand that, but what was the anxiety attack about?"

"Nothing, don't worry about it—it was a one time thing. Go ahead and watch the game." She walked over to the closet to find something to wear.

"Lisa, I feel guilty about what happened yesterday. I think your attack had something to do with Jason. I feel I pushed this all on you pretty fast and it overwhelmed you. Are you sure you're okay with this?"

"Yes, I'm fine with it. Stop asking me that. I am a little scared, but that's only because I don't have any kids or any experience with them. As far as him living here I don't have any problem with that. This is your home and he belongs here with his family. Do you know how many families let their blood go into the foster care system? What you're doing is the right thing."

"I've noticed that you haven't been acting like yourself lately. I thought it would pass, but it seems to me like it's getting worst."

"It's nothing, Darnel. I'm fine—don't worry about me. Why don't you go and watch the game with Jason. I'm sure he's lonely."

"I'm going, but it seems to me like you're avoiding the issue. We need to talk Lisa. It's your call now."

"Okay Darnel, go on."

Lisa knew that things were getting worst, but just couldn't stop the dominoes from falling. These days, all she thought about was Mike. She felt like he could take her away from all of this. But she loved Darnel. Why would she want to be with someone else? Lisa kept flashing back to the conversation she'd had with Natasha. She knew she needed some help. She would have to call that therapist soon before she lost everything that was dear to her. God help her!

21

Later in the week, Lisa placed a call to Natasha's therapist, who in turn recommended someone else. Things seemed to be going pretty well with Jason. Darnel had registered him in school. With more than a half a year of school left, Darnel didn't think it was necessary for Jason to stay at his old school. Besides, the schools around them had a better academic program and that's where Darnel wanted him. Theresa had been showing signs of improvement, but not enough for Darnel's family. Jason had been enjoying his time with her. Somehow, Lisa had been delegated the responsibility of taking Jason to see his mother. If she didn't, she knew no one else would.

When Lisa arrived at the therapist's office, she turned around nearly three times before she finally decided to go in. The room was so hip and funky she knew the therapist had to be a musician on the side. At any moment she felt like someone was going to ask her if she wanted a drink. When the therapist finally emerged from her office, the first thing Lisa noticed were her feet. She was tall and lanky like a basketball player. Her handshake was that of a man's; it was firm with no feminine feel to it. Her nails weren't painted and her makeup wasn't heavy. She wore slacks and comfortable shoes, and all those things made Lisa feel right at home.

For the first few minutes the therapist asked Lisa general questions. Lisa didn't pay as much attention to her as she did to the paintings on the wall. At one point, the therapist noticed Lisa staring at a painting and asked her what she felt. Lisa said she didn't feel much, except that it was hypnotizing. She couldn't take her eyes off of it. The therapist asked her about Darnel. All Lisa could remember telling her was that he was a good man, trustworthy, loving and so forth. Later the thing she remembered most was that she'd told the therapist that he was damn near perfect. It's funny because when she said it, it struck a chord with her. At first she laughed, and then she felt like, "Yeah, he is damn near perfect." They talked about Darnel a little further and it came out that Lisa felt intimidated by Darnel because he chose to do the right things. Her relationship would be a lot easier if he was like her father. She would have been prepared for it. She became numb to the things that her father used to do to her mother. That would have been easier to deal with then the fact that Darnel never fucked up; he just never did. So, if he wasn't the one who fucked up, then Lisa guessed it would have to be her. Right? Lisa said that it was sad to admit, but she was the one causing the most trouble in the relationship. "To be perfectly honest," she admitted to the therapist, "a lot of the things I've done to cause arguments could have been avoided." Lisa said she knew what things bothered Darnel and did them anyway. She thought he expected her to do them. Lisa thought Darnel knew she had to mess up in order to feel control. He had to prove to her that he'd love her no matter what.

Lisa told the therapist that she knew one day her luck was going to run out and that's why she's prepared herself for him leaving her. The therapist asked her when was she going to stop testing his love. Lisa looked at her and confessed she honestly didn't know. That's what stuck with Lisa about her first session later on. As she drove home, it just kept replaying itself. "When are you going to stop, Lisa? When are you going to stop?"

***

Lisa was busy at her desk working when Andre came in. "Hey girl, how ya doing?"

"Fine, what's going on?"

"I have that research you wanted. Also, I want to thank you for sending me to the library."

"Why, did you meet someone?" Lisa looked at him and saw that devilish grin on his face. "You did meet someone. Who is it?"

"It's the new librarian; he works on the third floor."

"Who? Describe him to me."

"He's tall with olive skin and dark features. He looks like a Greek god."

"I know you don't mean the one with a butt chiseled out in stone."

"Yes, that's him."

"I've seen all the female law students spending an awful lot of time on the third floor lately. So I checked it out, and thought I'd give you an early birthday present," she teased smiling.

"It's nice to see you smiling again. I bet you haven't even noticed that I haven't been around lately."

"Oh I noticed, and I figured that it was something I did or said again. I knew in time you would either forgive me or you wouldn't."

"Well Lisa, you know you're a bitch sometimes. But I'm a bitch also, and I really can't have you stealing the spotlight from me. But I love you anyway."

"I'm glad you do. I'm sorry, but I've been going through a lot of things lately."

"I know sweetheart, but tonight is my birthday party. Don't say anything—I know you forgot. I'm having a big shindig at LaFox and I want you to come."

"Oh Andre, not tonight. I'm swamped."

"Lisa, this is the least you can do for all the weeks of pain and suffering you've put me through. Please!" Andre clasped his hands together and got down on one knee.

"Okay, I'll come, but I'm not staying long."

"That's fine. And bring your beautiful fiancé too I would love to see that. It will be a hoot." As soon as Andre left Lisa called Darnel to see if he would go to the party. She knew there was no way he would, but she thought she'd try asking instead of just going by herself.

Just as she'd thought, Darnel refused to step a foot in a gay club, and he wasn't too happy about her going. He finally agreed to back off because he knew how close Andre was to Lisa. And how he helped her through her time off. Darnel said he was taking Jason over to his mother's for dinner and that he would see her when she got in.

That night Lisa went home to find her most outrageous outfit so that she could blend in. Andre begged her to wear a platinum blonde wig that she'd bought over two Halloweens ago. She promised she would, so she had to find something bold and funky to wear with it.

By the time Lisa arrived at the club, she knew there was no way she was going to get home at a decent hour. The club was already bumping. Lisa wandered in, said a few hellos, and went straight for the bar. Andre found her through the crowd and yelled, "Diva you look fabulous!" She looked at him and said, "But I can't hold a candle to you."

Andre did a three sixty so that she could admire him from all sides. "Thank you, darling," he said. Then he leaned over and whispered, "You won't believe who showed up." She looked around thinking maybe Darnel had surprised her, but she didn't see him. Andre said, "Look over there, in the corner where that red strobe light is." Lisa was surprised to see Mike sitting there, talking to this great big ole drag queen. She nearly fell off the stool.

"What the hell is he doing here?"

"I think he's here to see you."

"What? "How did he know I was going to be here?"

"Well, when I invited him he made a point to ask three or four times whether or not you would be here? When I told him you'd promised, I think that's when he made up his mind to come. That man wants you, baby. If he has to spend the whole night with a bunch of queers and dikes then he'll do it. I know what's going on, Lisa. I just hope you do too. Bye." Andre vanished into the crowd.

Lisa didn't know if Mike had seen her yet, but hoped he hadn't. She knew that from a distance he wouldn't recognize her in the wig, but if he saw her face he would. She turned to the lady sitting next to her and asked if she could borrow her Mardi Gras mask.

Lisa worked her way over to Mike's table and just stood there. Mike looked up and said, "Hello." Lisa grabbed his hand and pulled him in the direction of the dance floor. He pulled his hand back and said, "No thanks man, I'll sit this one out." Lisa grabbed his hand again and before he could pull it away, there was Andre.

He held both of their hands and said to Mike, "I think this is the dance you've been waiting for. So go ahead and have a good time." Mike reluctantly got up and followed Lisa to the dance floor.

Mike wouldn't dance too close to her since he thought she was a man in drag. Lisa laughed the whole time and that made him even more uncomfortable. She tried to lean in, but the strength in his arms held her at a distance. Finally, she let go of his hands and pushed into his chest, then grabbed his ass and squeezed it. He pushed her off and balled up his fist, about to deck her, when Lisa yelled, "It's me!"

His eyes popped out. "Lisa, is that you?" Pulling off the mask, she started laughing hysterically. Mike turned around and stormed away.

Through her laughter she managed to follow him. When she caught up to him, she tried to apologize. But he couldn't really hear her so Lisa took him into a room and closed the door. She said, "I was just playing Mike; it was a joke." He gave her those elevator eyes. "Say something, Mike!" she insisted. Unexpectedly, he grabbed her and kissed her. Lisa's mind began to whirl, she knew she wasn't drunk, but she was filled with lust.

He let go and said, "I put up with a lot of bullshit tonight just so I could spend some time with you."

She grabbed him and kissed him back. He began to say something, but Lisa said, "Don't say anything, just let it happen."

Mike pinned her up against the wall; it was as though they couldn't get enough of each other. He pulled her skirt up. He was going to take her right there in that room. She unbuckled his pants and just then Andre walked in. "OOPS, excuse me. I'm so sorry," he muttered, then turned around and left. Lisa felt like her parents had just walked in on her first kiss. She was so ashamed that she pulled her skirt back down and ran out of the room.

When she entered the dance room, the lights were flashing everywhere. She felt like the spotlight was on her. She covered her head with her hand to shield herself from the light. Lisa just knew that everyone knew what she'd been doing in that room. She felt like a whore, a whore who had been caught. If Andre hadn't walked in, would she have gone through with it? My God, what was happening to her? Lisa went to the bar, ordered a cosmopolitan and gulped it down. "Give me another one," she yelled. That one was gone quicker than she could blink an eye.

She turned around and Mike was right behind her. "We need to talk, Lisa."

"Not now Mike, I can't handle this right now."

"We need to do this now, Lisa!" He leaned his head to the side, pointing towards the door.

"Okay, let's go and get this over with." She followed him out of the club. When they got outside it was too noisy to talk. He told her he didn't live too far away and convinced her to go to his house where they could talk.

Lisa walked into his house and immediately wanted to turn around. She was surrounded by perfection. His Italian leather sofas looked as if they'd been delivered yesterday. Along one wall was his entertainment center. She'd never seen that much equipment gathered in one place outside of a music studio. It was the type of home where your parents hated to take you because if you broke one thing it would cost them a month's salary. He walked over to her and holding her arm said, "Sit down. It will be all right."

Lisa sat there for a few minutes wondering what the hell she was doing there? She had to break the silence because it was killing her. "Look Mike, I don't know what came over me tonight. It was wrong and I feel really bad about it. I feel my life is spinning out of control. Kissing you made me feel like I had some control. I know that wasn't the way to go about getting it, and it won't happen again."

"Lisa, I can understand how you feel, but that has nothing to do with why I kissed you. I'm attracted to you. I did something that I've been wanting to do for a long time. I'm not sorry anything happened. I'll take you any way I can get you."

"That's pathetic. There are too many available women out there who would take me out just to get you."

He got up and moved over to where she was sitting. "You see, that is what I love about you. There's no holds barred with you."

"Love, I think you've had too much to drink," she said.

"I don't think so," he said as he leaned in to kiss her. Lisa grabbed the back of his head and kissed him passionately, then pushed him away. "I thought we came here to talk."

"Don't be a tease, I know you're not naïve. You know why I want you here. You're not going to play games are you? I know you want this just as much as I do."

"Fine, a real man would have..." He grabbed her and lifted her up in his arms and carried her to the bedroom.

Her body yearned for his touch as he laid her down on the bed. She grabbed the rim of his pants and pulled him towards her, then lifted his shirt out of his pants. She kissed his stomach gently. Rapidly she unbuckled his belt and the button to his pants. Mike pushed her wig backwards and it fell down her back. She released her hair so it hung down on the sides of her face. Sweeping it up in one hand, Mike tugged on it and pulled her up. She stood in front of him. His eyes glared; they were hot as fire. He held her hair to the back of her head, balled up in a fist. Lisa wanted to taste the sweetness of his mouth and drew him closer. She took his lips in. They were sweet as nectar from a fruit. She bit him and felt him wince. Mike turned her around so she had her back to him and was facing the bed. She leaned into him. His hands crept up her blouse, squeezing her breasts as if they were ripe melons. She felt sweat trickle down her forehead. Her breathing increased. As his manhood rubbed against her buttocks, she thought she would faint. Moaning with delight, she glided her hand toward her sweetness. It ached for him. His hand joined hers. His fingers could stretch for an eternity.

Mike pushed Lisa toward the bed. Her ass arched up begging for entry. He lifted her skirt and ripped her pantyhose in half. Sitting on the floor, he pulled her back to his face. His tongue was cold. She stumbled forward, grabbing the covers to help her maintain her balance. He was lost inside of her. Pleasuring her over and over again. Lisa took her blouse off. The sweat trickled down her body. Then Mike stood up and took her from behind. Grabbing a fistful of hair, he yanked it every now and them. He slapped her ass and the sting sent shivers up her body. She begged him for more. Just before she thought he would cum, she made him stop. She threw him on the bed and licked his stomach and sucked on his nipples. She climbed on top. The head of his penis was so big it made a popping noise when it entered. It filled her up. So strong and hard. Up and down. She gyrated her hips. Up and down. Smack! The sound of their bodies hitting one another. "Give it to me!" she yelled. Faster and faster she went. Sucking in all the air she could get; his body jerking under hers. Mike sat up and she pulled his head to her breast, then he put her nipple in his mouth. Both exhausted, he fell back and she lay on top of him. Their bodies drenched. Lisa's hair was soaked and began to curl from the perspiration. She wiped the sweat from his forehead. He kissed her hand. Lisa rolled off of him and lay on her side. He turned around towards her and they fell asleep, his body fitting to her curves, spoonlike.

That night Lisa was gone as soon as she could get out of there. She had to get home quickly before Darnel had a chance to miss her. Lisa arrived home at about five in the morning. Passing Jason's room she looked in on him. He looked so sweet and innocent. She walked in, pulled the covers over him and pulled the door closed behind her. She walked in the bedroom and found Darnel was asleep. She didn't want to get in the bed with him. She sat down in the chair and drifted off.

22

A few hours later Darnel woke Lisa. "Lisa you must have had a good time last night look at you. I didn't know you were going in costume. I wish I had seen you last night. Are you going to work? You look exhausted?"

"No, I'll call Andre and let him know. That's even if he makes it in."

"Why don't you take those clothes off and get in the bed?" He lifted her up and placed her on the bed, pulled the wig off and laughed. Covering her up with the sheets, he kissed her forehead and left the room.

Lisa fell asleep for an hour or two. She called in and spoke to Andre. He asked if everything was okay? She told him everything was fine and not to worry that she would be in on Monday. "Lisa," he said, "did you do anything that you regret?"

"Andre, I've done plenty of things that I regret. Do you have time for me to name them all?"

Around one Darnel called from work to see how Lisa was doing. He wanted to meet for lunch, but she declined. She just couldn't face him. She told him she would pick Jason up from school and take him to the hospital. They agreed they'd sit down and have dinner as a family.

Lisa called Andre and had some of her work messengered over so that she wouldn't be too far behind on Monday. She threw herself into her work for about an hour. Pretty soon it was time to pick up Jason. When Lisa arrived at the school, Jason seemed like he was happy to see her. He jumped in the car and they went to the hospital. Lisa sat in the room for awhile then decided to wait in the waiting area. Lisa had her head buried in a magazine when she noticed someone standing over her. Looking up she saw it was Mike. Her heart almost jumped out of her chest. "What are you doing here?"

He sat down on the couch beside her, "I was worried because of the way you left last night without even saying goodbye.

"I'm fine Mike. I was a little tired and decided to take a personal day. How did you know I was here?"

"I have my sources."

"What are you following me or have you been following me?"

"No, nothing like that. Relax. Why are you acting so anxious?"

"Because you shouldn't be here. Darnel could show up here at any time. He knows where I am. It is a possibility." She turned around and looked over her shoulder.

"Well, he didn't know where you were last night."

Lisa looked at him. He had a cocky grin on his face. "What the hell are you smiling about? You're acting as if you won something. What we did was wrong and you know it."

"I don't regret it at all. In fact, I want it to happen again."

"Well it won't. I think it would be best if we kept our relationship strictly professional from now on."

"Lisa, don't be naïve. It will never be on a strictly professional level. We made love last night; that changes everything."

"No Mike, we had sex and that doesn't change a damn thing." Lisa turned around and saw Jason standing there. She didn't know what to do or say. She didn't know how long he had been standing there. Mike jumped up and introduced himself and told Jason that they were co-workers.

Mike turned towards Lisa and said, "It was nice running into you, Lisa. I'll see you at the office." She breathed a sigh of relief grabbed her purse and headed home.

When they got home Darnel was in the kitchen cooking. He was making nachos; his specialty. As Lisa walked by the kitchen, he ran over and grabbed her. "Hey you, not so fast I haven't spent any quality time with you all week. I've missed you." Then he laid a big sloppy one on her. Jason was over in the corner laughing. Lisa wiggled her way out of his arms and told Jason to go upstairs and wash up for dinner. When she turned to go do the same, Darnel slapped her on the butt.

They sat down for dinner and Darnel said the prayer—and Lisa said one of her own. Everyone dug into the nachos. While they were eating, Darnel was busy asking Jason how his day had been. Lisa got up briefly to get some hot sauce, and Jason called over to her, "Lisa, who was that man at the hospital, I forgot what he said his name was?" Lisa dropped the bottle on the floor and stood still.

"Are you all right?" Darnel yelled.

"Fine," Lisa said picking up the bottle, then wiping the floor. She thought if she stayed quiet, Jason would forget his question.

"So who was he talking about, Lisa?" Darnel asked.

She looked at Jason because she felt he'd deliberately mentioned that Mike was at the hospital. Lisa watched Jason closely to see if he was watching her. She tried to compose herself and focus her attention back to Darnel. "Oh, it was Mike; we ran into each other at the hospital. He stopped and we chatted for a few minutes." She looked over at Jason to see if he was going to add anything, but he continued to eat. After she cleaned up the mess, she sat back down and finished her dinner.

Jason was watching the X-Files when Lisa decided to go to bed. She hadn't caught up on any of the sleep she'd missed so she decided to retire early. She had already taken her shower and put on her pajamas. As she was pulling the sheets up to her neck, Darnel walked in. He came over to the bed and embraced her from behind. "Hey, what do you think you're doing? I know you don't plan on going to bed this early."

"Why Darnel, what did you have in mind?" He kissed her and said, "I love you. I think things are going pretty well with us. I love it when you act maternal; it turns me on."

"You're so silly D."

"You know I want to marry you girl and I want you to have my babies?"

"Yes Darnel, I'm fully aware of that."

"Lisa, you know we are already a family and I'm not going anywhere." He looked her in the eyes. "There's no reason to wait; we've waited long enough."

Lisa sat up in the bed and looked him straight in the eye and said, "Do you really mean that?"

"Of course I mean it." Her head swayed back and forth—she felt choked up. It hurt too much to form words then they finally came out. "Darnel, you won't leave me no matter what, right?"

"Lisa, I'm not going anywhere. I'm where I want to be."

"Darnel, I love you and I finally realize what you mean to me. I don't know what I would do if you ever turned your back on me."

"You have nothing to worry about."

"Darnel, I'm sorry, I'm so sorry," she cried as the tears flowed. Darnel wiped them away with his hands.

"Lisa, what are you talking about?"

"Nothing, just tell me there's nothing I could ever do to make you stop loving me."

"There's nothing you could do." He gently kissed her and caressed her. He walked over to the door to make sure it was locked and they made love all night long.

***

On Saturday Natasha called Lisa to see how she was doing. Lisa told her everything was fine. Natasha said she was coming over to borrow a dress for a date she had that night. Lisa tried to talk her out of it; she didn't want to see her. She came up with every excuse there was, but Natasha was not going to be persuaded. That dress had her name on it and she was coming to claim it.

Darnel took Jason to the park to play some ball, so Lisa had the house to herself. She pretty much laid around the house.

She wasn't feeling too good—the guilt was eating at her. It was different this time. She'd never regretted anything she had done with a man before. If they got hurt, it was their fault for getting too close.

Lisa was jolted back to the present by the ringing of the phone. She wasn't eager to pick it up so she decided to let the answering machine get it. She recognized the voice, but she couldn't believe it. Lisa's mouth dropped to the floor. Mike was leaving a message saying that it was very important that she contact him. Grabbing the phone off the hook knocking everything off of the nightstand she yelled, "What the hell is wrong with you? Why are you leaving a message on my machine?"

"Ah, so you are home. Why didn't you just answer the phone? I hope you're not trying to avoid me."

"Look, I don't have time to avoid you, but you don't have any business calling my house. You never called it before, so don't start now."

"I just wanted to talk to you about the other night."

"Look, save the speech Mike. I know the script. It will never happen again. I don't want a relationship blah blah blah."

"I guess you've been there, done that. But that's not at all what I wanted to say. In fact, I want to see you again and not in a professional capacity."

"You know that is not going to happen again. I'm deeply involved with someone. We had sex that's it. It doesn't mean that I don't love Darnel anymore. I fucked up big time is what it means."

"Lisa, when I first met you, you didn't even stare at me crossways. You can't sit there and tell me that something is not happening between us."

"Mike, you're acting like you planned this. It just happened."

"Nothing ever just happens; we make things possible. I knew I wanted to be with you a long time ago and I went for it. I still want to be with you, so I'm not about to stop now."

"I can't believe you. You're acting like what I did was only natural. It was low down and dirty."

"Well, I'm not going to beat myself up about it. Lisa, you and I are alike in many ways and different in others. I just want to let life be no more rings on my finger. Nothing that's going to suffocate me and that's what you need. You know Darnel wants more, and you're simply not ready for that."

"Well maybe I think I am. I think I can handle that family now."

"Oh, so your feelings have changed in just a few weeks. Give me a break! You need to stop fooling yourself." There was a long silence on the phone.

"Mike, I don't know what you want from me, but there is nothing I can give you. Actually being with you has been the best thing for my relationship. I realize now that I can make a family and that it's not all that bad. I'm just sorry that it took me doing something so foolish to wake up."

"Do you think Darnel will think what we did helped your relationship?"

"Are you trying to say something to me, Mike?"

"No."

"Are you threatening me?"

"Of course not. I don't have anything to gain from it. I don't have to do anything. I just have to trust that you're going to be you."

"Don't call me here anymore," she said as she slammed the phone down. She was pissed. Mike acted as if he knew her so well. She was even angrier with herself for ever confiding in him. This wouldn't have happened if she had talked to the person she needed to talk to in the first place. She should have turned to Darnel if she had any doubts.

A few hours later Darnel and Jason returned, with Tasha pulling up right behind them. They were outside horsing around for awhile. Tasha was shooting her mouth off about ball. They came in and were just as rowdy. Lisa yelled downstairs for them to knock it off. When she came downstairs, Darnel and Jason were busy raiding the refrigerator. She yelled at them to get out of her refrigerator. "Go take showers and I will make you some sandwiches." Darnel kissed her when he passed.

Natasha said, "Look at Ms. Suzy Homemaker—that sure is a sweet picture."

"Shut up and tell me where you're going tonight."

"Well, I met this professor at school."

"You're the only one I know who goes to college to meet men."

"Girl it's nothing like that; I met him after I went to register."

"That reminds me do you need any money?"

"No, I have it covered. Now, would you shut up and let me finish. Well, I went to the cafeteria to get me something to eat. I was so hungry. You know I had to get my grub on. It was so crowded and I saw this guy sitting at a table for two, alone, so I sat down."

"You didn't?"

"Yup, I sure did. I didn't ask him if he was alone or anything. I sat there looked him straight in his face and started biting my burger. He looked at me like I was crazy and that's just what I wanted because I wanted the table for myself. He started laughing so I looked at him like what the hell is his problem."

"Tasha, stop cursing you know Jason is here."

"Girl, it's not like he hasn't heard worse in school."

"That doesn't mean he has to hear it here."

"Okay mother just let me finish."

"Go ahead then."

"So I'm munching on my fries and I tell him, 'Look I've had a long day. I'm an old woman trying to get back in school and that if you have a problem, I will end your college career.'

Lisa looked over at Tasha. Tasha never ceases to amaze her. "What did he say?"

"He started laughing. So I smiled at him and told him that I was serious as a heart attack. After that he started asking me questions and I thought I'd amuse him until my food was gone. You know play along with those psychotics. Well eventually, he told me that he wasn't a student and that this was his first year teaching there. So I needed proof of course, and it turned out he was a professor. He looked so young, Lisa. He's actually a year younger than I am. Well anyway, we exchanged numbers and we've been talking for a couple of weeks now. He invited me to some formal dinner. Now, how do you like that?" she winked.

"Girl, if you would have met him any other way I wouldn't have believed you," Lisa laughed.

"Okay girl, let's go through my closet to see if we can find what you're looking for?" They went up the stairs as Darnel and Jason were on their way down. "The sandwiches are on the counter and sit at the table not on the couch."

Darnel said, "Yes dear." When Lisa turned around Natasha was already gone. She wasn't about to waste any time. A free reign on Lisa's closet was just what she wanted. When Lisa opened the door Natasha was already in it. She strolled over to the bed and flopped down. "Natasha don't even think about that one. Get your grubby little paws off of it."

"I was just admiring it, Lisa."

"I'm sure you were, now let it go." She turned her head and heard Tasha laughing. She turned around to see what was happening. Lisa looked at Tasha's hand and saw she was holding her Halloween wig. "Lisa, you wore this to Andre's party didn't you?"

"Yes, I did."

"This used to be a bad Halloween wig, now it's a hoochies best accessory. They say a platinum blond wig takes over some people's minds. They think their invincible and the sexiest thing on this damn earth. I hope you didn't let this wig get the best of you." Then she threw it up on the shelf and starting laughing. If she only knew the half of it, Lisa thought.

Natasha found what she wanted and decided to leave. She volunteered to take Jason with her for a couple of hours so that Lisa and Darnel could be alone and Jason took her up on it. Lisa wasn't thrilled by the idea. Once Natasha and Jason left, Darnel attacked Lisa. "I've been wanting to do this all day," he whispered in her ear. "It feels so good to just hold you." Then he swept her off her feet and carried her upstairs.

23

When Lisa walked in her office on Monday morning, Andre was sitting there waiting for her. She sighed as she walked in. "What are you doing in here so early?"

Sitting there like fox who has just outsmarted the farmer, he replied, "I'm here to catch you up on all your work. There's nothing wrong with that is there?"

Lisa looked at him and rolled her eyes. She knew he wasn't there for that. He just wanted the dirt and he was going to make her life a living hell until he got it. Lisa got up from her desk and went over to her door and closed it. "What do you want to know Andre, and I haven't got all day."

"Well for one, I want to know what was going on in that room?"

"You're not blind. What do you think was going on in that room? We got caught up in the moment and we were kissing as you could see. Now did you really need me to explain that to you? Is that it, Andre?"

"Lisa, I know you don't expect me to believe that."

"Why shouldn't you? Did you see anything after that? I'm sure your nosy ass noticed that we came out right after you. Plus I left shortly after that."

"Well, that sure is strange because so did Mike."

"I went home alone Andre and stop being so fucking nosy. You make me sick. I don't know why the hell I'm explaining this to you. Do you have any business to discuss with me?"

"The cases are on your desk. You don't have to bite my head off. I wasn't the one caught in the closet."

Lisa gave him a look that could rival a stare from O.J. He got the hint because he got up, turned around and walked out the office.

Lisa sat there twisting her hair. Darnel had only been treating her better lately.

Sometimes she felt that she deserved what she was going to get. How can she despise her father so much and then turn out to be just like him.

Last night Lisa had been tempted to call her mother and tell her what she'd done. She knew she was the one person who wouldn't tell. Natasha wouldn't either, but she would have judged her. She'd also contemplated telling Darnel. Give him the chance to walk away if he wanted to. Shit, who was she kidding. She didn't want him to know. She'd must be crazy to think that he could forgive her. She'd do anything to protect this secret and she'll be damned if Mike was going to drive her to do something that she didn't want to do. And that's exactly what she's going to tell him.

After work Lisa decided to go straight to Mike's house. She pulled up in his driveway, walked up to the door, and rang the bell. When he came to the door he seemed surprised. Stepping aside, he motioned for her to come in. She walked through the door and sat down on the couch. He sat in the recliner across from her.

"Mike, I really don't have time for pleasantries. I came to say something and that's what I'm going to do. I don't want to be bothered by you anymore. I want to be with Darnel. I don't need you lurking around in the background."

"Lisa, you make me sound like a vampire. Lurking around? Come on you're exaggerating."

"I really don't care how it sounds. I just want you to know where I stand, and I would like you to respect that. What I need from you is a promise that you will never let what happened between us leave this room."

He looked around for a few minutes and said, "I won't tell anyone what happened. You can trust me."

"Thank you."

"Lisa, we don't have to be enemies now that this has happened."

"Mike, I think that it would be better if we see as little of each other as we possibly can."

Mike got up and walked over to sit on the couch next to her. "Why is that Lisa? Are you afraid that it can happen again?"

"No, I'm not afraid of that. That's just the way things are going to have to be." Slowly, he started inching towards her.

Lisa looked at him and said, "What the hell are you doing?"

"I just wanted to kiss you one last time."

"Are you out of your mind? Have you been listening? This will never happen again Mike. Never." As Lisa went to get up, he grabbed her.

"Lisa, why did you come back here? You could have talked to me all day at work. I believe I passed you maybe twice in the halls today. Why didn't you talk to me there?"

Lisa jumped up and turned to him. "Well, if you must know I didn't want anyone accidentally overhearing—like say Andre. I didn't come here for one last time. To be honest with you, I really don't remember the first time."

Mike started laughing and said, "If you aim that bullet any higher you'd be sure to take me out." Mike got up and came close to her face as if he was going to kiss her. Instead, he rubbed his cheek against hers then walked behind her and put his hands on her shoulders. Lisa started to quiver. He stopped and said, "Now, you tell me that you don't remember the first time."

Lisa took a deep breath and licked her lips, "I have to get out of here." She started walking to the door. Mike walked behind her, put his hand above her shoulder and held the door shut. Lisa closed her eyes and bit her lip. "Lisa, I know you don't want to leave. I may have been coming at you the wrong way. I do care that you are hurting over this. I don't know what to do because I want you too. I can't just walk away. Right now I need to hold you. All I think about is that night; all I think about is you. I don't want to be the bad guy. I'm just the other guy who wants to be with you." He started to kiss her neck and she moaned with pleasure.

Turning around, she said, "Mike, I don't know what I feel for you. It's mixed with so many wrong emotions. I don't want to hurt Darnel. I'm just another conquest for you."

"Don't be too sure, Lisa. You have no idea what I feel on the inside."

"You're right, but I'm in a relationship. I have a family now, and I don't want to throw that all away."

"Lisa all I know right now is that I don't want you to walk out that door." He kissed her again.

"Mike, please don't."

"I won't if you can honestly tell me that you don't want me to touch you."

She closed her eyes. "You know I can't tell you that," she whispered.

"Don't fight it, Lisa." Before she realized it the tears began to flow. "Lisa, don't cry. I don't want to be with you if you don't want to be with me."

"It's not that. It's the fact that I do want to be with you. Right now, more than anything I want to be with you."

He wiped away the tears and held her face. "I want you so badly."

"I want you too." She kissed him. He looked as if her kissing him first meant everything to him. Picking her up, he carried her into the bedroom and lay her on the bed. He undressed her while she tenderly kissed him. Lisa turned over and lay on her stomach, while he kissed her from head to toe. Turning over, she looked up in his eyes and felt as if she would stop breathing. He had never looked at her like this before. He kissed her forehead, then her nose and then her lips. He didn't stop there; he tongued her breast ever so gently and kissed her stomach and then he went down. His tongue was the longest tongue she ever had the pleasure of being acquainted with. The rest of the night was magical. Lisa felt so comfortable with him and that's exactly where she wanted to be, so help her God.

They lay in the bed and he held her against his chest Lisa looked up at Mike to see he had a smile on his face. "Why are you smiling?"

"I'm just glad that you're here."

Sitting, Lisa turned around and looked at him. "Mike, what do you expect to come from this?"

"I really don't know."

"Never mind," she snapped. "It's not up to you anyway. I have to make a decision and stick to it. I'm not going to continue to cheat on Darnel. He deserves better than that."

"Lisa, I'm not pressuring you into anything."

"Look, don't worry about it. I'm definitely not coming over here with my suitcases."

"That's not what I meant. I just want you to be sure of what you're doing, and if that takes time then I'm willing to give it to you."

She wanted to spit on him. How dare he be so understanding. He had nothing to do with her decision. She got out of the bed, got dressed and left. Lisa knew she had to get home. She had to get home before she was missed.

When she walked into the house the lights were off. Everyone was in bed. It was after three in the morning. She went in the kitchen to fix something to eat. She was starving. "What are you doing?" Darnel asked.

Lisa jumped, "I'm just fixing me something to eat. What are you still doing up?"

"What am I doing up? How about where the hell have you been?"

She looked at the ham on her bread for a sign to get her out of this mess. It stared up at her like "You fool, what can I do?" She composed herself and replied, "I went out for a drink I had a hard day."

"Where did you go?"

"I don't know—some little bar off the freeway?"

"On the south or the north side?"

"I think it was on the north or maybe it was on the south."

"Well, which one is it Lisa?"

She felt crowded so she pushed her way past him, but he caught her arm. "What Darnel?" she asked, trying to pull away.

"So Lisa if, I wanted to go could you give me directions?"

"Yeah, I sure could. What is this anyway twenty questions? If you want to ask me something then ask it. Don't beat around the fucking bush."

"What would I want to ask you?"

"Well if you can't figure it out then let me go," she said as she wiggled out of his grip.

"This is bullshit!"

"Lower your voice Darnel. You're going to wake Jason up."

"I don't give a damn. What the hell is going on? Do you think I'm some sort of fool? No decent woman strolls in the house at three o'clock in the morning."

"Darnel, don't start with me. I'm a grown woman. I can come and go as I please."

"Not in this house you can't."

"Well, what are you going to do?" He turned around and punched a hole right through the wall. She looked at him wide eyed. She couldn't believe he'd done that. Darnel had been mad before, but he'd never done anything like that. Lisa didn't know what to do. She wanted to go over to him and see if his hand was all right but something wouldn't let her move. She felt if she touched him she would be next. His face was to the wall the whole time. "Darnel, are you all right?" He didn't answer. "I don't see what you're getting worked up about I was just late." Her voice shook. He still didn't bother to respond. She walked over to him and grabbed his hand and said, "Let me see." He pushed Lisa so hard she fell to the floor. Grabbing his keys, he walked out the door and slammed it behind him. Lisa just sat there and begun to cry.

He didn't know anything, she thought. He doesn't have any proof. She wiped her eyes. Holding onto the rim of the kitchen sink, she pulled herself up. Deny everything was all she thought.

Walking towards the staircase, she looked up and saw Jason standing there. She lowered her head then looked at him again. She could have sworn she saw herself when she was his age, watching her father walk up the stairs. She closed her eyes again and it was Jason standing there. Lisa walked up, turned him around, and walked him to his bedroom. "Go to sleep. I'll talk to you in the morning." He got under his covers. When she tried to tuck him in he pulled away.

Darnel didn't come home that night. However, he did show up in the morning. He had to get some blue prints for an important meeting. He walked past her and didn't say anything. Lisa had nothing to say to him. She'd concentrate on getting Jason ready for school. She fixed Jason some breakfast and walked him to the bus stop. When she returned home Darnel was still there, taking a shower. When she walked into the bathroom, he peeped out from the shower curtain like he didn't know who it could be. "Do you mind?" he said. Lisa rolled her eyes at him, then flushed the toilet on purpose and slammed the door. She heard him yell "oh shit" and that put a smile on her face.

She was about to walk out the door when he came up behind her. He asked her if she was coming home tonight. She rolled her eyes and said, "I don't know, maybe."

Brushing past her, he said, "Maybe you shouldn't." Then he walked out the door and jumped into his truck. Lisa stood there not knowing what to say or do. She still felt he didn't know anything and until he did she would deny everything.

24

When Lisa arrived at work there were a dozen yellow roses on her desk. She opened the card and it said, "You're always on my mind—M." All these different feelings welled up inside of her. She was flattered and at the same time confused. It was time to talk to someone and it had to be soon before she ruined her life.

After work she went straight to the mall hoping to find Natasha. She found her at the clearance rack ticketing clothing. When Natasha glanced looked up she looked as if she'd seen a ghost. "Hey girl, what are you doing here? You are aware that we do not sell Anne Klein or Donna Karan?" she laughed.

"I slept with Mike," Lisa blurted out.

"What did you say? Come again."

"You heard me. I don't want to repeat it."

Natasha stated at her and shook her head from side to side. "Typical," she said.

"What do you mean typical?"

"You know what I mean." She sucked her teeth and curled her upper lip. "What did Darnel ever do to you for you to betray him like that? Especially, with that piece of shit that calls himself a liar, I mean lawyer."

"I need to talk, Tasha." Lisa pleaded with her eyes. She wanted Tasha to understand. "You can pass judgment on me later."

"Come on, I'll take my break now." They walked over to the cafeteria area and sat down at a table. "So, what are you waiting for I'm listening."

"You don't have to make this hard for me, Tasha."

"Well, I sure as hell will not make it easy for you."

"Just listen. The first time I slept with Mike was the night of Andre's party. I felt afterward that I would keep it to myself. I thought I'd come to my senses and it was just a learning experience. I discovered how important my family was to me. But then, I went and slept with him again, and I don't know why. What I do know is that given a chance, I'll probably do it again. The bad part is that I came home late and now Darnel suspects something. There maybe a chance that I can correct this, possibly try to save what we have. In the meantime, I can't go on sleeping with Mike." She paused. "Stop staring at me like that Tasha."

"How do you want me to look at you? Just finish your story."

"Well, I don't know what I want with Mike either. There's a part of me that wouldn't mind spending some time with him."

"Oh, I think you've been spending quite enough time with Mike."

"I don't know what I want with him, but I don't want to give him up either."

"I see, we want a little something over here and a little something over there. Is that what I hear you saying?"

"No Tasha, it's not like that. What I'm saying is that I'm confused."

"Confused? Oh that's putting it nicely. I would say that you are out of your damn mind!"

"Tasha! Lower your voice."

"So now you don't want attention huh? What is wrong with you, Lisa? You couldn't forgive Daddy for what he'd done, but you go out and do it yourself. How does that sound?"

"Look Tasha, I know it's not right, but I'm not married to Darnel."

"That's just an excuse. It has nothing to do with a piece of paper. It's the commitment between two people. Besides you're engaged or did you over look that fact when you were opening your legs."

"You don't have to be so vulgar, Tasha."

"Oh you haven't heard vulgar yet. You better be glad we are here instead of somewhere else."

"Oh stop being so self-righteous; you aren't the Virgin Mary."

"No, but I ain't Jezebel either."

"I can't believe you, Tasha. Whose sister are you mine or Darnel's?"

"It doesn't matter whose sister I am. The point is that I can say these things to you because you are my sister. I know you didn't think that I was going to be like 'how was it?'

There was a long silence. Lisa bowed her head and stared at the floor. She was waiting for Tasha to say something.

"By the way, how was it?"

Lisa cracked a smile. "You're crazy girl. Believe it or not, it really is not about sex. You know Darnel had it going on in that department."

"Then why Lisa, why did you do it?"

"I don't know, Tasha. I really don't know."

That night Darnel called to tell Lisa he wasn't coming home. He didn't give her a chance to ask questions he hung up so quickly. Lisa was upset because he'd left Jason with her. She knew Jason thought it was all her fault.

They sat down to eat dinner. Lisa wanted to send him to his room to eat, so she didn't have to look at him. But they sat down anyway; she picked at her food. Looking over at him, she saw he was picking at his food too. After he'd finished, he looked at her and asked, "What did you do to him?"

"What are you talking about?"

"I heard you arguing last night."

"What makes you think I did something to him?"

"He was mad last night and it had something to do with you not being here."

"I really don't want to discuss this with you."

"Why are you kicking him out?"

"I'm not kicking anyone out."

"Then why isn't he coming home tonight," Jason said, his voiced raised.

"Who told you that?"

"He did."

"When?"

"He called me after school."

"And what did he tell you?" Jason sat there and looked through her as if she wasn't there.

"I asked you a question?"

"He said that you were having some problems and he wouldn't be coming home tonight."

"What else did he say?"

"He told me if you didn't get home by six thirty to call him at the number he gave me."

"He gave you a number?"

"Yes, I wrote it down on a piece of paper."

"Jason do me a favor and go and get me that number." He didn't move. "Did you hear what I said?"

"You're not my mother."

"I don't have to be your mother to tell you to go and get me something in my own house." She gave him that look her mother use to give her. "I'm not going to ask you twice."

He slowly pushed his chair from under the table and stomped to his bedroom. When he returned, he placed the number in front of her. Lisa picked up the piece of paper, and said, "Thank you."

She walked over to the telephone and dialed it. It rang two times and the voice said, "Economy Inn."

"Yes, hello. Can you tell me where you're located?"

"At 54th and 3rd Avenue."

"Thank you," Lisa said and hung up. "Jason! Get some clothes for school tomorrow and some pajamas and your toothbrush. You're spending the night at your grandparents'." She went to her bedroom, put her shoes on, and they were out the door.

When they got to Estelle's, Lisa told her an emergency had come up and she needed Jason to spend the night with her. Estelle looked at her and nodded; then Lisa turned around and jumped into her car. She didn't have time to wonder what Jason thought of her. That could be addressed at a later time. Right now she had to save her relationship.

Lisa pulled up in front of the registration area and went straight to the desk. She asked the young lady what room Darnel was staying in? The clerk gave her that mumbo jumbo about it being private. Lisa pulled out a fifty and then the clerk directed her to Darnel's room. She got in the elevator, shaking more than thc leaves on Labor Day.

Lisa knocked on the door and heard some rustling in the room.

"Who is it?"

"Lisa."

There was a brief pause and then she heard the door unlock. Standing behind the door, Darnel allowed her to walk in. When he closed the door she could see that he was in his boxers. The ones she had bought him for his birthday last year. She looked around and saw that he'd ordered some takeout, and there were blueprints all over the bed. Lisa sat down in a chair.

"Darnel, we need to talk." Darnel walked over to the closet and pulled out a pair of blue jeans and put them on.

She looked at him in amazement. "How long do you plan on staying here? It looks like you have a wardrobe in there."

"I picked up a few things this afternoon."

"Oh."

"Where is Jason?"

"I dropped him off at your mother's house."

He rolled his eyes and threw his arms up in the air. "Why did you do that? I don't want my family involved in this."

"I didn't tell them what was going on. I just explained to them that I had an emergency. What are you planning on doing, Darnel?"

"I don't know what I plan on doing. That's why I'm here, I need time to think."

"To think about what? You don't even know what happened. You're going to sit here and analyze a situation you know nothing about?"

"I know you didn't come home the other night that's what I do know."

"Nothing happened Darnel; I told you I was out getting a drink."

"If you came here to lie to me then you can turn around and walk out that door."

"Can you prove that I'm lying, Darnel?"

"I'm not in court. I don't have to prove anything."

"Well, you have to at least back your shit up."

"You sure have a lot of nerve. If I had done the same thing you're telling me, things would be all right with you? Then again, I wouldn't do something like that to you. On the other hand you would do it over and over again," he said as he pounded his fist in his hand.

"Well, what do you think happened Darnel?"

"I don't even want to say what I think happened."

Lisa sighed, and went over and sat down in the chair. She really didn't want to hear him say what he thought she'd done. She didn't know whether she would deny it. Maybe she wanted him to know the truth, and then she wouldn't have to carry it on her shoulders. Is that selfish? she thought. She felt numb like this was a scene in her life that she was always meant to play out. It didn't feel strange at all; it felt all too familiar. The scene was the same, the characters were the same, but the actors were different.

Lisa didn't move from her chair. She knew once she walked out that eventually it would be over. So she just sat and watched him, but Darnel wouldn't look at her.

When Lisa awoke it was dark, and Darnel was lying on the bed asleep with the TV still on. The room was cold; he had fallen asleep with the air conditioner on. Lisa knew in the morning he would wake up with a cold. She walked over to the air conditioner and turned it off. Tiptoeing over to the bed, she pulled the covers over Darnel. Lisa sat down on the edge of the bed and began to cry. She'd really messed up this time—no fast-talking was going to get her out of this one. She felt like shit; all she could think of was she wanted her mother. Laying her head on the pillow, she crawled into the fetal position and cried and cried. She felt Darnel stirring on his side of the bed.

All sorts of bad thoughts were running through her head; she was scaring herself. Lisa decided to get out before one of them came true. When she started to get up, Darnel grabbed her and held her, and she cried some more, like a three-year-old. He held her tighter and tighter and it seemed like an eternity had passed before she stopped crying. When she finally stopped, Darnel said to her, "I love you Lisa. I love you more than I've loved anybody else. But you're going to kill me, or I'm going to kill you. I think we need some time apart. You need to figure out what you want. You need to grow up. I don't want to know what you did. I don't need proof."

Lisa jumped out of the bed; she would have stabbed him if a knife had been available. Glaring at him, she hoped her eyes could set him on fire. But she caught herself because when she looked at him more closely, she saw his eyes were red. He had been crying too. "I'm sorry, Darnel. I didn't mean to hurt you. I didn't want it to be this way. I do love you."

"Lisa, I know you do."

She ran over to the bed and jumped on top of him. "Then please don't leave me," she cried as she started kissing him. He responded and she knew he wanted her badly.

He then grabbed her and said, "Lisa don't."

"Why?"

"Just don't do it. It's not going to work; it doesn't make any difference if we sleep together or not."

"I'm not doing this to try and stop you. I love you that's all. Please don't turn me away, Darnel." Grabbing a hold of her wrists real hard, he firmly pushed her away. The tightness of his hands around her wrists stung. He finally released her. Her wrists were red and throbbing and she knew she had to get out of there. She needed to get out of there. She ran to the door.

"I'm a man, Lisa, not a saint."

"I didn't do anything, Darnel. You're throwing away what we have for nothing. You're the one who's going to be sorry."

25

The last thing Lisa remembered was ordering a drink. She'd wanted to keep them coming. She had dozed off at the bar. When she woke up, the place was practically empty. "Hey lady, I called you a cab." The bartender hissed, "You can't drive in that condition."

"I'm not taking a cab," she said her words slurred. "Where's my pocketbook?" She rubbed her eyes to get them back in focus.

"I have it here behind the counter."

"Well, what are you waiting for? Give it to me." He threw it at her. She looked inside and found one of Darnel's business cards. She handed it to the bartender. "Here, call him. He'll come and get me."

"Darnel Harvin?" he asked.

"OOPS. That's not my man anymore—he quit me." Then she started laughing; the bartender looked at her like he had no time for this tonight.

"Hey lady," he said annoyed.

"It's Lisa. Lee-sah, say it with me Lee-sah."

"Well Lisa, is there someone else I can call?"

"Wait let me check." She fished around in her purse some more. "Here, call him."

"Mike Wilson?"

"Yes, call him he'll come and get me."

It seemed like forever before Mike arrived. It was a sobering experience. The barkeep wouldn't serve anymore. He'd cut her off and she thought that was the funniest thing she'd ever heard.

When Mike arrived he walked over to Lisa and said, "It's going to be all right."

Lisa smiled at him and told him to take her to his place. When she tried to get up, she fell off the bar stool. Looking up at him she said, "Hey, you were supposed to catch me." He picked her up and carried her out, as she waved good-bye to the bartender. He threw her in the back seat and then sped off. She threw up, said "sorry," and fell asleep.

By the time they arrived at Mike's apartment Lisa was awake. When they got inside he took her straight to his bathroom and began undressing her. Lisa told him that she didn't want to have sex. He told her she had nothing to worry about. She laughed, "Hey that's a good one." Lisa sat on the toilet in her bra and panties with her head between her legs. Looking over at him, she saw he was running the water in the shower. He came back over to her and stood over her. "What are you going to do with me?" she asked.

"I'm going to clean you up so you can go home."

"Home?"

"Yes home. I'm pretty sure Darnel is worried about you."

She started whimpering, "I don't have a home anymore. I ain't got nowhere to go." She was still talking when Mike put her in the shower. She started yelling and screaming that the water was cold as ice. He blocked the exit to the shower, so she sank to the bottom of the tub and just sat there. After awhile he let her out and dried her off. Then he carried her to bed. He told her to lie down and he would go and make some coffee. Lisa mumbled, "I don't want any." But he was gone before he could even hear it.

She was feeling a little bit better when he came in with the coffee. She drank some and spit it out. "This is awful. What are you trying to do kill me?"

"I guess you must be feeling better; you sound like your old self."

Lisa just looked at him as if he didn't exist. She felt the top of her hair and it was wet. "Why did you let me get my hair wet? I just got my hair done."

"I wasn't thinking about that."

Rolling her eyes, she said, "It takes two seconds to put on a shower cap, two seconds."

"Look Lisa, don't come in here bossing me around. I'm tired. I have to be in court in the morning."

"I'm sorry. I guess I'm not in a great mood."

"Are you ever?"

"Ha Ha—very funny." She stood up and took her wet bra and panties off. Glancing at Mike from the corner of her eye, she noted he was watching her. She went over to his drawer and found a T-shirt and some boxers. She could feel his eyes on her the whole time. She put on the T-shirt and started pulling on the boxers then glared at him. "Do you mind?" Turning around, she pulled them all the way up. "So, what do you have to eat around here?"

"Not much. I am a bachelor you know."

"Are you trying to tell me something, Mike? Don't worry I'm not moving in."

"So you think all of this is going to be that easy Lisa?"

"What did you say you had to eat?"

"Answer the question, Lisa."

"I don't know what it's going to be like. I'll just have to make it easy and not dwell on it. Come with me to the kitchen; I'm so hungry."

"I guess I will, but I would like to know what happened."

"Aren't you nosy? I think men are actually the nosiest people on the planet."

"Oh, you think so?"

"Well, it's been my experience. Come on. What are you waiting for? I'm hungry." She grabbed his hand and led him to the kitchen. The cabinets were bare, and the refrigerator was empty. Sitting down at the table, she ate a peanut butter sandwich with a glass of water. She knew Mike was dying to know what had happened. "Nothing happened. We're just having some problems now. I'm sure we'll work them out. I exaggerated at the bar. I had a little too much to drink."

"You're lying through your pretty white teeth. I know you're smarter than that. You're caught. Have enough sense to realize that."

"Oh, bite me. I'm not caught. I'll get Darnel back. You just wait and see. You're just jealous, because you can't have me."

"Oh I had you, Lisa." She slapped him across the face.

Laughing, he backed away from her and taunted, "Touchy subject huh? I'll leave you alone. Good night, Lisa." Watching him leave, she decided her sandwich was more important to her at the moment.

26

In the morning Mike drove Lisa to get her car then she went home for some clothes. No one was there. She suspected Darnel hadn't been by yet. She got enough things so she wouldn't have to come back for a couple of days. She put the things in the back seat of her car. Lisa showered and changed and headed for work. When she got there she threw herself into her work.

After a few hours Andre barged into her office. She looked straight up at him like he'd lost his mind.

"Hello Lisa, how are you?"

"I'm fine, Andre, and you?"

"I'm doing pretty good. Are you planning on doing any traveling soon?"

"What?" she asked annoyed.

"Are you getting ready to take a trip?"

She had no idea what he was talking about and why he had that notion. "No Andre, I'm not going anywhere. Why?"

"Well, I seen all those clothes in the back of your car. I just thought maybe you were going on vacation or something."

Now she knew what this fool was getting at. "Why were you looking in the back of my car, Andre? Don't we have enough work around here to keep you busy without you having to resort to that? Now, since you have all this free time to be in my business, I think I'll give you some work."

"Ah come on Lisa, I just passed your car when I was getting something in mine."

"Really, well take these files and do what you do best." She got up and shoved them into his arms, she turned him around, opened the door and pushed him out.

Around that time she began to feel hungry. She wasn't in the mood to go out so she thought she'd order in. She was rummaging through her desk drawer for some menus, her head practically in her desk, when someone walked in. It was Mike and he had food in his hands. "So, I guess you can read my mind now," she quipped.

"I guess I can."

"It smells so good. You have excellent timing."

"I thought the way you were eating last night that you'd still be hungry today."

"Very funny. Have a seat."

"Who would have thought that all this time the key to your heart was food." Mike teased. Lisa dug right into the food. They didn't talk much. After they'd finished eating, he just sat there staring at her. "What are you staring at?"

"You. I like the way you look in my underwear. I was just trying to picture it again."

They were engrossed in their conversation when she heard a knock on the door. She wasn't really paying too much attention, but she told the person to come in. Her mouth dropped to the floor. It was Darnel, standing there looking taller than Mt. Everest. She jumped up and said, "Darnel, what are you doing here?"

Mike stood up, "How have you been, Darnel?"

She closed her eyes and waited for the earthquake to start. Then she blinked and things were still very still.

Darnel's eyes were cold, cold like ice picks. Mike stood his ground and walked past him. Darnel grabbed Mike by his throat, yelling, "I should break your neck motherfucker." Mike's arms flailed around. "Stand still! Give me one more reason to break your fucking neck!"

Lisa ran around from behind her desk and grabbed Darnel's hands, trying to loosen his grip. "Darnel, let him go!" Mike's face was turning red. "He can't breathe, Darnel. You're going to kill him!" she screamed as tears began to fall from her eyes.

"Tell me the truth, Lisa. Did you sleep with him?"

"What?" she stuttered.

"I will break his neck, Lisa." Mike's eyes were bulging out of his head.

"Stop Darnel! What do you think you're doing?"

"I'm only going to ask you this one last time."

"I don't know what you're talking about. Are you crazy? Stop this! Please Darnel, let him go." Mike started to turn a deep shade of purple. "Darnel please," she sobbed. Lisa looked at Mike; his eyes pleaded for her to help him. "Darnel stop!"

"Did you?"

"No."

"Did you?"

"No Darnel."

"You're lying for this piece of shit."

"I'm telling you the truth."

"I'm going to kill him!" Darnel yelled and began squeezing even harder.

"Yes!" I did it. I'm sorry." A look of utter disbelief came over Darnel's face. He froze in his place. Grasping his fingers, she pulled them one by one from around Mike's throat. He slumped to the floor, gasping for air. Lisa's mascara was running down her face. She had broken two nails, trying to get Darnel off of Mike.

Darnel looked at her and started laughing a strange laugh. "I came here to see if you wanted to figure out some kind of schedule to see Jason. He's really attached to you which I'm sure you already know." He looked at his hands, then at her. "I don't ever want to see you again. I'll have your things packed and you can have someone pick them up." He walked towards the door. "I mean it Lisa; I don't want you any where near my property."

She choked up and tried to swallow hard to get the words out. "What about Jason?"

"He'll have to get over it." Darnel slammed the door and left.

27

That night Lisa went over Natasha's house. She picked up the key from her at work. When she got there she began to feel a little stir crazy and decided to go for a ride. As Lisa was walking out, Natasha was coming in. Before Natasha could even ask Lisa told her she'd be back later and walked off. Lisa heard Natasha yell down the hall, "Don't do anything stupid!" Lisa was gone.

She drove and drove and finally ended up where she wanted to go in the first place, Mike's house. After she'd entered his apartment, she continually apologized for what had happened in her office. Finger marks were still visible around his neck, and every so often he would touch his neck. The way he looked made her think Darnel's hands were still around his throat.

"You know Lisa, I'd better stay away from you before somebody gets hurt."

"I know you're not going to try and put this on me. You knew my situation. So, now that you been roughed up a little... Are you going to disappear into the woodwork?" She laughed at him saying, "Now, I've never seen that side of Darnel before. You think you know a person. Come to think of it, I've never seen that side of you. You have to laugh." Mike's face was red as a beet.

"I don't find anything humorous about it. I'm not embarrassed. Am I supposed to be ashamed that your barbaric boyfriend lost control?"

"Well, what would you have done? Can you blame him? Quit feeling sorry for yourself."

"Lisa ,you are so heartless."

"Oh, because you got your little neck choked, the world stops. What about me, you selfish bastard. I just lost the person whom I love more than anything. My relationship is ruined not yours. You didn't have anyone to answer to, but I did."

"You're a grown woman. Nobody made you do anything."

"You know what? You can go to hell. I'm out of here."

***

Lisa walked up to the door. She couldn't remember the last time that she'd been there. It seemed so long ago. She rang the bell and waited. A few minutes later the porch light came on. It was shining so bright, she felt like she was on stage.

"Who is it?"

"Ma, it's me."

"Is that you Lisa?" her mother asked.

"Yeah Ma, cut off the light and open the door." Her mother opened the door slowly and Lisa walked in. "I'm not going to rob you Ma, relax."

"Lisa, do you know what time it is?"

"No."

"Well what's wrong?"

"I cheated on Darnel. He almost killed Mike, and he doesn't want to see me anymore."

"Oh child, what's wrong with you?"

"I don't know."

"Why did you do it?"

"I don't even know that." She leaned up against the wall and slowly slid down it. "What is that you're wearing?" her mother asked her.

"It's Natasha's clothes; I'm supposed to be staying with her."

"Where did you just come from?" Lisa looked down at the floor because she didn't want to say. "I guess you came from that fella's house."

Lisa started laughing she couldn't believe she called him a fella. She got up and walked to her old room. She opened the door. It still looked pretty much the same. She fell on her bed and fell asleep.

When Lisa woke up she took a shower. She put on the same clothes she had on yesterday. "Now," she thought, "I can leave." She thought she would say good-bye first. As she went past the kitchen she saw her mother had already cooked some breakfast. Looking up at her, her mother said, "Where do you think you're sneaking off to?" She pointed to Lisa's old seat and told her to sit down and eat. Lisa walked over to the chair as if she were five years old. She had to admit that food sure smelled good and recently, it seemed like she was hungry all the time. Sitting down at the table, she began to eat like she hadn't eaten in days. Her mother watched in astonishment, saying, "What's wrong with you? Have you been living on the streets?

Lisa laughed, "No Ma, I haven't. "I'm just hungry that's all."

"Natasha called this morning. She was worried about you. She had no idea you'd be here. I must admit I was taken aback? But I thought I would wait for you to tell me. Go ahead, I'm waiting," Sandra said as she sat down at the table.

Lisa debated about what she was going to tell her. She was irritated, but wanted to say the right thing and not offend her. She thought about several nice things to say, but her mother would have seen through them quicker than Lisa could have told another lie. So Lisa decided to let her mouth just flow and see what happened. "Ma, I don't really know why I came here. I thought I would come and think things over, but I just wound up falling fast asleep. I could have stayed at Tasha's place, but I just wasn't comfortable there. I went by to see my friend... Let's just say things didn't go to well." Lisa looked at her mother who cocked her eyebrow, but didn't say anything. "I felt like the wind was knocked out of me when Darnel said he didn't want to see me again. He meant it, Ma. I think that's when it dawned on me that maybe he'll never take me back. That's if I wanted to go back. Somewhere in the back of my head I thought that if I made the wrong decision that I would still be able to go back. He would understand, you know."

"Girl, have you gone plum crazy? He's a man isn't he?"

"Yes."

"I hope you don't think because I took your father back that I understood."

"Well if you didn't Ma why did you take him back?"

"For a lot of reasons. Men will be men, Lisa, and that's how I saw it."

"Ma, you know that is a bunch of crap. Men can be monogamous if they choose to be. They just don't make that choice."

"So what's your reason, Lisa? You didn't choose to be monogamous?"

"I really don't know what the hell was going through my head. I could have made the right choice, but I chose to jump into something. Now I don't want to be held accountable."

"And you think it's that easy?"

"I don't know what I think, Ma. I feel that I have to find out who I want to be with. And that Darnel should be there waiting for me if I decide it's him that I love."

"Oh really! If you decide? Did you think that's what happened between me and your father? He had no choices after he'd done what he did. I was the only one making any decisions around here. The first time he cheated it hurt a lot. It hurt like hell, and I thought I wouldn't ever let him back in my life again. It seems like love won out, and practicality. I wanted my marriage to work. I wanted to be with him. I made the decision to let him back into my life. Darnel will be making all the decisions now. It's up to him as to whether or not he wants you back in his life. I'm going to tell you this Lisa, it's hard for a man. No matter how much he loves you, that will not affect his decision. You have to think about his pride, and his manhood. And whether or not he could ever look at you without hating you. Do you think that's gonna happen?"

"I'm not sure. Why aren't you asking me about the other man?"

"If he was that important you'd be worrying about what was going to happen with ya'll next. I think you and Darnel belong together. He's a good man. You've gone and done something foolish that he may never forgive you for. Was it worth it?"

"I don't know yet."

"And what about that boy that is staying with you?"

"Jason?"

"Yes, Darnel's nephew, don't you think that this might affect him. He's been through so much you know. I always thought it was better for you and Natasha that your father and I stayed together. Children should have both parents and that's what I gave you."

"Well Ma, I guess we totally disagree on that one. I think it would have been better if you and Dad had gone your separate ways. Your being together was a great disservice to me. I've had tremendous difficulties with relationships because of your unhealthy one. Maybe if I had seen you be strong, I would see life a little differently."

"That's a bunch of hogwash, Lisa. I never cheated on your father. Why did you cheat on Darnel?"

"I did it to him before he could do it to me."

"There was no cause for you to think he was going to cheat on you."

"Hey, you never know."

"Now you're grasping at straws. I guess if you need to believe that you will. Your father had a lot of things he needed to believe in order to look at himself in the mirror."

"I've never heard you talk about him like that before."

"There were many reasons for that. I believe he was a good father; he just wasn't a good husband. I played a part in that too. I could have left him, but I didn't. I didn't think there was a reason to badmouth him to you and Tasha. You already were starting to be disrespectful. If I had given you any more ammunition, things would have really gotten crazy around here. He apologized and we worked things out to the best of our abilities."

"He never apologized to us."

"What do you mean he never apologized to you?"

"It wasn't only against you Ma. What he did was against the family. He hurt us all. It was like he tarnished our union and it wasn't special anymore. I couldn't understand how he let someone enter our circle and then tore us apart. I think if maybe once he had said to me, 'Lisa I'm sorry,' I wouldn't hate him as much as I do now."

"You don't hate him Lisa."

"Oh yeah? I think I do."

"You just don't know what to do with the love you have for him inside. You call it hate, but it's only your way of holding onto the love you have for him."

Lisa sank into her chair, and looked at this woman and said to herself, you know she might be right.

28

Lisa didn't quite know what to do with herself; she felt like she had no where to go. She just wanted to go home, lay down, and get in her bed. She didn't want to go to Tasha's place or Mike's place. She wanted to go home! Damn she needed to go home. She needed to at least get some clothes. There, that was her excuse. So that's where she headed.

Lisa pulled up in the driveway and sat there for a few minutes. She knew Darnel was home because his truck was in the driveway. She just didn't know how she was going to get in there. She had no game plan. Could she just waltz in like she still lived there? Or should she knock like a guest? Her head was spinning trying to figure out what to do. Spinning so badly she felt like she had to throw up, and that's just what she did. She opened the door and threw up right there on the pavement. Getting out of her car, she went to the door and opened it with her key. She walked in. Darnel and Jason were sitting on the couch. She looked at them and felt dizzy all over again. She ran to the bathroom holding her mouth. Luckily, she made it in time. She started washing up and brushing her teeth when she heard Darnel approach the door. "Lisa, are you okay?" She didn't answer him because she had a toothbrush in her mouth. He barged in the door knocking her against the wall. She looked at him in sheer horror, thinking maybe he was truly serious about not seeing her again.

"Whaaaaat?" she yelled.

"I didn't know if you were all right. Do you know how it looked—you barging in here then running in the bathroom and throwing up? And then you didn't answer."

"I was brushing my teeth."

"I can see that. I'm sorry, are you all right?"

"Yeah, I'm fine but it hurt."

"Yeah okay, what are you doing here, Lisa?"

"I came to get some clothes."

"You could have called."

She looked at him and rolled her eyes, then she pushed him out of the way. She went to the living room to see Jason.

"Hi there. How are you doing?"

"Fine," he said, but he wouldn't look at her.

"You're not so talkative today. What's wrong?"

"Nothing."

"Is that all your going to say to me?"

"I haven't been doing anything."

Backing away, she walked up the stairs. She went to the bedroom, and sat on the bed she had to absorb some of the pain. She didn't quite know how to react. Walking over to the closet, she pulled out a small bag, stuffing things in—it was all a blur. She didn't realize it was because she was crying until Darnel walked in. He handed her a tissue and she snatched it from him. He just sighed and turned around. "What did you tell him, Darnel?"

"Lisa, what are you talking about?"

"Why is he acting like that towards me?"

"I don't know."

"Oh yes you do. Stop lying!"

"Lisa, don't come over here acting crazy. All he knows is that you're moving out; he just feels uncomfortable about the situation. Are you finished packing?"

"Why are you hovering over me? I'm not going to steal anything."

"Lisa, come on, I've already asked you nicely."

"You asked me nicely what? Do you want me to leave?"

"Yes, I do."

"Well tough, I'm not finished."

"I can't believe you. You come over here causing trouble when you were the one out there cheating on me. Woman you have nerve. This is my house—don't make me physically remove you."

"Remove me? Remove me? I want to see you try it," she challenged, walking over and pushing him. "Go ahead Darnel, do it."

"Woman take your hands off of me."

"Why, what are you going to do? Are you going to choke me too?" Darnel grabbed her, trying to restrain her. Lisa hadn't had enough because next she tried to punch him. Fortunately, she missed.

"Okay, it's time for you to go," Darnel said, taking her by the arm and pulling her towards the door.

"I'm not going anywhere!" she screamed as she broke free, ran in the bathroom, and locked the door.

"Lisa, come out of there," Darnel yelled.

"If you want me out, you're going to have to break down your precious door." Lisa looked around and decided she'd sit right there on the toilet. She didn't hear anything so she assumed Darnel had left her alone. He'd been gone for about fifteen minutes, when all of a sudden she heard him fidgeting with the door. She looked at the doorknob, but it wasn't moving. So she stepped back and tried to figure out what he was up to. Then it came to her—he wasn't going to mess up his precious door. That motherfucker was taking it off its hinges. Lisa sat back and thought, "Let him."

He finished with the first one when Lisa heard Tasha's voice. "Lisa, what are you doing in there?"

"I live here. What the hell are you doing here?"

"Darnel called me. Why don't you come out of that bathroom."

"No, I'm not coming out. Let him finish with the door. Tasha, do me a favor go and see if Jason's hungry."

"Okay Lisa." She heard her leave the room and close the door. A few minutes later Darnel finished taking the door off the hinges. She looked directly at him and he looked at her. She sat there on the toilet for a few seconds and then got up. When she walked past him, she thought she heard him say something. She turned around because she really hadn't heard him. "Lisa, is this what it's going to be like?"

"I want to see Jason. If you let me see him, I'll try to leave you alone."

"Lisa, you have no rights to Jason he's not your flesh and blood."

"It doesn't matter. I'm the one who helped your family with the legal matters when you needed it. I've become attached to him. I'm always wondering how he's doing? We did spend a lot of time together. It's mainly me who takes him to see his mother."

"I will take him to see her now."

"That's not the point; I want to see him now."

"Okay, I'll work something out with you only if you stop pulling these stunts."

"Okay fine. I'll go."

"I don't want it to be like this Lisa. You need to give me time. I really cannot be around you right now. I'm trying my best to control my temper. Don't make me lose it in front of him."

"Well at least you have one. You act so cold towards me."

"What did you expect?"

"I didn't think past what I did. You don't miss me, Darnel?"

"I really don't want to talk about it."

"Well, do you at least want to hold me."

"Not really."

"I guess that's my cue to get the hell out of here."

"I guess it is."

"I'll call you tomorrow."

"No, let's go through Natasha or my mother." She jumped right in and said she'd go through Natasha. He said fine and then she turned around and left.

While she was downstairs, she said a few things to Jason. She told him she would still like them to spend some time together. He didn't respond, which made her feel a lot worse. Natasha walked with her out of the door. When Lisa got in her car, Natasha leaned in the window and told her to follow her home—like she was her mother. Lisa just looked at her and nodded. She knew she needed to go there eventually. So she might as well go ahead and get it over with.

When they got to Natasha's place Lisa went straight to the kitchen and fixed herself a drink. They both sat down in the living room. Natasha took a deep breath and said, "So, are you losing your mind?" Lisa merely looked at her and rolled her eyes. "What the hell do you think you were doing over there? I know that after what you did, you can't possibly think that you have a right to be over there? You can jump in anytime because I'm on a roll. I won't be stopping any time soon. What is wrong with you, Lisa?"

"Did you pick up those clothes for me at the cleaners?"

"What?"

"I need that black pantsuit for next week."

"You're just using that kid to drive Darnel crazy. This is not a game anymore, Lisa. Don't put that kid in the middle of this. So you're just going to ignore..." Lisa looked over at Natasha and tuned her out; she really didn't have anything to say. She knew what she felt wasn't normal, but there was no changing it. She wanted her way and she was going to get it eventually, or at least die trying.

29

Later on in the evening Natasha woke Lisa up to tell her that someone was on the phone. Lisa asked who it was, but Natasha didn't answer. She yelled, "You better pick it up before I hang it up." Lisa picked it up and it was Mike on the other end. They said their hellos then he asked her where had she been. She mumbled something and he seemed like he was satisfied with the answer. Things were positively not going the way she'd expected. Mike ended up talking her into coming over to his place. So she hung up and got ready.

Mike arrived about forty five minutes later to pick her up. When he drove up, she jumped in the car. He was smiling from ear to ear. She looked over at him and told him it was a sin to be that happy. He touched her face and said, "You are so beautiful, Lisa. Let's call a truce."

"Okay. I don't want to fight."

"I know you think things are getting out of hand. A little bit crazy. But I know we can have fun together." He put his hand on her thigh. He glanced over quickly, while trying to keep his eyes on the road. "It's up to you."

Lisa leaned back and ran her fingers through her hair, then scrunched up her face. "You're serious aren't you?"

"Yes, I am."

"I can't promise you anything, Darnel." She covered her mouth quickly. She was so embarrassed. "I mean, Mike. I'm not looking to jump into anything. I don't really know how you feel about me. I still love Darnel. You need to know that."

"I just don't want to fight with you, Lisa. I want to enjoy the time we spend together. I don't expect you to stop loving Darnel overnight." She looked over at him and he had an expression on his face that she couldn't quite describe. "You like me?" she said half surprised. He didn't respond. "You really like me, Mike. I didn't know."

"We'll talk about that at a later time. Let's just enjoy this evening."

Mike must have taken some time planning the evening because everything seemed to go so smoothly. He was really into it. Lisa would look over at his face and it seemed to her like it was glowing.

The first place they went was the comedy show. A good laugh was what she needed, to get her mind off of other things. Afterwards Mike took her to a four-star restaurant. They were seated immediately and a complementary bottle of champagne was sent to their table. Mike could be quite charming when he wanted to be. The way he glided into a room without effort. He took charge and things started happening. He was a beautiful thing to look at, pretty boy, but very masculine looking. He had natural curly hair, the kind where he would have to ask you nicely, Please stop running your fingers through my hair." His skin was cocoa caramel and he was broad like a football player. Darnel was tall and thin, and chocolate like a Hershey's kiss. He was strong looking, a fine brother. Muscular with no help from dumbbells, he had a washboard stomach. Darnel's face was chiseled; there was nothing pretty about it. It was a man's face and there was no mistaking that. They were two very handsome men in different ways.

Lisa's eyes came back into focus. She could see she'd just agreed to do something which she knew nothing about. He had taken the liberty of ordering dessert for her. He was now reading her mind. She was like a little kid when she saw the cheesecake covered with fresh strawberries. It was "ooh wee" bring it here. Mike was enjoying this, she could tell because that smile never left his face.

After she'd finished eating, she sat for awhile patting her stomach because she had eaten too much. She felt like a pig and thought she must have looked like one too. But the way Mike looked at her, you would think she was the most beautiful thing in the room. He slid over next to her in the booth and gently kissed her on her cheek. It felt good. She looked at him and smiled, and kind of laid her head on his shoulders. He asked her how the evening was so far. "Pretty good," she replied.

"How would you like to make it a little better?"

"I'm game."

"I want to take you home and make love to you, Lisa."

"Whoa! Slow down cowboy. You want to make love to me?"

"I wanna take you right here in the restaurant, but I don't think that would be appropriate."

"So you wanna take me right now?" she said blushing.

"I guess what I really want to say to you is that life is short, and I don't want to waste any of it." Who could argue with that?

"Okay Mike, let's go."

She started moving out of her seat, when he grabbed her arm and said, "I also wanted to tell you that I'm in love with you." She blinked her eyes twice and took a deep breath. It felt like the room was spinning out of control.

"Don't say anything, Lisa. I know you're still in love with Darnel, but I needed to tell you. I don't want you thinking that this is just an affair for me, it's more than that. I want to make love to you and I want you to know it. I want you to let me make love to you." Then he kissed her on her lips. "Do you think you can handle that Lisa?"

She kissed him back, grabbed his hand and pulled him along behind her. When they got to his car, she pushed him against the car and started to kiss him. He held her very tightly as she looked up into his eyes. For a minute she felt secure, right there in his arms. She let all thoughts of Darnel fade away. Mike whispered in her ear, "Are you ready?"

She said, "Yes, I am."

"Are you sure Lisa?"

"Yes, I'm sure." He kissed her on her forehead and opened the car door.

As they sped off he reached out and held her hand and it felt nice. For a minute, she gave into the idea that there could be life after Darnel, and maybe it could be nice. It sure felt nice. Mike popped in a R. Kelly CD and let the music play. The ride home was pretty quiet; no one was really on the road that night. He was singing along to one of the songs. She'd never seen this side of him and it was sure a fun side. She started laughing. Glancing over at her, he said, "I know you're not laughing at this beautiful singing."

"Why of course not Mike. You sound just like the record."

He smiled, "You know I like it when you lie to me." He took her hand and squeezed it gently. "Girl, you know I can make you happy."

"Really?"

"Yes, I know I can."

"You want to make me happy?"

"That's all I think about. Keeping you with me."

"You know it might be hard to keep me."

"I don't think about that. Thinking about you staying with me is a much nicer thought."

All of a sudden they saw a big rig bearing down on them. The lights were so bright. Mike started beeping the horn and switching lanes, but it seemed as if the truck took up the entire highway. Mike tried speeding up, but that didn't slow the truck down; he just came up behind them faster. "Mike, we need to get off this road!" Lisa yelled. Mike was so busy trying to avoid the truck that he didn't respond. They spotted the next off ramp and Lisa could tell that as soon as they got near it they would get off. All of sudden her body jerked forward. The bastard had hit them from behind. She started to panic, but Mike seemed to be under control.

"We're almost there," he said. Bang! The truck hit them again and this time they seemed to be attached to it. Mike lost control of the wheel. Lisa was screaming. Somehow they were let loose, and for a second, they thought things were going to be okay. Lisa looked back at the truck and when she turned around, they were headed straight for a wall and everything went blank.

PART TWO

1

Lisa slowly opened her eyes, her mouth felt dry and nasty. She tried to sit up but couldn't she was in so much pain. "Relax" was all she heard. Her eyes weren't focusing properly. "Mike! Mike!" Was all Lisa could say, then everything went blank.

***

It seemed like only a few minutes before she had been calling out Mike's name. She wasn't quite sure, but she thought she saw her mother sitting there. "Ma," she said softly. She had to say it a few times before she finally got her mother's attention.

When Sandra noticed Lisa, she soothed her, saying, "Ssssh Lisa, don't try to talk."

Lisa ignored her mother's advice. "Ma, what's going on? What happened?"

"Well, let's not talk about that right now. I'll go and get the doctor." A few minutes later the doctor came into the room. Right behind him were Natasha and Darnel. The doctor checked her vitals and had the nurse come in and do some things.

"Is she going to be all right?" Sandra asked anxiously. "Will she be unconscious again? What should we tell her?" The doctor moved Sandra out of Lisa's earshot. Natasha who was holding Lisa's hand, squeezed it gently. Lisa saw Darnel standing over in the corner. There was something wrong with this picture she thought to herself. What was it? Where was Mike?

"Natasha, where is Mike? Is he all right?" Lisa asked.

"We'll talk about that later."

"Natasha, where is he?" Lisa insisted in a strained voice. Natasha looked over at Darnel, and then she turned around to get the doctor's attention. Lisa couldn't understand what the hell was going on. Why couldn't Natasha just answer the question? While their backs were turned, Lisa started to get out of the bed.

She wasn't watching what she was doing and accidentally pulled the IV out of her arm. A loud beeping noise went off, sending everyone in the room into a panic.

"She's trying to hurt herself," Sandra yelled.

"It was an accident," Lisa tried to explain. But no one could hear her over all the hysteria in the room.

"I knew this was going to happen. I think she needs something to calm her down."

"I don't need anything!" Lisa yelled, confused by all the commotion. "Just tell me where he is?" But nobody would say anything. Lisa tried to get up again so the doctor called for the nurse and they both held her down. Lisa saw the nurse coming towards her with a needle and started to scream, trying to break free. "Darnel help me!" Darnel looked like he felt sorry for her. "Darnel, tell them I'm okay," she implored him.

Coming over to the bed, he asked, "Do you have to be so rough?"

She looked in his eyes, pleading for him to help—"Darnel pleaaasssse…"

When Lisa awoke later she remained still; she didn't want to ask any more questions. Her mother motioned for Tasha to do something. Lisa shut her eyes.

"Lisa." She opened her eyes. "My name is Doctor Green; I'm a psychiatrist." Lisa looked at her wondering, *so what?* Dr. Green motioned for whoever was in the room to gather around. Lisa saw her mother, Natasha and Darnel. She had to do a doubletake, but, yes, it was her father in the far corner. "What we have to tell you might be hard to take at first. But we are all here for you. Your family and friends will be here to support you." Right then she knew. Mike was dead—he had to be. Tears started to roll down her face, and whatever that lady was saying just faded into the background. She looked around—looked at all these faces staring at her. She wanted them out of her room. She didn't want to see any of them.

"I want to be alone," is all she said to them.

Dr. Green said, "There is some good news."

Lisa stared at her like she had two heads. "Good news? What could you possibly have to say to me that could be construed as good news?"

The doctor replied, "Well, the baby is fine, and with some work there shouldn't be any complications."

"What baby?" Lisa asked sharply, now paying attention.

Everyone looked around puzzled? "She doesn't know?" Dr. Green asked. She gathered herself up and took a deep breath, but before she could utter anything, Natasha cut in, "Lisa you're pregnant."

"What?"

"You're about three months pregnant." Lisa immediately looked at Darnel. The room was silent. Grabbing her stomach, she started crying uncontrollably.

"Are you sure?" she muttered through her sobs.

"Yes. In fact, a sonogram was done on you the first night you were here. Your mother has the photo. Ms. Munroe, I think now would be a good time to show her."

Sandra pulled a piece of paper out of her purse and handed it to Lisa. Lisa looked at it and saw a little alien-looking thing with a head, a big head. She just started crying again.

Natasha bent down and kissed her. "Lisa, it's going to be all right. You have to be strong for the baby." Lisa let out a yell that could have awakened the dead. Then Natasha started crying too. All Lisa remembered was crying and eventually falling asleep.

2

The next day the nurse woke Lisa up at an ungodly hour. They had stopped feeding Lisa intravenously, and the nurse was mumbling something about breakfast, "It's six in the morning. I'm not hungry yet," Lisa grumbled.

"Well, this is the time we serve breakfast dear. Why don't you sit up? Or do you need to use the bathroom?"

"Yes, I do need to use one," Lisa said as she started to get out of the bed.

"Hold on," the nurse said restraining her. She went into Lisa's bathroom and returned with a bedpan.

"I'm not going in that," Lisa said scrunching up her nose. "I want to use the bathroom."

"Fine, Wonder Woman. Let's see what you can do."

It took about fifty maneuvers and twenty twists to end up right where she'd started. When Lisa saw that smirk on the nurse's face, she wanted to smack it right off of her. "I need that pan!" Lisa snapped at her. The nurse helped her up and that was the end of that.

While she cleared a space for Lisa to eat, she started talking. "I'm really sorry about your friend. He was on the news for the first couple of nights. I believe the services are going to be tomorrow."

"Where?" Lisa whispered.

"It's in New York, dear. That's where he was from and that is where his family is."

"Oh." Lisa looked down at her food and thought it was lemonade in a dish.

The nurse seeing the expression on her face, said, "It's broth dear; I'm afraid you're on a liquid diet."

"I'm really not that hungry."

"Well, what about that baby you're carrying? I suppose he has to eat."

"He?"

"It's just an expression, don't get excited."

"There's nothing to get excited about."

"A baby is a blessing. Of course there's something to be excited about."

"You tell that to my waistline. Just leave it there I'll eat later."

"Well, the doctor said if you didn't cooperate that it would have to be intravenously. So what's it going to be?" Lisa grabbed her plastic spoon and started to dip in it. Her face was so scrunched and contorted, that she looked like she was having a convulsion. "Delicious, isn't it? Don't eat so fast—there's more." The nurse laughed as her belly vibrated right over Lisa's broth.

Lisa had been watching TV all morning. Around ten o'clock she heard a knock on the door and then it slowly opened. Looking up, she saw it was Darnel. He walked over to the bed and squeezed her hand, then he sat down in a chair. Lisa was neither glad nor upset that he was there. He didn't say anything and neither did she. They both continued to watch the television. About a half-hour later the nurse came in and said, "Here Ms. Munroe, here's your vitamin."

"What is this for?" But before the nurse could answer, Lisa said, "Oh, it's a pre-natal vitamin." She glanced at Darnel, but he acted as if he was engrossed in the television program. When the nurse left Lisa sat up and said, "Darnel, I really appreciate this visit, but what are you really here for?"

"I just wanted to make sure you're all right. I had some time this morning so I thought I'd stop by."

"And that's it?"

"That's it for now, the most important thing is that you get better."

"So, when I'm better, you're going to tear me apart."

"I'm going to make sure you have a full recovery and that's all I can do for now."

"How are you going to do that? You know I don't need you financially. Emotionally? I don't think so. You hate me right now. What's the real reason?"

Darnel stood up. "I'm here for that baby. That's why I'm here. There is a fifty percent chance that it's mine. I did the math. There is still a strong possibility that it's mine. As long as I know that, I'm going to be here whether you like it or not. You owe me at least that."

"I don't owe you anything," Lisa said defiantly. "What about Mike? What if it's his? If anybody is owed something, it would be him."

"I'm not concerned about him right now. All I care is if it is mine!"

"I don't expect for you to have any sympathy for me. But I don't expect you to be cruel either. I have some grieving to do. I just lost..."

"Oh say it Lisa, it's no secret. You just lost a lover."

"You don't have to be ugly about it. We've already established that," she retorted and turned towards the window.

"Lisa?"

"Look, I'm not having some mock custody battle over someone whom we don't even know is yours. For your information, I haven't decided what I'm going to do about it."

A vein popped out of his head. "You're evil, Lisa. You have always been selfish and I've put up with it. You know that I've been pleading with you to have a child. And if it's mine, you're going to kill it?"

"It doesn't matter whose it is. It's a decision I have the right to make." She looked over at his face and his eyes were watery.

"If you do that I'll kill you and send you to be with that man!"

"Get out!" she yelled. Darnel didn't move. "I said, get the hell out of here."

Just then Natasha walked in the room. "What's going on in here?"

"I want him out of here," Lisa moaned holding her stomach.

Natasha pulled on Darnel's arm, and urged, "Come on Darnel, you need to leave." He pulled away from Natasha and stormed out of the room.

"What just happened in here?" Natasha asked.

"Nothing. I don't want to talk about it."

"Well, ya'll can't carry on like that in a hospital. Do you want to get kicked out?"

"It won't happen again because I don't want him here anymore."

"You don't mean that Lisa. He's the only one you've got now."

"Why? Because Mike's dead? Haven't I taught you anything about settling. Besides, he didn't want anything to do with me before the accident. So he doesn't need to start now."

"I think you might have hit your head a little bit harder than we all thought. He didn't want anything to do with you because you were cheating on him with a coworker. Um—hello. Does that ring any bells? My God Lisa, you can be a real dope sometimes."

"Natasha, I don't want to talk about this with you. But there are some things that I need to talk to you about. Pull that chair over here close to me. I wanna know if that was really Daddy here the other day."

"Yes it was."

"Well, is he still here?"

"He is, but I think he's leaving tomorrow night. I guess he just wanted to make sure everything was going to be all right."

"Well, is he coming back to the hospital?"

"I guess that's up to you. He was here all the time when you were unconscious. Him and Mommie spent the night with you. So did Darnel."

"I don't want to hear about Darnel's good gestures. He had a motive."

"I know what you're getting at. He spent the night before he knew anything about the baby. Darnel still loves you even though he probably wants to wring your neck. Personally, I think that's all understandable."

"When did ya'll find out that I was pregnant?"

"Mother already knew. When we arrived at the hospital, she told the doctor that she believed you were pregnant. Of course they check all that stuff out. So, they were way ahead of the game. Mother and I were in the waiting room when the doctor came out. Darnel was there too; Daddy hadn't arrived yet. The doctor gave us an update and said that the baby was fine. Come on Lisa, you really didn't know?"

"No, I didn't. I had no idea. I don't think it's possible for someone to wake up from unconsciousness and know to lie right away to save their ass."

"You work in the criminal justice system that shouldn't come as a surprise to you."

"Whatever. I guess mother was very embarrassed. With me being an unwed mother and all."

"She wasn't concerned with that. I would like to ask you a question though. Deep down inside whose baby do you think it is?"

Lisa took a long deep breath and sighed. She thought long and hard and came up with nothing. Absolutely nothing. She wasn't really concerned at this point because she hadn't decided whether or not she wanted to keep it. She knew that thought must have at least crossed Tasha's mind. If it was Mike's, she felt she had an obligation to keep it. On the other hand, she knew how much Darnel wanted children. Lisa wanted to blame everyone else. The more she thought about it the more she knew she didn't want to make a decision. She just didn't want to think about it any longer and that's what she did—put it right out of her mind.

3

The next day Lisa's mother was at the hospital early in the morning. She really didn't say much about anything. She just sort of stared at Lisa. Lisa tried to ignore her. She knew her mother was dying for Lisa to ask her opinion about the situation. She knew the speech was ready. Whenever did she not have an opinion? Lisa thought to herself. However, Sandra surprised her by keeping her thoughts to herself and for that Lisa was truly grateful.

Later on that day, while the nurse was taking Lisa's blood pressure, over the nurse's shoulder Lisa could see the door open. She couldn't quite make out who it was. The nurse motioned for her to sit still and stop making it so difficult. Lisa sat still and when the nurse had finished, Lisa looked up. It was Darnel. The nurse took the cuff off of her arm, wrote down her reading on the clipboard and left.

Lisa waited for Darnel to say something first. He held her gaze. Lisa turned away and mumbled, "What are you doing here?"

"I just wanted to see how you and the baby were doing?"

"Well, so far so good. My back is still bothering me, and my neck. But they say that the fetus that I'm carrying is fine."

"Fetus? Is that how you refer to it. It seems as if you've already made a decision."

"I haven't given it much thought really. I'm just concentrating on getting better."

"I understand that Lisa. I know that you know I've been going crazy wondering whose baby it is." He paused and then continued, "I was hoping you could give me some help with that.

Lisa turned to stare out of the window. "I'm afraid I can't help you with that right now."

"You can't help me or you don't want to help me ?"

"I said I can't. Don't make me keep repeating it. You don't want me to keep saying that."

Darnel sat down in the chair exhausted. "Lisa, I want to know how it ever got to this point? Did you ever think the day would come when you would have to wonder whose baby you were carrying?"

"Is that your polite way of calling me a whore?"

"I didn't come here to fight or for name calling. I'm concerned about something that I think may be mine. I don't want to put any pressure on you that will cause you to make a rash decision. I know how impulsive and reckless you can be. If it's mine and you are not ready to be a mother, I want to raise it." He paused, trying to choose his words carefully. "I felt I had to say that before you made any decisions that you couldn't change. I'm willing to take full custody of it."

Lisa was turning red. She'd thought maybe he was there because he cared about her and all he wanted was dibs on the baby.

"So Darnel, what are you saying? You want to take my baby away from me? Or are you trying to say I'm not capable of raising a child? What the hell is it that you are trying to say to me, you snake?"

Darnel got up out of his seat and said, "Why are you being irrational? I wanted you to know you had another option?"

"Option? What makes you think I would let you raise anything that came out of me. You're a self-righteous, unforgiving person. The almighty Darnel has come to let me know that he will do right by his child. What a saint you are. You can leave now!" she shouted. Darnel turned around and walked towards the door. "Hey Darnel!" she yelled. "Don't come back here—I could do without the headache." She turned her back to him and heard the door swing shut. A tear rolled down her cheek. She shut her eyes so hard, determined not to let any others fall.

4

A week later they finally let Lisa out of the hospital. Fortunately, there were no more visits from Darnel. Natasha visited almost every day, as well as her mother. Since Lisa was trying so hard not to think about Darnel, her thoughts kept turning to Mike. But whenever she thought about him, all she could think was that she might be carrying a dead man's baby. The thought of it made her cringe.

Lisa never really sorted out her feelings for Mike. She was more confused than ever, but her survivalist's instinct told her that she had to focus on what was now. And what was now was Darnel. She knew deep down she still loved him but she just couldn't stand him right now. For the most part, that was because she was guilty as hell. Darnel was different somehow. He was cold.

***

Lisa woke up screaming, dreaming about the accident. She saw the horror in her face as they hit the wall. "I love you, Lisa," kept playing in her head over and over again. Had Mike really loved her? The pain inside was unbearable. Lisa searched all of her mother's cabinets looking for something—anything that would help her forget. She found a bottle of Puerto Rican rum, her father's favorite. Her mother must have kept the bottle for a reason. Oh well. She poured it into her glass. "Cheers Daddy," she whispered, lifting her glass.

Lisa picked up the phone and started to dial. She didn't know what number she was going to dial; but she felt possessed.

"Hello," he answered.

She was silent and he repeated it over and over again. He was getting ready to hang up. "Darnel, it's me." He was silent. "Are you going to talk to me?"

"I don't know what you want me to say to you, Lisa."

"I just want you to talk to me."

"The other week you were kicking me out of the hospital."

"I didn't say I wanted to see you. I said, I wanted to talk."

"Where are you staying?"

"I'm staying with my mother. She's at church right now so I'm all alone." He got silent again. "I'm not coming on to you Darnel, so don't get worried."

"Why are you talking so slow, Lisa?"

"It's probably those drinks. Yeah, I think that's what it is," she slurred.

"Are you supposed to be drinking?"

"Why can't I drink?"

"You're still pregnant right?"

"Oh yeah, I am ain't I," she chirped. Then started laughing.

"What's so funny?"

"Nothing. Do you miss me, Darnel?"

"I don't want to talk about that."

"Just answer the question; I need to know. Do you ever think you can forgive me? Do you think that's a possibility?"

"I don't trust you Lisa, that's all I know. I don't respect the things you've done."

"So Darnel, if this baby is yours, I bet you want joint custody."

"Yes, you're right."

"Is that the way you thought your baby would be raised?"

"No, that's not what I wanted for my family, but sometimes there are things we cannot control. This is one of them."

"Why do you have to be such a goody two shoes? I know you still love me." No one spoke for a moment, and then Lisa said mockingly, "Can't answer that one can you?"

"Lisa, is there something you wanted?"

"No, not in particular. I kinda just wanted to hear your voice."

"This is not doing either one of us any good. Things are over between us, I'm just concerned about the baby."

"Yeah Darnel, I know," Lisa admitted, then hung up.

Why did she expect things to be different? She knew what she'd done. What made it so hard was that Mike was gone. She didn't have anyone to fall back on. All her life she'd had a spare. A spare man that is. But now she was totally alone. She couldn't lie to herself—she missed Darnel. She missed him a whole lot. She didn't want to be alone while she carried this baby. Was that too much to ask for?

5

"So how are you doing, Lisa?"

"I'm fine. What are you doing here? I thought you had to work today?"

"Yes, I thought I did too. So I called in sick." Natasha smiled.

"No—you are sick," Lisa teased.

"So how are things otherwise?"

"I guess I'm fine physically. I'm on bed rest for another week."

"What do you plan to do after that?"

"I want to go back to work; I have bills to pay."

"Girl, you know you don't have to worry about that. If I know you, which I do, you have a stash in the bank. What's the real reason you want to go back."

"Laying around this house is driving me crazy. Ma's been all right; she has her own life. But being here just gives me too much time to think."

"Which one are you thinking about?"

"Both of them actually."

"Did you love Mike?"

"No, I don't think I did, but I liked him a lot. He was fun to be with and adventurous. That's what made him so attractive to me, that dangerous element you know. The night of the accident he told me he loved me."

"Ain't that some shit?" Tasha said. "Did you believe him?"

"Well, I guess I did. He had nothing to gain from telling me. Darnel and I had already broken up. If it was just about sex, he could have kept it that way. You know what I mean?"

"I guess you're right. But he was no good, Lisa. A rich kid with too much time on his hands. Playing with people's lives, that isn't exactly a great quality."

"I'm a grown woman. He didn't make me do anything I didn't want to. And I wanted to."

"That's nothing to gloat about."

"I'm not gloating. I'm just being honest. I figure from now on that's what I'm going to try to do."

"You sure picked a fine time to start."

"What is that supposed to mean?"

"If you were honest before, a whole lot of people wouldn't be hurt now."

"Get off of your sermon box, Tasha. And I suppose I'm responsible for JFK's death too."

"Oh stop being so melodramatic. I feel bad for Darnel; he's a good person. There's a lot of us single women out there who would kill for a man like him. Women like you break their hearts and then throw them out to us with a chip on their shoulder."

"Now I'm responsible for the whole dating population."

"You aren't taking this seriously, Lisa. I know you. I just bet you think with your charms that you can have him back anytime you want to."

Lisa raised her eyes to Natasha because she knew she was right.

Natasha shook her head and said, "Well, it's not going to happen, Lisa."

"How do you know? Just because you don't have a man, don't be wishing I won't have one either."

"Looks aren't everything."

"Here we go with that again. You have always had a problem with the way that I look. You think it's why I have what I have. I don't understand why it's so hard for you to believe that a man could possibly like me for what is on the inside."

Natasha looked at Lisa and nothing came out of her mouth.

"Well do you?" she asked waiting. "Well, forget you then. I thought you were supposed to be my sister."

"I am your sister, but it doesn't mean I have to like everything about you."

"Touché. So now what's my problem?"

"You're conceited, self-centered, domineering, unfaithful, and sometimes you are just plain evil."

"Evil? Did you say evil?"

"Damn right."

"I'm going to have to disagree with that one."

"You can disagree all you like, but it's true."

"Would an evil person pay for you to go back to school?"

"Yes, an evil person would. It's only money, Lisa."

"You know that hurts, Tasha. I'm tired of you misjudging me."

"I'm not saying you don't do nice things. That's a part of you also."

"So I'm good and evil. Make up your mind, Tasha. I can't be both."

"You're missing the point."

"No, I'm not getting the point. You know what you can do for me?"

"You want me to go to hell huh? But, isn't that where you're living right now?"

Rolling her eyes at her sister, Lisa snatched the spread off of the couch, went into her bedroom, and slammed the door behind her. Ooh—I hate her sometimes, she thought. Natasha and Darnel belong together—they're both so damned self-righteous.

6

When Lisa walked into her office, she found a big bouquet of flowers on her desk, with a sympathy card signed by the staff. She knew Andre had to be behind it. He already knew too much. He had been at the hospital practically every night. Andre knew she was pregnant, but never once had he asked who the father was. Lisa knew he was dying to know; she could see it in his eyes. Andre had never been one to be shy so Lisa assumed that he thought she didn't know either.

Her body ached. She wondered if she'd made the right decision in coming back so soon. She was four and a half months now and it seemed as if she were eight. The accident surely took a toll on her body.

Lisa's desk was clear. She couldn't remember the last time she'd seen it like that. She rubbed her hand across it—it felt empty just like her life.

But overall, it was good to be back. She had to get on with her life. It was just her and this baby now. She rubbed her stomach and smiled, and for the first time she felt something—really felt something. Like a flutter. She was amazed. She smiled as a tear rolled down her cheek.

***

"Ma, I'm going to be looking for a place soon."

"What's your hurry? You know I said you can stay here as long as you like."

"I know Ma, but..."

"But what? You know you have gestational diabetes. Do you pay attention to what your doctor says? I know if I don't cook for you, you won't eat right. Just wait until after the baby's born. Have you heard from Darnel?"

"No, I haven't."

"What are you going to do about it?"

"I'm not going to do anything. He wants me to leave him alone so I will." She turned around quickly. She heard footsteps from behind and looked back and saw Natasha.

"I don't believe that. Do you Mama? Don't let Lisa sit here and lie to you. You know she's sitting there planning and plotting," Natasha said with a grin on her face.

They laughed at her. "Hey, that's not fair. I really am trying to stay out of trouble. Don't say anything to encourage me."

"How's the bun in the oven?"

"The bun is fine. Are you still seeing that professor?"

"From time to time. A little oil change and tire rotating here and there."

"I know what you two are talking about." They started laughing again. "I was young once too. I just hope, Natasha, that you're practicing safe sex."

"You mean with a condom, Mama?" Lisa said, her eyes open wide.

"Hush up, Lisa. If you did the same you wouldn't be in the situation you are in now."

"Ooh," Natasha hissed. "That's one for Ma."

"Oh shut up, Tasha!" Lisa barked back at her.

"When is the last time you saw that little boy?"

"It's been awhile, Ma."

"Well, the circus is in town. I have two tickets I won in a raffle. Why don't you go pick him up and take him."

Lisa thought about it and said, "Okay, I haven't got anything else to do. I do want to see him. Fine, I'll go." She jumped out of her chair and headed for her room.

"That's a good one, Ma."

"A good one what?"

"We both know you don't put any money in raffles." Lisa's mother winked and went on talking.

Lisa called Darnel and arranged to pick up Jason. They went to the circus and had a pretty good time.

When Lisa pulled up in the driveway Jason was asleep. She grabbed all his souvenirs, walked to his side of the car and opened the door. Lisa shook him gently, and his big brown eyes stared up at her. "Come on get out. We're here."

"Okay," he said sleepily.

When she opened the front door, he made a mad dash for the stairs. "Good night Lisa!" he yelled.

"Did you say thank you?" Darnel said as he entered from the kitchen.

"Thank you, Lisa!" Jason yelled.

"Good night!" she yelled back.

Lisa turned to Darnel and asked, "What are you still doing up?"

"Couldn't sleep."

"Is it your back?"

"No, no it's fine," he tried to say as convincingly as possible.

"It is your back. Come here I'll do it."

"No, that's not necessary."

"Look, Darnel, I have to go soon. Get over here and let me do it." Lisa sat down on the couch. He walked over and sat down in front of her. She placed her hands on his shoulders at the base of his neck and began massaging, trying to work out some of the knots. "Does that feel better?"

"Mm, that feels good."

She continued to work her way down his back. "Lift your arms up." He reluctantly lifted them up. She rubbed down his sides. There's this thing that he'd loved for her to do at the end of a massage. He would stretch out his arms and she would come up behind him and pull them back as far as she could. When he'd had enough, he would overpower her and bring his arms forward. Routinely, she would end up falling on his back and so she did this time. His skin felt so soft. Her lips were drawn to it like a magnet. She kissed the back of his neck. While her hands massaged his chest, she kissed her way up his neck landing on his cheeks. He turned his head towards her and their lips touched. The warmth of his breath could have melted her heart. He grabbed her and pulled her around to the front of him. Their tongues intertwined. Pushing her down on the floor, he put his head under her blouse. He unsnapped her bra with his teeth and out fell her swollen bosom. And he tasted them, one after another with his tongue. He sucked them as if they would produce milk. Her head writhed around in pleasure. He kissed his way down and kissed her stomach. He felt it under his fingertips. It was firm and protruding a little. Abruptly, he got up and sat on the floor next to the couch.

"Why did you stop?" Lisa asked. He shook his head, closed his eyes so tight you could see the lines in his face. She backed away, trying to cover herself up. Turning around, she hooked her bra and pulled down her blouse. Quickly as she could, she ran for the door, stopped, and turned around to see Darnel. He was just where she'd left him. He didn't move or say anything. She felt her belly and cursed the baby. She hated it. She wanted it out.

7

"Natasha, don't argue with me. I need you now. Can you just help me with this?" The silence lasted a dozen heart beats.

"What do you need me to do?"

"I need you to go with me to the Clinic."

"Okay, I'll do it. When is the appointment?"

"Saturday." Sandra walked into the room with a basket of folded clothes. "I'll talk to you later." Lisa hung up the phone as quickly as she could. Sandra took Lisa's clothes out of the basket and placed them on her bed.

"What clinic were you talking about? You have a private doctor." Lisa didn't say anything. "Lisa, do you hear me talking to you?"

"Yes, I hear you. I'm not deaf. It's something I have to take care of."

"Something like what?"

"It's nothing, Ma. Why don't you stop eavesdropping?"

Sandra looked hurt. "Are you going to do what I think you're going to do?"

"Yes!" Lisa yelled. "Ma, please just mind your business. Stay out of this."

Her mother's voice was even and calm. It was sort of eerie. This was not the woman Lisa grew up with. "What brought this on, Lisa?"

"I don't want it. I can't do this by myself."

"Oh, so now you're a quitter. You're a lot of things, but I would have never thought you were that."

"It's a mistake, Mother. This is the wrong time for me to have a child. I need to get my life in order."

"You know this is something that you can't take back."

"Mother. Don't you think I know that?"

"You're very reckless at times. If you make the wrong decision, nobody can fix this for you."

"I've had one before," Lisa blurted out. Sandra looked horrified. She grabbed her stomach in mock pain.

"Ma, sit down on the bed." Her mother sat there shaking her head in disbelief.

"When Lisa?"

"In college."

"I didn't know."

"I didn't tell you."

"I can't believe this. Oh my God," she cried, covering her mouth. Her hand slowly fell to her lap. "What happened?"

Lisa took a deep breath and explained, "I was dating this basketball player. He was as much in love with himself as I was with myself. But I thought I was in love. And I thought he loved me too.

"During my junior year I found out that I was pregnant. I remember it was cold and I had spent the entire day looking for him. I finally caught up with him that night. He had been drinking with some of the guys in his dorm. I told him I needed to speak to him so we went into his room. Immediately, he tried to kiss me. I pulled away and blurted out that I was pregnant. He was so angry. He acted as if I had done it on purpose. He started yelling things like, 'You're trying to trap me.' And said that I wanted to hold him back. He started acting crazy. I'd never seen him act like that before. I started backing up. I tried to get out of that room as quickly as I could. As I was walking towards the door, he grabbed me by the back of my hair and slammed my head against the door. He kept yelling, 'bitch you better not have this baby'.

"If he would have let me finish, he would have known I needed money. I had to finish school. I had law schools to apply to. I didn't want any baby.

"So I sold the TV and stereo you bought me for my room. And along with some money I had, I went and did it by myself. That was the one summer in college that I spent home. I never spoke to him after that.

"The following semester is when I hooked up with that poetry guy. One night I mentioned what had happened. So he asked me what would be the ultimate pay back. I said hit him where it hurts. There's nothing he loved more than basketball. He smiled at me and I shrugged my shoulders. So I left it at that.

"The following week he broke the basketball player's hand. He was kicked out of school and I never seen him again. He used to send me a lot of poetry. He was talented, but also crazy."

"Lisa, you're not in college anymore. You're a grown woman now. You're not alone; you have family that will support you."

"Ma, I don't want to hear this. Let me do what I have to do."

Sandra got up from the bed and walked towards the door. "Lisa, I usually stay out of your business. But if you do this, I promise you—you will regret it."

"Ma, I know what..."

"Just listen for a change. Damn! It's not about you anymore. You have a life growing inside of you. Isn't that precious to you? The miracle of life. Do you ever sit back and marvel at that? I know you, Lisa. You're going to do what you want to do. Please, think about this. Will you do that for me?"

"I'm sorry Ma, my mind's already made up." Sandra shook her head in disbelief. She left the room and slammed the door so hard some of Lisa's perfume bottles fell off the dresser.

8

Darnel's family made several attempts to help Theresa for Jason's sake. When she was released from the hospital, Darnel's family forced her into rehab. It was a thirty-day treatment program. She managed to make it through three weeks but at the end of the third week she checked herself out. No one was able to find her. Two weeks later her body was found in an alley. She had overdosed on heroin.

Sandra hadn't spoken to Lisa for days. Lisa missed her Saturday appointment and knew her mother was secretly happy.

Sandra decided to go with Lisa to the funeral. Even though Lisa still was not speaking to her. Jason sat with Darnel's family in the front of the church. He kept turning around to make sure Lisa was there.

Darnel's family looked like they always looked. Pillars of the community. Estelle sat there stiff as a board. Lisa couldn't help but wonder if Estelle was happy about what had happened to Theresa. She wanted Jason with her family. Lisa knew it was going to be hard to let him go. The service was brief and to the point. Afterwards, everyone expressed how beautiful it had been. Sounding like a record stuck in that one groove.

Often times Jason had confided in Lisa that he didn't like going to Estelle's house. He said she stared at him all the time. Once she had made a mistake and called him David. Jason wanted to say she was crazy, but he didn't. Estelle never acknowledged Theresa's existence, which Lisa knew hurt Jason. Estelle would never talk about Theresa with Jason. That's why he liked spending time with Lisa. She was the only one who would let him talk about his mother. Lisa could relate; she was an outsider too—someone who'd broken the heart of one of the Harvin Boys.

After the service Lisa dropped her mother home and went on to Estelle's house to pay her respects and to drop off some of the food her mother had cooked.

When she pulled up around the house, Jason was on the porch sitting in a rocking chair. He ran over to the car. She gave him the food and told him to take it in the house. He started to run and almost dropped the food. "Walk!" she yelled. He turned around and smiled.

Most of the grandchildren were in the bedrooms watching TV. Lisa walked towards the back of the house where she knew the rest of the family was.

It smelled of bacon fried up in some greens. She could detect the sweet fragrance of corn coming from the cornbread. Her mouth watered and her belly ached for some. Lisa walked past the kitchen towards the den, where most of the adults were gathered. She stopped short in the hallway when Lisa noticed Jason standing right outside the door. What is he doing there? she wondered. As she drew closer, she heard voices. "She was nothing but a junkie."

"I believe she's the one who got David hooked on that stuff."

Lisa wasn't sure, but the second voice sounded like Estelle's.

"Jason will be better off without her."

As Lisa approached Jason she could see the tears streaming down his face. Her appearance in the doorway startled everyone. They all turned around and stared at her. Jason brushed past Lisa and ran down the hall.

"Jason!" she called after him, but he didn't answer. He kept running until he was no longer in sight.

The room was silent. Some faces were turned down, while others glanced at one another. Lisa noticed Darnel in a far corner sitting alone. She walked into the room, with her back straight and stomach poked out, determined to give them a piece of her mind.

"She hasn't even been in the ground twenty-four hours. I guess what you had to say couldn't wait. She's dead—what more do you want from her? You could have at least had the decency to pretend a little while longer."

"Lisa, we didn't mean it the way it sounded," said Darnel's older sister.

"No, you didn't mean for Jason to overhear you. But he did."

"Lisa, we're sorry he overheard, but don't come in here with a sanctimonious attitude. You should be the last one to talk. I'm surprised you're even showing your face around here. After what you did."

Lisa was taken aback. She couldn't believe his sister was bringing that up at a time like this. Lisa glanced in Darnel's direction and he just stared right back at her.

"You're nothing but a whore," his sister announced. She was on a roll now.

"Well, isn't that the pot calling the kettle black. Does your husband know that your fat ass slept with the trainer at the gym?" Mouths flew open. You could hear chatter throughout the room. Darnel's sister cut her eyes across the room towards Darnel. Darnel looked at Lisa as if she'd betrayed him for letting out something he'd told her in confidence. Darnel's sister's husband Earl stood up and asked her if it was true. Later, all Lisa remembered was hearing his sister crying as she left the room.

When she came out of the house, she saw Jason waiting in her car on the passenger side. She walked around the car and climbed in. Taking a piece of tissue out of her purse, she wiped his face. She put the key in the ignition and took him home.

Lisa opened the door then stepped aside. Darnel walked in and asked, "Where's Jason?"

"He's outside playing." She walked over to the couch and sat down, leaving him standing in the doorway. Darnel walked around the couch and sat beside her.

"You know, Lisa, you can't take him whenever you want to." She sat there with her fist balled up under her chin and her elbow embedded in the arm of the sofa. "I apologize for the way my sister attacked you today. I wanted to say something, but my lips wouldn't move. It wasn't her place. She shouldn't have done it." Lisa stared straight ahead. She didn't move an inch, nor did her eyes blink. "Are you going to say anything?"

"I have nothing to say to you. You've made your apologies. What do you want me to do?"

"You're not going to guilt me, Lisa."

"I'll go and tell Jason you're here." She inched towards the edge of the couch so she could get up but he took a hold of her arm to prevent her from leaving. "Today's service brought a lot of things to my attention, Lisa. One, how precious life is and two, how short it is. We take things for granted. We take people for granted. One day when we wake up they might not be there."

"I know what you mean," she said as she laid back on the couch. "It's funny how someone or something can be taken from you in the blink of an eye. And when they're gone, you realize how much you need them in your life. I made an appointment to terminate this pregnancy two weeks ago. And for some reason or another I kept missing the appointments. Three times the preacher said: 'Hold on to what is dear to you.' This is a part of me. It's a part of my life now. It's time to grow up and make some changes. I'm not running from this anymore."

"Truce?" he asked extending his hand.

"Truce," she said sticking her hand out. "I'll go get Jason."

As Lisa approached the back door, something felt strange. In one glance you could see the entire backyard. Something was wrong—she couldn't see Jason anywhere. Opening the screen door, she called out his name, but there was no answer.

She raced upstairs to see if he was in the guest bedroom. Nothing. There was no sign of him. She ran downstairs and bumped into Darnel. "Lisa, what's wrong?"

Barely able to catch her breath, she gasped, "He's gone!"

"What did you say?"

"I said, he's gone. Jason's gone.

They rode in Darnel's truck as Lisa repeated what Jason's note said:

I'm leaving
I hate your family
I'm going to be with my mother
I'm going back home
Jason

"What do you think he meant about going to be with his mother? You don't think he's talking about suicide?" Darnel asked.

"I hope not. Maybe he means he just wants to be near her."

"And how is he supposed to do that. She's dead, damn it. Do you think he went to the cemetery? If so, I need to get off at this exit."

"No, keep driving. He didn't go to the cemetery. Young kids don't go to cemeteries. It's too scary. He left a map on the note."

"Where? I didn't see any map."

"The last line is the map. 'I'm going home.' He can't make it any clearer than that."

"You're right." Darnel sighed a breath of relief. "Wait until I get my hands on that kid. I don't know what he was thinking. Running off…"

"Darnel, do you hear yourself? You just skipped the most important part of the story. Did you forget what happened at your mother's house?"

He rolled his eyes and said, "Of course I didn't forget. Is that what you're going to do—start placing blame?"

"I'm not pointing any fingers. You just said you didn't know what he was thinking. Well now you know."

Lisa followed Darnel as he walked up to the door. There were beer cans, cigarette butts, and trash scattered in grass that was in desperate need of care.

Darnel knocked, but didn't wait for a response. He pulled the screen door open and stepped inside. The kitchen was to the right of them. Dishes were everywhere. There were too many for the sink to hold, so they ran over onto the counters and even the stove. When Lisa turned around Darnel was gone. "Darnel," she whispered. But there was no response. She started moving as fast as she could, stumbling into the living room, where she saw Jason fast asleep on the couch. Darnel was standing over him. Within a matter of seconds, Darnel grabbed Jason by his arms and started to lift him off the couch. Jason awoke screaming. "What are you doing? Let go of him," Lisa cried as she ran over to them. She pried open Darnel's fingers and Jason fell to the couch, with a look of horror on his face. When she looked back at Darnel she saw he shared the same expression.

"Are you going to be a junkie too?" Darnel shouted.

"What are you talking about, Darnel?" Lisa asked.

"Look at the table."

There was a spoon, a lighter, a syringe, and an empty dime bag. "Is that what you came back here for?" Darnel said.

"No," Jason muttered as he lowered his head.

"Are you crazy? Don't you realize what this has done to your father and mother." Darnel picked up the end table and threw it against the wall. Jason slid over to the other end of the couch. Lisa waited to see what Darnel was going to do next. He turned around and stormed out of the house. Jason looked at her and she looked at him. Pulling a chair from under the table, she sat down. They sat in silence until Darnel returned.

"Let's go," Darnel barked. Jason didn't move. "Let's go," he repeated.

"You better listen to your uncle."

"Don't tell me what to do. You're not my mother."

"No, I'm not, and I don't want to be. I have enough problems of my own. What do I need with a kid that sticks needles in his arm?" she rolled her eyes at him. "So was this your first time?" Lisa asked as she got up from the chair. "For somebody who thinks they're so tough, you sure have done some stupid things today." Darnel looked puzzled. "So, Darnel's family was talking about your mother. So what."

"Shut up!" Jason yelled.

"Don't you speak..." Darnel started.

"Darnel don't interfere. This is between me and him." Lisa got right in Jason's face. "Your mother was a junkie, your father was a junkie, so what are you going to be?" He tried to look away, but she grabbed his jaw and turned him towards her. "What are you going to be, Jason?"

"I'm not going to be a junkie!" he yelled. "I didn't even do those drugs." His eyes welled up with tears.

"Oh, so you're ambitious, huh? Maybe you're going to sell them."

"Lisa that's enough," Darnel said.

"Stay out of this Darnel! Who are you going to sell them to? Are you going to sell them to mothers who eventually overdose and are found dead in alleys with needles sticking out of their arms?"

"No."

"Then who Jason? Maybe to men who then contract A.I.D.S. and never get to be fathers to their children."

The tears ran down his face, as he pulled out of her grip and laid back on the couch. Darnel pulled Lisa away from Jason and asked, "What are you doing?"

She looked back at Jason through the tears in her eyes.

"I would never sell drugs," Jason sobbed.

"I believe you," Lisa said quietly as she walked over to him and sat down next to him on the couch.

"I didn't do those drugs."

"I know you didn't." She reached over, took his hand into hers, and squeezed it gently. "Our parents make mistakes, Jason. It doesn't mean we're destined to repeat them. We can make our own way. If you want I'll help you."

He squeezed her hand. Wiping her eyes, she looked at Darnel. "For the record Darnel, Jason doesn't do drugs."

"Fine," he said.

"Darnel, you both need to sit down and discuss what happened at your mother's house today. Jason go wash your face so we can go."

Jason headed for the bathroom and Darnel whispered, "How do you know he didn't do those drugs?"

"I've been a prosecutor long enough to know when someone's lying to me. My gut says he's telling the truth."

"That's it? You're belief is based on your gut."

"Plus, if you look down at your feet, you'll notice he spilled it all over the floor."

9

It hadn't been too bad at work, in fact, Lisa felt good about it. The baby wouldn't stop kicking. It learned it could and was determined to keep getting her attention. Up to then, Lisa never really had touched her stomach that way before. She really hadn't shown this baby any love—she was just carrying it.

Lisa started for home, but somehow ended up in Darnel's driveway. She saw his truck outside so she knew he was home. She walked around to the back of the house because he generally left the back door open. She could see him in the kitchen cutting up some fruit. Darnel looked very surprised to see her. Not waiting for him to motion her inside, she just went in. "Look, I'm not here to cause any trouble. I just ended up here somehow." Lisa walked over to him and put his hand on her stomach. "He's been kicking all day. He started earlier and he just won't stop."

"He? Do you know something I don't know?"

"Well, not really, but it just sounds right to call him a he. Do you feel anything?"

"No, not really."

"Here—you have to press a little harder. Go on. You're not going to hurt me." She grabbed his hand and found the spot.

"Hey, I think I did feel something," he said smiling as he looked into her eyes.

"It's amazing isn't it, Darnel?"

"It sure is." Lisa didn't know what had come over her, but it was just instinctual for her to touch his face. And he let her. She really felt great at that moment.

Unexpectedly, around the corner came Natasha. She stopped dead in her tracks. Darnel had his hand on Lisa's stomach and Lisa had her hand on his face. Seeing Natasha, he pulled away from Lisa like he was doing something wrong. Natasha looked at Lisa like she was surprised to see her there.

Before either one of them could say anything, Lisa calmly said, "What the hell are you doing here?"

"I came over to help Darnel with Jason."

"He's ten; what kind of help does he need? I know he's not still wearing diapers. Wait a minute, why didn't I see your car in the driveway?"

"Darnel picked me up."

"Oh really. So I guess you two have been becoming close. Well, isn't that special."

"I'm just helping him out with..."

"With what Tasha? Why haven't you mentioned this to me? I just saw you a week ago. You didn't say anything? Why didn't you say anything?" They were both silent then Darnel said, "You're overreacting, Lisa."

"I find my sister in my house with you and I'm overreacting." Lisa started laughing. "I can't believe this. I know this is not happening to me. Are you sleeping with him, Tasha?" Before Natasha could reply Lisa said, "Is this what you have resorted to? You can't do any better than my leftovers?"

"Lisa, you're overreacting; this is not what it looks like. I've been helping Darnel with Jason."

"Well, if he needed help he could have asked me."

"Don't be ridiculous. I've been helping him since you've been in the hospital. And you know the doctor said you needed some time to heal. Darnel has a busy schedule and he needed the help."

"If he needed the help, why didn't he ask his family. Why did it have to be my family."

Natasha looked over at Darned. "I guess that means you should answer that one Darnel," Lisa snapped, turning to him and waiting for his response.

"Lisa, there's no particular reason that I asked her. She offered to help and I took her up on it."

"Why didn't you tell me Natasha?"

"Because I didn't want to be a go between—between the two of you."

"Oh I see. I'm out of here." Lisa started backing up towards the door, but tripped over a ball that was lying on the floor. She almost fell, but caught her balance just in time. Natasha and Darnel raced over to try and help her. "Get away from me!" she yelled. Darnel held her anyway, but she snatched her arm from him and pushed him away. Opening the back door, she went out, leaving it open behind her.

When Lisa arrived home her mother was in the kitchen cooking dinner. "Ma!" she yelled. "You won't believe what I just saw. Natasha was at Darnel's house and apparently she's been spending some time there. She claims it's to help out with Jason, but there's something about that—that just doesn't sit right with me. It's like it's all been a big secret. She could have told me if she picked up Jason from school occasionally. I wouldn't have had a problem with that. But Darnel is going out of his way to pick her up so she can spend some time at his house. If I find out that she's sleeping with him, I'll kill them both."

"Lisa, calm down. You're talking crazy. There's no way that Natasha and Darnel are sleeping together. It's your hormones getting the best of you. I know it can't be as bad as you're making it out to be."

"Oh, because I'm pregnant that means I'm crazy. If there were nothing wrong with it then they would have told me up front. But no, Tasha lied about it. Believe me if I know one thing it's that when you lie you're up to no good."

10

All day at work the next day Lisa couldn't manage to get the image of Natasha and Darnel out of her mind. It just kept repeating itself like a bad record. Maybe she was overreacting. It is possible that it's innocent, she tried to convince herself. Every time Lisa thought about it, something kept telling her—if you want him back, you'll have to keep them apart. What nonsense! she thought. They weren't together. Or were they? It's impossible. It's too soon for Darnel to be in another relationship. And Natasha wouldn't do that to me, Lisa told herself. However, lately all she can do is blame me for the breakup and go on and on about how good a man Darnel is. And how bad I hurt him. Was she feeling sorry for him? Or was she trying to rationalize her actions. Lisa didn't have any of the answers but was determined to get to the bottom of this. And if she found out that it was true, they'd both be sorry. Very sorry.

Lisa was exhausted; her day had been non-stop. She felt like she was on a rollercoaster. All she could think about was food. Thank goodness staying with her mother meant a home-cooked meal every night. Sandra was preparing the food according to Lisa's new diet. Unfortunately Lisa's sugar was high. To be honest, she had no time to prepare meals that were nutritionally sound. She was sitting down at the dining room table eating when Natasha walked in. "Look Lisa, we have to talk!"

"I'm eating—I don't want to be bothered." Lisa lifted her fork to her mouth as if Natasha wasn't there. "Ma, did you call her and tell her I was home?" Lisa yelled from the dining room. There was no answer from the living room.

Natasha sat down at the table. "Look, I don't appreciate what you said at Darnel's house yesterday."

"Oh, so now its Darnel's house. You use to call it my house."

"Whatever Lisa. You're being paranoid."

Lisa looked at her and rolled her eyes. "Okay, you said your piece; you can go now."

"I don't know who you think you're talking to Lisa."

Lisa jumped up knocking her glass of milk over. "I'm talking to you bitch! If you think you're going to have some sort of relationship with Darnel you're wrong. It's a rebound Tasha. He wants me but he's settling for you."

"You can't have him anymore, Lisa, because you're a whore. I know it, you know it, and he knows it. Because of your selfish nature you lost him. You want it all, but you can't have it all. It was so typical of you to sleep with Mike. Practice some self-control!" Natasha yelled. "You and your hang-ups. You'll never hold on to a decent man. You need to be with someone who'll treat you bad. You're pathetic. A successful attorney who can't even keep her personal life together. Oh wait now, did I forget? You don't even know whose bastard you're carrying."

That was it. That was all Lisa could take. She lunged at Natasha and started beating her in the head. She was crying uncontrollably. Natasha was trying to hold her back.

Natasha yelled, "Don't make me hit you while you're pregnant!"

Their mother ran into the kitchen screaming. She tried to get in between the two of them. "I said stop it—God damn it!" she screeched. At the top of her lungs she yelled, "So help me God—I'll knock the hell out of both of you." That shrill made them shudder, and it stopped Lisa dead in her tracks. They both looked at their mother in disbelief.

Lisa glared at Natasha and said, "I'm not through with you. You'll get yours bitch!"

"Lisa, you watch your mouth," Sandra said.

As Lisa walked out of the dining room, she heard Natasha yell, "Not if you get yours first."

Lisa had fallen asleep crying on her bed and woke up hours later. She needed someone to talk to, so she decided to call

Andre. When she picked up the receiver, she could hear her mother on the phone. She wondered who in the hell could she be on the phone with at this hour. Lisa didn't put the receiver down, instead she held it to her ear and covered the mouthpiece.

"I don't know what's wrong with her, Natasha. This can't be the pregnancy; she's over the edge. She's been this way ever since the accident."

"Ma, I don't know what's wrong with her either. She needs help. We can't help her."

"Well, maybe she needs to go back to church."

"Ma, I'm not saying she shouldn't, but I think maybe she needs some professional help. I was talking about her with that guy I'm dating and he said something about her not getting over the accident yet. He said it seemed to him that she'd never grieved for Mike…" Lisa put the phone down, shut off the light and went to sleep.

***

A few days passed and Lisa had been very successful in avoiding her mother. She was up early in the morning and came home late at night. Sandra always left her something to eat. At least Lisa knew her mother was thinking about her.

One night after taking a shower, Lisa happened to catch a glimpse of herself. She couldn't believe what she was seeing; she had to look twice. She stood there and looked directly at herself. Her eyes roamed over her body, starting with her feet. She couldn't help but conclude that she had been neglecting herself. A pedicure was needed and she vowed to get on it right away. Her legs looked to be about the same size as before. Her thighs were getting a little bit bigger. She looked at her stomach and it was poking out, more towards the bottom than anything. She turned sideways so she could see it from that angle also.

She didn't know what kind of denial she was in. Her suits were getting a little bit harder to fasten, but she always figured a way to get her big behind in them. She didn't like it, not one bit—not having any control over her body. Lisa felt her breasts and they felt heavier. They also looked fuller, not to mention her bras were a little too tight. She held her hair up above her head to look at her face to see if her neck was getting fatter. It appeared to be the same size. She knew she had to do it, she had to take a look at her behind. What if it had spread? She didn't think she would be able to take it. Here goes, one, two, three—"Oh my God!" she gasped. "That's not my behind." She thought, how can I expect any man to want to look at that? Grabbing her panties, she put them on as fast as she could and pulled her nightgown down over her head. As she walked away from the mirror, she caught a glimpse and could still see her belly protruding through the nightgown. She cringed and decided the only thing that would make her feel better was a peanut butter and jelly sandwich.

11

Dear Ms. Munroe,

I know we haven't spoken in the past. Due to the circumstances, we weren't able to meet thereafter. The death of my son was devastating for me. I have since spent much of my time out of the States. Upon returning a month ago, I have had the opportunity to track you down. I would very much like to meet you and discuss a very important matter.

Sincerely,

Mrs. Wilson

Lisa had to sit down before she fell. She kept re-reading the letter. She couldn't imagine what Mike's mother wanted with her now. Mrs. Wilson had never come to see her in the hospital or responded to the flowers Lisa had sent after her recovery. Lisa figured Mrs. Wilson thought she really was no one of importance in Mike's life. Mrs. Wilson didn't even acknowledge that Lisa had been the one in the vehicle with her son. All Lisa wanted to do was express her condolences, but receiving no response, she'd eventually given up.

Now all this time had passed and Mrs. Wilson wanted to meet her. And to discuss what? This woman knew absolutely nothing about her. Lisa decided she wasn't going to meet with her and that was that.

The next day at work Lisa decided she needed someone to talk to and it turned out, as usual, to be Andre.

"Aren't you curious about what she wants, Lisa?"

"Of course, I'm curious. I just don't want to meet her. I wish you could go for me."

"I wish I could go for you too. This is a great opportunity. I would never pass up this kind of information. I don't think so, honey." It slurred off his tongue. "Well, I suppose I could go in drag. She doesn't know how you look does she?" Lisa started laughing. "Good, a smile on that face; life isn't that hard you know. I think you're scared to meet her."

"I wouldn't say scared, Andre. But I don't know what I would say to her."

"Apparently, you don't have to worry about doing any of the talking. It looks like she has an agenda. You should go girl. She's in town just to see you."

"How do you know that? She could be in town for some other reason and just decided she wanted to meet me."

"Well, that could be true, but think about this for a minute. If you flew to another part of the country to see someone and they decided that they couldn't talk to you, would you (A) get back on the plane, or (B) see that person no matter what it took?"

Lisa snorted at him because she knew he was right. There was no way in hell she would get back on that plane without saying her piece. "I guess I better get it over with. I'll do it for Mike."

Lisa called Mrs. Wilson on the phone and they set up a time to meet. That morning Lisa was nervous. She didn't know what to wear. She could have really used Tasha's help, but she wasn't speaking to her. She wanted to look intelligent, strong and assertive. At the same time, she wanted to look sweet, kind and caring. The one thing she didn't want to look was pregnant.

Lisa arrived at the Hotel Wellington ahead of time due to her nervousness. She had never been there before. A huge fountain stood in the middle of the floor of the lobby. The patrons looked like mice scurrying here and there. Luggage racks zoomed across the floor like trolley cars. When Lisa looked down at her feet, she could see her reflection in the floor. She wanted to turn around and get the hell out of there. "Lisa, go up and ask for her room," the little Lisa on her shoulder said. It was literally a struggle. But she knew she looked like a fool standing in the middle of the floor.

"Excuse me ma'am, do you need some assistance?"

"No, I'm fine," Lisa replied and headed straight for the desk. "I'm here to see Mrs. Wilson. Her room number is 20C. Can you please call her and tell her I'm here."

"Yes, madam." After a few seconds, Lisa was instructed that Mrs. Wilson was expecting her. The front desk clerk pointed to a bank of elevators. She stepped into the elevator and found she was the only one in it besides the attendant. She decided to sit on the sofa for the ride. The elevator operator stared at her reflection on the elevator doors. He was beginning to annoy her. Thankfully, they had arrived at her stop before she had a chance to say something to him.

"Have a nice day, ma'am."

"Yeah whatever," she replied. Walking towards Mrs. Wilson's room, Lisa felt her chest begin to pound so hard she thought it would reach out and knock for her. Taking a deep breath, she braced herself and knocked on the door. A lanky gentleman answered the door.

"I'm Lisa Munroe. I'm here to see Mrs. Wilson."

"Yes," he said stepping back and gesturing for her to enter.

The room was beautiful; the lobby couldn't compare to this room for luxuriousness. It looked like a piece of paradise bottled up in one room. Lisa walked around the corner and there appeared to be an elegant, full-figured, Nubian Princess sitting on the couch drinking tea. Her essence was the South. Lisa could picture her sitting under a magnolia tree sipping mint juleps. When she walked in, Mrs. Wilson lifted her head up and smiled. "Come in. Have a seat. Well, well, I've been looking forward to this. You're quite beautiful. I can see why Mike was fond of you. He's always been a sucker for beautiful women."

Timidly Lisa said, "Thank you."

"Relax you look so nervous. I'm not going to bite you. So how are you doing today?"

"I'm fine and yourself."

"Well, I could be better; I think I've been overdoing it. I've got my pressure up a little. Speaking of pressure. Milton!" she yelled. Out of nowhere the lanky gentleman was back again. "I need to take my medicine. Bring me a small glass of orange juice with it please." He disappeared as quickly as he came. Before she could even begin to speak again, he was there with her order.

Lisa looked around and thought, "hey I could get used to this."

"I'm sorry we haven't spoken before. I couldn't bring myself to do it. Michael was my only child. It was tremendously hard on me and it still is. I had to get away, so I left the States right after his funeral. I needed time to deal with it on my own."

"That's understandable—no one can blame you for that."

"Well, I blame me. I should have visited you in the hospital. Obviously, you were someone important in his life. He'll never forgive me for that."

"No Mrs. Wilson, he understands, I understand. I'm fine now. This is a better time to meet anyway. I was a real bitch in the hospital," Lisa said laughing. Lisa's stomach began to growl. "Mrs. Wilson, I know you have something in that kitchen for me to eat. I didn't really eat anything this morning. And if I don't get anything, I'm going to be sick."

"Oh excuse me. Where are my manners? It seems like I'm a little bit nervous too. I'll have Milton fix you up something quick." Before she could call Milton he was there. He brought out a tray of finger sandwiches. Lisa asked for a diet coke. Mrs. Wilson said, "You probably should have some juice, dear."

Lisa thought that actually she needed the soda without the sugar. "No, diet coke is just fine thank you. I don't mean to be impatient, but I know you didn't want to see me to chitchat. There has to be something you want to talk about."

"Well, I was getting around to that," she said as she took a deep breath. "This is how it happened." Then she brought her teacup to her mouth and took a sip. "When I was in Antigua one night, I had fallen asleep on the verandah of my summer home. I had been thinking about Michael all day. As soon as I closed my eyes, it was like he was instantly there. He said to me, 'Mama I'm all right. Stop this! Get on with your life. I'm happy, Ma. I'm here with Darlene.' That's his late wife, Lisa." Lisa shook her head in understanding. "I reached out to him, but he said 'No mother, it's not your time yet.' I said, 'Baby take your mother's hand.' He answered, 'No mother, you still have a life to live. You have some work to do.'

'What work Michael?' I asked. He replied, "Mama, she needs help; you have to help her.' 'Who Michael?' I yelled. 'You'll know. Just help her.' Then he started walking away. 'Wait Michael!' I cried. 'Don't leave me, baby.' He turned around and said, 'I love you, Mama.' Then I woke up.

"Now, I'm not one to believe in horoscopes, psychics and so on. But I'm from the South, honey, and I do believe in dreams. I knew it had to mean something. I really needed to stop moping around. I had to thank God for what time I'd had with him and be thankful that he's at a place where he has love. The only thing I didn't understand was who was this 'she' who needed help. I walked around for days in that house, racking my brain trying to figure out whom he could be talking about. It was beginning to be a bit much. Poor Milton thought I was losing my mind. I decided that I would confide in him about my dream. He didn't question my sanity but he listened attentively. Then he stood up and said, 'Perhaps you should start by looking for the young woman who was in the accident with him.' As soon as he said it, it was like it had been there all the time. I knew it had to be you. When I returned to the States, I decided to look you up first thing. I hired a private investigator to find you. He was successful and here I am."

"You mean to tell me you did this all because of that one dream."

"Yes, I did."

"Well, I don't know what Mike was trying to tell you, but I'm fine."

"Are you child?"

"To my knowledge I am. Unless you had some other dream that tells you I'm not."

"You have a sense of humor. I like that," Mrs. Wilson chuckled. "During the investigation, I found out some other things also. I know the nature of your relationship with my son. All I can say is it wasn't the best way to start any kind of relationship."

"You had a private investigator dig into my personal life?"

"These other facts were incidentals. All I was interested in knowing was where I could locate you. Unfortunately, more information was given than was necessary." Lisa began looking at Mrs. Wilson in disbelief. But before Lisa could utter one word, Mrs. Wilson said, "Yes, I know you're pregnant."

"Well in that case, I can loosen this skirt to the third button. It's killing me."

"As soon as I heard that I was on the next plane out here. I knew we had to talk. I really don't know the details of your private life. I don't know whom you were seeing when or what. Help me out child; you know what I'm trying to say."

"No, I don't know who the father is."

"I was afraid of that." They both sat there in silence. Lisa didn't know what Mrs. Wilson was thinking about. All Lisa was thinking of was how she felt so violated. Yet, she didn't feel Mike's mother was judging her. She actually seemed concerned, but then Lisa didn't know her all that well. She felt like she had to get the hell out of there. Mrs. Wilson took a deep breath and said, "Well, what are we going to do now?"

"I don't know about you, but I'm getting out of here," Lisa said, standing up to go.

"Sit down!" Lisa slowly sat down. "I know you're wondering what I'm thinking. So instead of concocting something up in your head ask me what you need to know." Lisa stared at her without speaking. "Well, if you're not going to talk then I will. Of course I'm interested in knowing if that's my grandchild you're carrying. If it is, I most definitely want to be a part of its life. And that starts from now. I have the resources to give you all the help that you need financially. I can also be there for support emotionally. I think that's what he meant by helping you. I'm not judging you—we all make mistakes. In fact, I married Mr. Wilson while I was carrying another man's child. It's a long story. The fact is that I never told either one of them. May they rest in peace. I've carried this secret around with me for thirty-three years. You're the first person I've told. It's a lot to hold in. I don't know if what I did was wrong. All I do know is that Mike loved his father and his father loved him. They had a beautiful relationship. If they had been flesh and blood, they couldn't have loved each other any more. I've made peace with what I did and I hope that they both forgive me. I know what it's like to be scared and do things that, no matter how hard you try, you can't change."

"You sure hit that one on the head, Mrs. Wilson," Lisa finally remarked.

"Oh don't be silly; call me Althea."

"There's nothing I can do about my situation. I can't go back and change anything. What's funny is I think that's what people hate me for. Not being able to take it back."

"What people?"

"Mainly Darnel. He'll never get over this. There's no way for us to start over. This baby is a constant reminder of my infidelity."

"You shouldn't think of it that way, dear. It should be a constant reminder of love. I'm assuming you cared for both of them."

"I think I did. But this baby is like wearing the scarlet letter. I'm marked. I look in Darnel's eyes—I see it. I look at my mother—I see it. I look in my sister's face—I see it. It hurts so much. At times I truly resent being pregnant. If I weren't pregnant, I feel it would be easier for people to forgive me."

"Who are these people that you're talking about, honey?"

"Darnel."

"Then say Darnel, honey; I won't be offended."

"I just don't know why everything keeps coming back to him. The old me wouldn't care. He would just have to deal with it."

"Take it or leave it, huh?"

"Exactly."

"It seems like you want his respect and it bothers you that you don't have."

"That might be it."

"Do you still love him?"

"I don't know. I'm not sure if it's him I want or if I just don't want to be alone."

"Naw, I don't buy that. If you didn't want to be alone, I'm sure you could have your pick from the lot of them. And the fact that you're pregnant would not stop some men. You want him and you want him for a reason."

"Maybe I just don't want him to be with anybody else."

"I know you're not talking about sex, honey. Oh, he's a man—he'll have sex. I don't think he'll be jumping into anything serious any time soon. If you want him back, you're going to have to fight for him."

"What if this is Mike's baby. Do you still want me to be with Darnel?"

"Child you're going to have to be with someone, sooner or later. If you're going to be with anyone, it should be someone you love."

"You don't mind someone else raising your grandchild?"

"Every child needs a father who loves them. If this Darnel person can give my grandchild that, then I don't have any problems. Besides, I've already done a thorough background check on Mr. Harvin, and he passed with flying colors."

"I don't think I can do it Althea. I won't beg for Darnel to take me back."

"Who said anything about begging, child? I know you didn't hear me say anything about begging. You just let an old pro help you out."

***

Later on that evening Lisa found herself craving beef. All she could think about was beef. She had already eaten and there was nothing left. She couldn't believe that she'd actually gotten dressed and headed for the supermarket. All she could envision was rows and rows of beef.

Lisa was in her own little world in the twenty-four hour supermarket. It amazed her how many other things they sold there. She became engrossed in the sugar and spices aisle; she wanted to bake. Lisa stood there with a box of cake mix in her hand, then she turned around because she thought she'd heard someone calling her name. "No one's there," it must have been my imagination, she said to herself. No one she knew could possibly be up at this ungodly hour. "Lisa!" There it goes again, she thought. Looking up, this time she saw Darnel walking towards her.

"What are you doing out this late?" he asked, obviously irritated.

"None of your business. I have nothing to say to you," Lisa snapped and proceeded to walk away. He was right behind her, on the back of her heels. He didn't say a word—he just followed her around the supermarket. He was irritating her at this point, so she turned around to give him a piece of her mind. Then she noticed that Jason wasn't with him. "Where is Jason?" she asked. "Oh, let me guess, he's at the house with Natasha."

"No, for your information he's spending the night at his grandparents' house."

"Oh," she said looking embarrassed. "Well anyway, I would appreciate it if you would stop following me."

"Don't flatter yourself. It doesn't make any sense that you're out this late. You're a single woman and you're pregnant at that. I would hope that you would take better care of yourself. At least for the baby's sake; it's not just you anymore you know."

"I'm fully aware of what's in my stomach. You've never been pregnant, so don't tell me you could withstand the power of a craving."

"Is that what this is? You're having cravings already?"

"Already! I'm five months, almost six."

"Look Lisa, knowing that you're out here this late is going to drive me crazy. If you have a craving, you can call me—day or nigh—I'll get it for you."

"Look, don't be doing me any favors. I got here just fine by myself, and I'll get home the same way."

"I know you're upset with me right now, but don't be foolish. I sincerely meant what I said."

"Whatever!" she snapped. Lisa walked away, but she wasn't finished with him yet. She turned back around and said, "You know Darnel, you really irk me. You get on my last nerve. You act like you're a fucking saint."

"Lisa, lower your voice."

"No. Who the hell is in this store at this hour? I'm a grown woman; I don't need your pity or your so-called generosity."

"You always have to make something into a battle. Why can't you just accept something without labeling it?"

"Because I can't that's why."

"That's your problem now. Oh, never mind."

"No, go ahead and finish, Darnel."

"Look, I had it with you woman. I said for you to call me and that's what you better do. When you finish shopping, I'll be out in the parking lot waiting for you." He practically mangled the cart trying to get away from her.

Lisa couldn't continue with her shopping now. Darnel had spoiled her mood. So she took what little she had in the cart and headed for the register. When she walked outside, she saw that Darnel had pulled up alongside her car. Without saying a word, he jumped out to help put the groceries in the car. Lisa sat down in her car, started the engine and pulled off. He pulled out right behind her.

Lisa didn't feel like cooking. It was crazy that she'd bought all these groceries which she had no intention of cooking herself. She decided to go to an all night-burger joint on the beach. Darnel kept following even though he probably knew she wasn't headed home. When Lisa got out of her car she walked over to his car and said, "Look, I'm hungry. If you're going to be my bodyguard, you might as well get out and get something too." He thought about it for a second. Lisa said, "Look sweetheart, you don't have to eat with me if you don't want to." Darnel got out of his car and followed her. She walked up to the window and ordered a Texas chiliburger with a side of chili cheese fries and a strawberry shake. Darnel ordered some coffee and that was it. Before she could get her wallet out, he'd already paid for it. Lisa sat down while he waited on the order. Darnel brought her meal over to her. "Hmm—that smells so good." He put it down in front of her. Lisa started sipping on her shake first, then took a huge bite out of her burger.

"Slow down Lisa; it isn't going anywhere."

Lisa had to laugh. If he only knew how out of control she felt about food these days. While she ate, neither of them spoke. Lisa noticed how often Darnel kept looking at his watch. "Do you have somewhere to go in the morning?"

"No."

"Then why do you keep staring down at your watch."

"I didn't plan on spending this much time out of the house."

"Well, I'm not holding you Darnel."

"No, it's all right."

She laughed at him, and teased, "You're nervous, aren't you?"

"Why would I be nervous?"

"I don't know you tell me. It's all right; I know you think I'm a vampire. I'm not going to bite you." He smiled. "Look Darnel; I'm tired too, but I'm also hungry. I'll be finished in just a bit; I'm not keeping you here on purpose." She started to eat her fries. After she'd gulped down her shake, she sat there for a minute to let her food digest a little. Lisa could see Darnel was about to fall asleep and didn't want him driving in that condition. She knew she hadn't really let everything settle yet, but got up anyway. "Come on sleepy, let's go." As they were walking to their cars, she felt a sharp pain right on the top of her stomach. It was so strong she thought that it would knock her over. She stumbled just a bit.

"Lisa, are you all right?" Darnel asked concerned.

"I'm fine. It's just a little gas, I think." When she got to her car the pains were getting stronger and weren't going away. Then she balled over in pain.

"Lisa, are you all right?"

"It's my stomach. Ow—it hurts. I feel like I can't breathe."

"Do you think you need to go to the hospital?"

She looked at him like he was stupid. "You think? Ow—damn it, will you hurry!" Darnel put her in his car and sped off. He was driving like a maniac. "Look Darnel, I'm not delivering; I'm just having some pain. Slow down!" she yelled. "I'm not too fond of cars these days." He slowed down just a little. She was breathing very hard and in spurts.

Looking over at her, he asked, "Why are you breathing like that? You sound like you're in the delivery room."

"I'm breathing like this because it's hard to catch my breath. Stop asking me stupid questions and get me to the hospital."

They pulled into the emergency room entrance, and he helped Lisa out of the car. "She can't breathe," he kept saying. Lisa had expected him to be calmer in this kind of situation. She wanted to panic, but thanks to him she had to be the sensible one.

"Look Darnel, I can talk. Back up please. Go on!" Then she turned to the nurse and explained, "I'm having these sharp pains in my upper abdomen. I'm five or so months pregnant. I have gestational diabetes also."

The nurse looked at Darnel and asked him if he would be able to fill out the paperwork while they got Lisa to a room right away. He nodded. The nurse whisked her into a wheelchair and they headed for an obstetric exam room.

Lisa was given a sonogram, her pressure was taken and her sugar levels were measured. She felt like she was being prodded, poked and pulled in every direction. The doctor told her to wait and he would be back in a few minutes.

When the doctor returned, Darnel was with him. Lisa wondered what he was doing in the exam room, but she didn't say anything. "Well, Ms. Munroe, I need to ask you a few questions. Could you tell me what you've eaten in the last twenty-four hours? Start with breakfast, please."

"I had a bowl of Crackling Oat Bran. Then around ten I had an apple— no a cheese danish with a cup of tea. At about eleven I got a hot dog from the cafeteria. On my way to Mrs. Wilson's I stopped by McDonald's and had some fries with some nuggets." She looked at the doctor's and Darnel's faces and they both looked at her like she was eating all that stuff right then and there.

"Is that all?" the doctor asked.

"Well no, I had some little sandwiches—I think I may have ate eight." She had to laugh at the rhyme. "My mother had something good for dinner. She had baked chicken without the skin, green beans and some boiled potatoes. Then at about two this morning I had a Texas chiliburger, chili cheese fries and a strawberry shake." She could have sworn the doctor's mouth dropped wide open.

Darnel said, "If I knew you ate all of that, I would have never let you go to that burger joint."

"I can't believe you honestly don't know why you're here, Ms. Munroe. Being pregnant doesn't give you a license to overeat. Your sugar was high. I looked up your records also. You know that you're a borderline diabetic and that it can be controlled by diet at this point. I don't know how many things you named in that diet of yours that consisted of sugar. I lost count after lunch. You need to take this a little bit more seriously. I know you don't want to have to start the insulin shots. Mr. Munroe, you need to keep an eye on her. It's obvious she needs help with her diet. I suggest you insist she doesn't go out for these late night snacks. Also, you need to start keeping a food diary starting tomorrow. Mr. Munroe, you should take a look at it at the end of the day. Maybe give her a call at work for some encouragement." He shook Darnel's hand. "Oh, I almost forgot, you have heartburn. Texas chili cheeseburger and chili cheese fries that's a new one. I'll send the nurse in here with a few antacids. This is going on your chart, Ms. Munroe. We'll be watching you."

"Ha ha—very funny," Lisa grumbled. The doctor turned around and walked out of the door. Lisa got up and started to get ready to leave.

"Oh, you think it's going to be that easy huh Lisa. You're moving in with me until you have that baby. You're going to have a healthy baby if it kills you. And I'm going to see to it. I don't even want to hear a word from you. We'll move you in tomorrow."

She grabbed her purse, shoved past him and turned around and said, "Okay." She didn't even turn around to see his expression. She could only imagine.

Darnel dropped her home and said he would make arrangements for her car to be picked up. Lisa couldn't muster up any energy to fight this time. She really needed some sleep. She nodded and said, "Okay," and went to bed.

12

At about nine o'clock in the morning, Lisa's mother came into her room. She opened the blinds and the rays of sunlight began to beat down on her face. "Lisa get up!" she yelled as she strolled over to the next window. "What are you going to do—sleep your life away?"

Lisa squinted to see her. "Oh Ma, please. Would you get out of here?"

"No can do. I'm going to make you something to eat. Besides, it's a sin to sleep this late. There are things to be done."

"Ma please, I was out really late last night."

"Sorry dear, you know it really bothers me when people sleep during the day. Go ahead and jump in the shower. I know you must be hungry."

"Ma, don't try to bribe me. I wanna sleep," Lisa whimpered. Her mother didn't say a word, but Lisa knew she was still in the room. She wouldn't leave until she saw Lisa's weary body in an upright position. Lisa should have known better, when it came to this her mother didn't play. Shoving off the covers, she sat up in the bed with her hair sticking straight up on her head. She looked over at her mother, trying to give her the evil eye.

She looked back and said, "Is that supposed to hurt me?"

Lisa sucked her teeth. "Ma, did Darnel call?"

"No, is he supposed to call?"

"Yes."

"Is there something going on that I should know about."

"I was at the hospital last night. Darnel pretty much didn't like what the doctor had to say about me. So, he insisted that I move in with him so he can keep an eye on me." Lisa got up and started looking for some underwear.

"So, you were in the hospital and didn't bother to mention that to me."

"It was no big deal, Ma. Sort of a false alarm. I thought I was having pain in my upper abdomen, but it was just heartburn."

Her mother started laughing and said, "It figures. I bet he said something about your eating habits. Who knows what junk you scarped down before you got there. And I bet you honestly couldn't put two and two together. Lisa, I have to say one thing about you—you're funny. I hope you don't put my grandchild down somewhere and forget where you left it."

"This is really funny to you, huh Ma?"

"I knew you and Darnel were getting back together."

"Oh no—don't you start. We're not back together! So when he gets here please don't act like that's what going on."

"Fine. I'm going to the kitchen now."

"Ma don't do it." Lisa shook her head at her. "I know you. Ma!" she yelled, but Sandra kept right on walking out of the room.

After Lisa took a long hot shower, she got dressed and did her hair. Maybe the thought of her and Darnel getting back together was having some effect on her. Usually she wouldn't have done her hair so early. She walked into the kitchen, made a plate and sat down at the dining room table. She was busy eating when Jason walked in. "Hi Lisa."

"Hey, how are you?" she said, glad to see him. He came up and gave her a kiss. She couldn't help but smile. He was the only person who ever seemed genuinely happy to see her. Behind him appeared Darnel.

"Hello," he said.

"Hi." Lisa couldn't help but notice how good Darnel was looking. She loved to look at him in jeans. His butt was just like she remembered it. She must truly be horny, she thought. She couldn't remember when was the last time. All of sudden she felt it. Yes, she felt that chill. It made her body shiver. She had to get a grip, before she wet her panties. A girl can dream can't she? When she stopped daydreaming, she heard Darnel saying her name. "What?" she said jumping back to the present.

"Well, are you packed?"

"No, I'm not packed. I didn't think you were serious." She cut her eyes over at her mama to make sure she wouldn't say a word.

"Well I'm here. I don't have much time I have plans tonight."

"I'll go and get some of my clothes then. Jason did you eat?"

"Yes, we went to McDonald's."

"Are you still hungry because that stuff goes right through you," she said smiling. Jason looked over at Darnel to get permission. Darnel nodded for him to go ahead. "Mama made some French toast; there's still some on the counter. Go heat it up in the microwave." Before she could even finish her sentence he was in the kitchen. Picking up her last piece, she put it in her mouth and then pushed herself away from the table. "I'm going to go and pack a suitcase. I'll be back in a few minutes. You can have a seat in the living room."

Why did he have to have that shirt on? she thought. Showing his muscular arms and the contour of his chest. He wasn't playing fair. How the hell was she supposed to live under the same roof as that and not be tempted for all the wrong reasons. She had to wipe her forehead and walk away.

It took Lisa about twenty minutes to pack. She called Darnel into the bedroom to get her luggage. He picked up the suitcase while flexing every possible muscle that could flex. "Are you coming now?"

"I don't see why not. I'll follow you in my car."

"Come on," he said huskily.

As soon as they got home, Jason immediately went outside to shoot that basketball. Darnel brought her suitcase into the guestroom. That irritated her in the worst way. She knew they weren't going to be sharing the same bedroom. Him doing that just said to her, "I don't want you in my life lady." Her defenses went up. Maybe this was a mistake, she thought to herself. She didn't really know what she expected. She was trying to throw him off balance. She had to prove to him that she was still in control of some aspect of her life. Lisa wanted him to feel like she did, that he wasn't needed anymore. Not to mention there was this whole Natasha situation. She really didn't know what that was all about. They say keep your friends close, but your enemies even closer. She vowed to find out what was going on. It better not be any of the things she'd imagined. Sister or no sister, if Natasha betrayed her she'd be sorry.

***

The next day Lisa really didn't do too much. She stayed in the house since she was still tired from the night before. The most strenuous thing she did all day was make some sandwiches for Jason and herself. Darnel observed them out of the corner of his eye. She knew he was wondering if she was going to make him sandwich. Lisa kindly put all the ingredients away, grinned and sat down at the dining room table.

It turned out to be a night in. She thought what a couch potato she'd become. So Jason and she decided to rent some movies. When they returned, Darnel was in the shower. On their way home they'd picked up a pizza and Lisa began eating hers as soon as she could. She didn't want to hear Darnel's mouth. She ate her two slices and went to sit down on the couch. "Jason, put the first movie in." Lisa was stuffed—she couldn't move.

When they were deep into the previews Darnel moseyed downstairs. Lisa could smell the cologne from the couch. He didn't say a word but went straight into the kitchen. She knew his ritual; he always drank a glass of orange juice before he left the house. "It gives me energy," he would say. Coming into the living room, he said, "Lisa, I suppose you bought this pizza."

"Yes I did. I only had two slices. I've been eating well all day. Besides, I can have pizza—just in moderation."

"Well, I'm going out. I have a business dinner."

"On a Saturday?"

"Yes, on a Saturday?"

"Well, who's the cologne for?"

"Lisa, could I see you in the kitchen please." She inched her way to the edge of the couch, stood up and followed him into the kitchen.

"Look Lisa, I have a social engagement to attend."

"You mean a date."

"Something like that."

"Anyway, I don't want Jason to know. I don't think he'll understand the kind of arrangement we have here. And I don't want him to think it's all right to date other people when you're with someone."

"Well, if you want it to be believable, I suggest next time you put on the cologne in the car and carry a briefcase."

"You would know wouldn't you?"

She rolled her eyes. "Fine Darnel, I'm going to watch my movie." She couldn't come up with anything else to say. Was she supposed to say it was all right? She knew it wasn't. Besides, she had done it and felt too guilty to say anything. Darnel grabbed his jacket and briefcase and was out the door.

That evening seemed to drag on forever. Jason seemed to be enjoying the movies. At one point, Lisa had to take the popcorn from him before he made himself sick. Every time she saw a light shine into the living room, she hoped that it was Darnel coming home and that his evening hadn't gone like he planned. Hell, she wanted him to have a terrible time.

Lisa sent Jason to bed around eleven thirty and soon followed. But she was very agitated and couldn't get to sleep. She felt suffocated. She couldn't stay in there. She needed some kind of homemade remedy to get to sleep and decided to heat up some milk.

As Lisa was placing the pot in the sink, she heard Darnel put the key in the door. She dropped the pot, grabbed the milk, and ran to her bedroom. She was running around the corner, sprinting to the guest bedroom, when her nightgown got caught on the hinge of the hallway closet. There she stood frozen like a deer caught in a hunter's headlights. Darnel calmly walked in while she was fumbling to get herself unhooked. He put his jacket in the closet along with his briefcase. "You're up pretty late, Lisa."

"I couldn't sleep; I was just getting a glass of milk," she mumbled.

"You must have been in a big hurry to get back into bed."

"What? What are you talking about?"

"Your gown, it's caught on the hinge."

"That doesn't mean I was in a hurry," she said quickly. "Anyway how was your evening? It's still pretty early. Didn't go too good did it?" she said smirking.

"No, I had a good time; I just decided to come home early."

"So how was she?"

"I don't think we should be talking about that?"

"Go ahead. It doesn't bother me. I'm so over you." It sounded so untrue she couldn't even convince herself. "Come on—I'm interested. Give me the scoop."

"I'm going to bed."

"It was just a question. You don't have to ignore me."

"What Lisa?" he sighed. "What do you want to know? Her age, height, weight? What? Why would you want to know?"

Defeated Lisa said, "Good night, Darnel," and went in her bedroom and closed the door. She heard Darnel call her name outside of the door. She leaned against the door, wondering what he wanted to say. She couldn't answer him; her throat was all choked up and the tears began to well up in her eyes. Lying down on the bed, she tried to push the thought of him with another woman out of her mind.

***

Lisa met Mrs. Wilson for lunch one day. She was always delighted to see her. Milton and she had even become pals. "So how are things going, my dear?"

"Oh, they're fine."

"Next time say it like you believe it. There's no reason for you to lie to me. What's ailing you child?"

"Darnel's dating. I don't think I can stay under the same roof with him while he does this? I feel like I can't object because we aren't together. It's making me sick. I know me. I'll let this fester inside of me until I blow up."

"Well, the way I see it is that it's bringing a lot of stress on you. Now, we both know Darnel wants you to have a healthy baby. Somehow it should come to his attention that this is very stressful situation." She gave Lisa a long look.

A light bulb clicked on. Why hadn't she thought of that? Was she losing her touch? She couldn't help but to smile from ear-to-ear. Mrs. Wilson looked at her and said, "Go ahead and finish your salad, dear."

That evening Lisa got home a little late. She had spent the afternoon with her mother. Sandra had her all over town in all the baby shops she'd heard of. Lisa was so amazed by how little the outfits were. They were so cute and tiny. It finally hit her she really was going to have a baby and it would be that small. She was overwhelmed. She found a little pink sleeper and had to have it now. Her mother kept saying, "Buy it in a neutral color." Lisa ignored her; she had to have it in pink. Walking up to the counter she pulled out her wallet and said, "Charge it."

When Lisa pulled up in the driveway she saw, Darnel's truck and knew he would be home. She went straight up to Jason's room. First she knocked on his door, and then opened it. He was the first person she wanted to show the baby sleeper. Looking at his bed, she noticed it was still made up. She walked down the hall to Darnel's room, knocked on the door and walked right in. He was on the telephone and he looked surprised to see her.

"I have to go," he said quickly, "I'll see you soon." Then he hung up the phone. "Lisa, you ever heard of waiting for someone to tell you to come in."

"I just wanted to know where Jason was."

"He's spending the night at my brother's house. He got a hold of some tickets for the game so he took his son and Jason."

"Oh okay," she said disappointed. "I guess I'll go ahead and get ready for bed."

"What did you want with him?"

"I wanted to show him something."

"What is it?"

"It's nothing," she said backing out of the room.

"It must have been something for you to come barging in here. Come on let me see it. What is it some video game you bought for him?"

"No, it's not." She hesitated and then walked over to Darnel and held the sleeper up against her stomach. She looked at his expression as hard as she could. He reached out his hand and took the sleeper from her. "It's so small," she said. "I couldn't believe it when I saw it." She sat down in the chair in the corner. "It's all becoming so real to me. I don't think I fully grasped it before. I thought when I first felt this baby kick that that had made it real. But it didn't really. Seeing that and knowing that the baby's going to be that small—that's what I'll be dressing it with. Do you believe that? I don't know if I'm ready for this. I know one thing; I can't raise this baby alone."

"If it's mine, you know I'll be there for you."

"That's a nice gesture, but what if it's not? What then? I can't raise this baby with my mother. I always knew that if I was going to have a baby, that I would have to be with a man who was the primary parent. I need my space. I need someone else to get the baby in the night. Because I can't do it every night." She looked over at him and he was laughing.

"Lisa, you'll have to do it. Babies are unpredictable. They don't know when you've had a hard day and to stay out of your way."

"It's not fair. Maybe I made the wrong decision. I don't want this baby to be a project. This isn't trial and error. I need to be focused in some kind of way."

"You'll be fine, I'm sure of it. You've always managed to land on your feet."

"You think so. That's real nice of you to say. Thanks, that really means a lot to me." She got up out of the chair, walked over to him and took the sleeper from his hand. He followed her to the door. On her way out, she turned around and kissed him. She saw his mouth open to say something, but before he could speak she put her finger on his lips. "It's all right; you don't have to say anything." He closed his eyes and didn't say a word.

Lisa left the bedroom thinking there was more that she could have said to him. The conversation didn't have to end that quickly. He wasn't asking her to leave, so why didn't she stay. Why didn't she stay?

***

A few weeks later Lisa ran into Natasha at her mother's. When Lisa came in, Natasha decided to leave. She walked right past Lisa without saying a word. It didn't really bother Lisa. As far as she was concerned, Natasha hadn't proven herself. There was still a reasonable doubt. When Lisa thought about it, she realized that was not like Natasha. Usually, if Natasha was right, she couldn't wait to rub it in your face. She didn't just walk away from things; there had to be something behind it—a motive, a reason. There had to be something. Lisa decided not to worry about it too much. As long as Natasha stayed away from Darnel she'd be fine. Ever since Lisa moved in, there hadn't been any contact between the two of them. And she liked it just fine like that. Just fine.

Lisa had wanted to spend a little time with her mother. However, her mother's church had some outing planned and she was on her way out. Lisa helped her lock up and then went on her way. She had nothing to do and no one to spend time with. It seemed like Jason had really adapted to Darnel's family. Every time she turned around, he was at some other relative's house. She was happy for him. He really needed that. But she still missed him.

For a while there she'd thought he wasn't going to come out of his shell, but he'd proven her wrong. One good thing was that all this other activity took up so much of his time he didn't have time to get into any kind of trouble. The Harvin family was very big on keeping their children into something. They always had family events; the children were always involved in some after-school activity. There was no time to hang on the street corners. Darnel's mother always said that after all the things she had planned for them if they still had time to hang on the corner then they must belong there. Lisa thought, I'll do that with this one. It doesn't seem like bad advice.

***

From down the block Lisa noticed Natasha's convertible in her driveway. Her first instinct was to cut off her lights and park on the street instead of the driveway. Her heart started pounding. She couldn't believe it. Had Natasha rushed over here thinking Lisa was going to be at her mother's for a while? Lisa got out of the car, grabbed her pocketbook, and headed for the house. Instead of walking up the driveway, she decided to walk on the grass so no one could hear her heels on the pavement. She positioned herself close to the window to see if she could hear anything. She heard absolutely nothing. She decided to go around back. Jackpot! There they were in the kitchen. She noticed they hadn't pulled the doors fully closed, which made eavesdropping a little bit easier. Lisa heard Darnel telling Natasha that she was taking everything the wrong way.

"How could I have possibly misinterpreted that Darnel?" Tasha said.

"I don't think it would be fair to Lisa," he replied.

"Fair to Lisa after what she's done to you. You're good Darnel, real good."

"You know how she gets. She wouldn't understand how close we've become."

"I guess not." Lisa stood there hesitating. Reluctantly she started to move. "Let me get out of here," she whispered to herself.

"I really had a good time the other night though," Natasha said.

"Me too. Get home safe." Lisa heard Darnel walking her out. She went in the back door while he was occupied. Then, she headed straight for her bedroom and closed the door. She had to sit down real quick before she passed out.

How close had they become? So, it was Natasha he went out with the other night. Is he dating her? What's going on? Lisa couldn't believe this was happening to her. She was possibly carrying his child, and he was dating her sister behind her back. That bitch! What had gotten into her? In all the years they'd never had a problem with men. They were never attracted to the same people. There was no stealing of boyfriends. Lisa always thought that was a line they would never cross. Natasha broke the secret oath. You know the oath you take when you're born. You don't mess with your sister's man, —the end.

Lisa's head was spinning. Darnel sneaking around like that. She never thought he would do something like that. It wasn't in his character. It was in hers, but not his. Maybe, he really was getting on with his life. But why did it have to be with her sister? Lisa's throat was getting dry; she needed some water. She had to go to the kitchen to get something to drink. She felt dizzy and lightheaded. She started for the kitchen and then all she saw was darkness.

When Lisa opened her eyes, she found she was lying on her bed. Since she appeared to be by herself, she thought that maybe she'd dreamt the whole thing. She felt a cold rag on her forehead and Darnel walked back into the room. "Are you all right? I found you lying in the hallway."

"I must have fainted. I need some orange juice or something."

"Lay down, I'll get it." He walked out of the room. She lay there trying to remember what she was doing before she'd fainted. And it all started to come back to her. Darnel came into the room holding the orange juice. "Here, sit up." Lisa obeyed. "What's going on with you, Lisa? You're determined to be hurt in some kind of way aren't you?"

"I'm fine. You can leave now," she answered, gesturing for him to hit the road.

"No, I'll stay right here and see if you're fine. If you don't mind?"

"Yes, I do mind. If I need your kind of help, I'll call you."

"My kind of help, what are you talking about?"

"Wouldn't you like to know?"

"Look Lisa, you're babbling. Did you hit your head when you fell?"

"Don't try to make it seem like I'm crazy. I know what you're doing and who you're doing it with. Asshole!"

"What the hell are you talking about?"

"Who did you go out with the other night, Darnel?"

Darnel avoided her eyes and didn't say anything right away. Then he took a deep breath and said, "I went out with a friend."

"Don't lie Darnel. You're no good at it. In order to be believable, it has to flow like water with no pauses."

"Who do you think I had dinner with the other night?"

"It's not who I think; I know who you had dinner with the other night."

"Who Lisa?" She said nothing. "Who Lisa?"

"Natasha—that's who damn it!" She threw her pillow at him and jumped up. "Oh, I'm sorry Darnel. I shouldn't have thrown that at you, especially when I knew it wouldn't hurt." She ran over to her dresser looking for something harder. The first thing that caught her eye was her hairbrush. She threw it as hard as she could. It knocked him right on the head.

"Lisa, what the hell is wrong with you?" She heard him mumble something to that effect while feeling his forehead for blood. She had no time to pay any attention to him. She picked up the bottle of hair grease and threw that also. While she was searching for something else, he came up behind her and held her arms.

"Calm down, Lisa!"

"Get off of me, Darnel!"

"I'm not letting you go until I think you're calm."

Lisa wasn't any fool. She knew she wasn't stronger than he was. She would pretend that she was calm and then he'd let her go. She took a few deep breaths and smiled. "Darnel, I'm calm. Let me go—you're hurting my wrists."

"Who do you think you're talking to? I know you—you are no where near calm. Besides, I'm not even holding your wrists that tight."

She started struggling to get lose, but to no avail. He wasn't letting her go. They just stood there with their reflections staring back at them from the mirror. She was breathing hard. She looked at Darnel's reflection. He just looked tired. "Why my sister, Darnel?" she whined.

"I'm not sleeping with her." he said.

She didn't know whether or not to believe him. "Well, do you want to?"

He didn't say anything. Before she could open her mouth, he said, "No, I don't."

"Then why all the sneaking around?"

"What did you expect her to do? You know how you reacted the last time you saw her here. I don't want to do anything that will make you get all crazy. You still think like a single woman. You need to watch what you do. You're carrying a baby."

"I know," she said softly. He decided to let go of her arms. He didn't move; he was still behind her. She turned around and they looked into each other's eyes. She felt there was still something there. She didn't know what to do with it, and neither did he. Her heart started to beat so fast; she felt so nervous. Putting her hand on the back of his head, she pulled him closer to her. She wanted to—so she had to go for it. Standing on her tiptoes she kissed him once. He didn't make any objections; it didn't seem like he wanted her to stop. She kissed him again, and he grabbed her like he had been wanting to for a long time. It felt so good, so right; she didn't want it to end. She wanted him to make love to her. If he wanted to she didn't have any objections. Darnel suddenly pulled away from her. "What?"

"I can't do this, Lisa?"

"Why?"

"I just can't. It's not going to change anything."

"Why does it have to? Why can't it just be? I need you now. You need me right? Stop analyzing it."

"It's not that easy."

"Sshh Darnel. I'm right here in front of you. You can do what you want. It's only one night it doesn't have to change anything if you don't want it to." He stood there as if he was struggling; he was in turmoil. She didn't push; she knew either way she would benefit. She knew he still cared. His eyes told her that. There was nothing else that he could say to her to make her think he didn't. If she played it right, he would come back around. She hoped.

"Lisa, this isn't right. I'm going up to my room."

"It use to be ours," she whispered. He stood there for a second and then walked out, closing the door behind him.

13

For the next two weeks Lisa was busy at work. She had a lot of things to do such as turning over her caseload. Her maternity leave was about to begin. Eight and a half months had gone by rather quickly. Darnel had been avoiding her, but she didn't mind because she knew that he was nervous. To her that meant she was on his mind and that was fine with her.

Lisa had also been spending a lot of time with Mike's mother. For the first time in her life she was really opening up to someone. It was so ironic that it would be Mike's mother. Spending time with her helped Lisa realize that she really did miss Mike. She hadn't taken the time to get over his death. She had spent too much time defending herself to other people. With dealing with being pregnant and trying to heal from the accident, she'd never talked to anyone about Mike's death. There had been no one to talk to. But she could talk to Althea. Althea had so many fascinating stories to tell her about Mike. Lisa hadn't really known him that well. He was really a good person; she confirmed that. Lisa had always felt he was, but that was not why she'd been with him. She'd been with him for all the wrong reasons. She was scared of the things in her life, so she ran to him instead of turning to Darnel. She hadn't known how to stay and work things out. She still didn't, but she was learning. She had no choice. Where does a big pregnant woman run?

***

One evening Lisa got off a little early, around the time Darnel and Jason were eating dinner. She walked in the living room and heard Jason call to her from the kitchen. "You just made it. We're about to eat dinner. Uncle Darnel made some steak."

"Hmm that sounds good," Lisa replied casually not wanting to invite herself to eat with them. They hadn't been doing it all along. It wasn't intentional, just conflicting schedules. Darnel always made sure she had a plate in the microwave. She looked over to him and he gave her a look that said he wouldn't mind. Lisa went to her room to put away her briefcase and wash her hands.

When she returned to the kitchen, Darnel and Jason were eating in the dining room. She sat across from Darnel and Jason sat in between them. She wasn't really hungry, but didn't want to pass up this opportunity. It had been a while since she had sat at the table with them. Jason was devouring his food. Lisa watched Darnel eat; he noticed she was watching him, but didn't say anything. She picked over her peas, ate a little of her potatoes, but she left the steak alone. Darnel looked up, "Is there something wrong?

"No, I guess I'm not that hungry tonight."

Jason started laughing. "But you're always hungry," he said. Darnel must have found that amusing because he was laughing too. Lisa nudged Jason in the head and also started to laugh.

"I'm tired and my feet are swollen. I think I'll go and lie down." While she was getting up, Jason asked if the baby was still kicking?

"I think it's too big to kick now. Mainly, she's just moving around. You can actually see her move from one side to the other."

"Really?" he asked puzzled.

"Yes, really."

"Will you call me the next time she does it?"

"Sure I will."

Darnel looked over at Lisa and said, "You both keep calling it a she. Is there something I don't know."

"Maybe," she answered smiling. "Good night, you two."

It hadn't been twenty minutes before Lisa heard a knock on her door. She had already undressed and was sitting up in bed. "Come in," she said. Darnel came in and closed the door. He came over and sat on the edge of the bed.

"Lisa, do you know the sex of the baby?"

"No, I don't. Why, what would you prefer?"

"You know I want a little man."

Lisa smiled. "I bet you do."

"Have you had a sonogram done yet?"

"Yes I did, but the baby had its legs crossed. They couldn't tell."

"Are you having anymore done?"

"I'm having the last one done next week."

"Do you mind if I come?"

"I have no problem with that. I never said you couldn't come. I thought it would be awkward for you. I know all you think about is becoming attached and wondering if she's yours. I don't blame you. I don't want to hurt you anymore. That's the only reason I haven't told you about any of my appointments."

"Well you're right that has been the reason I've been distancing myself from you and the baby. I don't want to miss out on the little things because I'm scared. It doesn't make sense that you and Jason share more about this baby than we do. The last time I felt it kick was months ago. Now you're talking about you can see it move from one side to the other. I've never heard of that."

"Me neither. I thought the only contact you could have was the kicking. I can be sitting still and I feel it moving—I can see it. Sometimes, she changes positions and wants to ball up on one side of my stomach. It looks like "aliens." It's so weird and fascinating at the same time. I can feel her head sometimes. I wanted to share it with you, but I didn't know if you wanted me to. Hey, could you do me a favor?"

"What?"

"My feet are killing me. Can you rub them for me, please?" He hesitated for a minute and then decided to do it. "Well, thank you—you make me feel like my feet are gross. They still look good."

"I'm not scared of your feet, Lisa."

"Oh I know what it is. You think I'm trying to seduce you." she laughed. "Sex is the furthest thing from my mind. My feet hurt. You try carrying a baby around all day, every day, and see what it does to your feet." She couldn't stop laughing. "You think I want to have sex with you. With you? I don't want any man anywhere near me. You have got to be kidding. I don't want to have sex with you."

Irritated he said, "Okay Lisa, I get the point."

"Oh, don't be offended." He started rubbing her feet too hard. "Ouch Darnel, that's enough. Obviously you're taking what I said too personally. What should you care? You've made it perfectly clear that you don't want me. You can stop now." She tried to pull her foot away. "I'll remind you about the appointment." He didn't move. "Let go of my foot, Darnel!" He dropped it. Lisa continued, "Sex with you? Have you seen me lately? Woo, I can't wait to tell Andre." She just lay there laughing at him. He got up and left the room. Boy that was a good one.

14

Lisa's office threw her a shower. Andre engineered the whole thing. She received some wonderful gifts and Hank even stopped by to wish her well. After everyone had gone it was just Andre and Lisa. He kept looking at her.

"What are you looking at Andre?"

"You. You're glowing girl. You actually look happy. Are things changing at home?"

"No, not really. But I'm glad this is almost over. I want this baby out. I'm giving it an eviction notice. Vacate premises immediately!"

He laughed, then a look of sadness came over his face. "You're not coming back are you, Lisa?"

"No, I don't think so. I don't think this is where I want to be anymore. I have to slow down some. While I was in college, I had such big ideals. I wanted to defend the little guys. I wanted to help people who couldn't afford legal help. Somewhere along the way it became more political than anything. How high could I go and how fast? It doesn't mean that much to me anymore. Besides, I'll need to spend more time at home. Lord knows I don't know anything about a baby."

"I think you'll make a great mother. I was worried at first, but you have changed so much. I didn't know if it was the accident or what? I know one thing if anybody messes with that baby they'll have hell to pay."

"Damn right!" Looking over at him, she said, "I'm going to miss you so much, Andre." She could feel the tears beginning to well up.

"Girl stop! You know I'm not going anywhere. Don't you make me start crying too." He held both of her hands and stared directly into her eyes. "There's something I want to share with you. I was here a long time before you came and I have worked with many people. But you are truly the best. You never gave me any problems with who I am. In fact, I could talk to you.

You were there for me when I needed you. You were sort of like my own personal crusader. I know a lot of people think you're a bitch around here. They're right, but you're a good bitch. Come on a give me a hug." Lisa stretched out her arms and gave him a nice long hug. "Well, I guess this is it, Ms. Munroe."

"So it is."

"Lisa, I hope things work out with Darnel. You belong together."

Lisa could barely see with all the tears in her eyes. She could barely speak she was all choked up. "Really, do you think we belong together?"

"I can't picture you with anyone else."

15

The day of Lisa's final check up, Darnel decided to take off of work and was really getting on her nerves. He was obsessed with being on time; he always had been. But she felt she didn't have to accommodate him. Her philosophy was that she would get there eventually. He was waiting in the living room for her. When she came out, she announced that she was ready. "Finally," he said.

When they went outside to the cars he expected her to get in the truck. She looked at him and said, "I can't get up in that thing."

"Lisa, you're not that big. You'll fit."

"I have no problem with fitting. It's the getting up there that's got me bothered."

"Come on—I'll help you." She walked over to the truck and said, "Now Darnel, when I grab on this handle, do you expect me to fall on my stomach and crush the baby." Grabbing her stomach with both hands she said, "Where do you want me to put this? Now can we go in my car?"

"Damn Lisa, I didn't know you were that big."

"I'm going to forget you said that. Here are my keys—we're going to be late."

When she arrived at the doctor's office she said hello to some of the women who she'd become acquainted with over the last five months. Darnel picked up a magazine to read. About fifteen minutes later, the nurse came out from the back and called Lisa's name. She looked over at Darnel and said, "Are you ready?" He shook his head and followed her back into the exam room.

The nurse said, "Take off your blouse and put the gown on. Just pull your skirt down a little. You don't have to take it all the way off." The nurse walked out of the room and closed the door behind her. Lisa began taking her blouse off and noticed Darnel was trying not to look. "Look Darnel, you've seen this before; would you stop acting silly."

"Things are different now."

"So you keep telling me. I'm not taking my bra off, so relax. Here put my blouse on that hanger and come and help me up on this table." He held her arm while she got her balance so that she could hop up on the table.

Darnel said, "What happened to all those sexy bra's you used wear."

"Well, my breasts are bigger as you can see. My mother bought these for me. My breasts were so tender. She said these bras would help some and they have. They're not exactly Victoria's Secret, but they do the job. Sorry, I couldn't give you a little peep show today."

"Don't you start that again, Lisa." She started laughing when she remembered that scene.

"Oh no, here we go again," he said.

"I'm okay. I'm not laughing at you." Lisa laid there with this big smile on her face.

There was a knock on the door and the technician walked in. "Are you ready, Ms. Munroe? Let's see if this baby is going to cooperate today? Go ahead and lay back. You know the drill this is going to be a little cold at first." She poured the gel on Lisa's belly. "How's that Mommie?"

"It's not that bad today."

"Hey that's a good sign." She turned on the monitor and said to Darnel, "Come around here Daddy if you expect to see anything. See the heartbeat, look at that big head. You're going to have a very smart baby," the technician joked, laughing. "She's sucking her thumb."

"She? Did you say she?" Darnel asked quickly.

"Just a general saying, Daddy. I didn't mean anything by it. Your wife and I have been calling it a she so far. Wait. Oh my goodness, this baby is determined to be a surprise—the legs are crossed again. I'll leave it on while I take the measurements, maybe she'll uncross her legs." They waited as Darnel inched closer. He was annoying Lisa so she grabbed him and pulled him closer so that he could see better. "Okay, that's it for today. I'm sorry we didn't find out the sex. The good news is the baby is progressing nicely. You two have a nice one."

"You too. And thank you," Lisa replied. Lisa looked over at Darnel and he was smiling. "Amazing isn't it?"

"It sure is. I think it's a boy," Darnel announced.

"Most fathers do." She flinched, almost biting her tongue off. "Sorry, I didn't mean that. Would you mind waiting in the waiting room until I get dressed."

"No."

"Wait. Before you go, can you help me down?" He helped her down," then put his hand on her stomach and held it there. He looked at her and asked her if she minded? Lisa said, "No. Go ahead." He knelt down and put his ear to her belly. It felt so right. She rubbed her hand on his head. He got up and he went to the waiting room.

Lisa had to sit down. Her head felt like it was spinning. She started crying. How could she do this to him? He loved her so much. He loved this baby. What if it wasn't his? It would kill him. Damn! How could she have been so cruel? Please God, let this baby be his. Not for my sake, but for his. I know you can look into the hearts of men. You know that Darnel is a good man. No one could possibly love this child more than he could. Lisa promised if God would help her out this one time she'd never do anything like this again. Amen.

On the drive home Darnel asked Lisa if she wanted to get something to eat?

"Are you kidding—of course I want something to eat." He took her to a café on the beach. She ordered a grilled chicken salad and he did the same. They ate in silence. She didn't know what Darnel was thinking about, but she could tell he was in deep thought. Lisa didn't want to pry so she left it alone. She was afraid he would say something that she didn't want to here. Lisa had been so emotional lately; she didn't want to lose it at this restaurant.

After they finished eating Darnel invited her to walk with him on the beach. It didn't seem like a bad idea so she accepted. They walked along side by side, him staring into the ocean, her staring straight ahead. It seemed like the perfect opportunity for her to talk to him freely.

"Darnel."

"Hmm."

"I need to ask you something?"

"Go ahead."

"Do you think there's any possibility of us getting back together?" He didn't say anything. "I know it's hard for you to think about. Things aren't exactly smooth between us and that's putting it lightly. But I still feel something. Something's there and you know it. I keep thinking about what happens next. I mean if it goes either way. If this child is yours, do I continue to live in the guestroom? And what if it's not? Do I get the boot and "it's nice knowing ya." What? What's going to happen to us?" He stared at the ocean. "Will you say something?"

"I don't know what to say. I'm taking this day by day." Lisa sucked her teeth. "Look Lisa, there aren't any easy answers. And I know you don't expect me to make any quick decisions."

"Okay Darnel, but what about me. I know I'm the one who screwed things up so I haven't said much, nor have I been demanding. But I'm human too. I'm not the unfeeling monster that everyone makes me out to be."

"No one thinks you're a monster. You're the one who does, and then you try to live up to it."

"That's how you see me?"

"I see you a lot of ways, Lisa. All that tough stuff you put on is a lot of bullshit. It doesn't bother me; it's your insecurity that worries me. Frankly, I don't think I could live with that. It makes you do stupid things that you can't change."

Lisa stopped dead in her tracks. She didn't say anything because deep down she knew he was right. "What is it going to take for us to get past this?" she asked.

"Both of us wanting back into this relationship."

"Whoa, I guess that was my hint. I sure as hell know that I can't make you do anything that you don't want to. Forget it then, I'll be fine by myself. I don't need anyone. I've been alone before, I can do it again," Lisa said, and then started walking a little faster. She wanted to get away from him. He caught up with her, grabbed her arm, and swung her around.

"See Lisa that is so like you. You don't like what you hear, so now you want to run away. The other day you said you couldn't do it alone. Now miraculously, you don't need anyone anymore. How about trying something new for a change. You used to be so exciting—now you're so predictable. Are you ever going to change?"

"You want something different? Do you want to hear something different?"

They were in each other's faces now. Nose-to-nose. "Yes, I do Lisa."

She felt so trapped she wanted to start yelling. "Here. How about this Darnel? I admit it—I fucked up. I fucked up big time. I was scared and I did the only thing I knew how to do. And that was to be self-destructive. I never meant to hurt you. I was really trying to hurt me. I know you can't understand this, but it's the truth. I love you Darnel and I've never stopped." She stood there and he looked into her eyes. She took his hand and held it. "Darnel, won't you please forgive me? Please, I'm so sorry. I'm so sorry." He pulled her close to him and hugged her, letting her cry in his arms. He didn't say anything, he just held her.

Nothing was really resolved between the two of them. She felt like she was walking around with an open wound. Her heart was on the line, and there was nothing she could do about it. For a moment she regretted telling Darnel anything. But then, all of a sudden, she felt free. She wasn't carrying around any secrets anymore. But she knew she needed to make some changes.

16

Days had passed and Lisa began to do some serious soul searching. Things were not turning out the way she'd hoped they would. Her future with Darnel began to seem bleak.

Lisa had her bags packed and waiting at the front door. She sat on the couch waiting for Darnel to come home. When he came in, he first spotted the suitcases. Walking around the sofa, he stood over her and asked, "Are you planning a trip Lisa?"

"Have a seat. We need to talk," she replied. He walked into the kitchen for a beer and headed for the sofa. Before he could say or ask anything, she began to speak. "I'm moving out."

Darnel cracked open the beer and lifted it to his mouth. Taking a long hard swallow, he put the can on the table and looked at her. "What's this about? I thought we settled all of this. What are you trying to pull now?"

"I'm not trying to pull anything. For once I'm being honest with myself. I don't belong here anymore. We're two strangers living under the same roof. I don't need room and board. I can get that anywhere."

"I never tried to make you feel like that."

"Are you kidding me? I sleep in the guestroom Darnel. It doesn't get much clearer than that. Besides that's just geography. It doesn't matter if we slept side by side. It still doesn't change a damn thing between us. Face it—it's over." She pulled her hair back away from her face. "I know you see it, Darnel."

"I've never asked you to leave, Lisa."

"You didn't have to."

"Is this about the other night?"

She took a deep breath and expelled all the air she possibly could. "I'm not going to lie. The other night has something to do with it."

"Before you go any further, think about this. You only have a few weeks left. There's no reason for you to move out now. Just stay until the baby is born and we'll take it from there."

"No," she said firmly.

"What do you mean no? You didn't even take the time to think about it?"

"I have been thinking about it. I don't want to stay here anymore."

"Why?"

"I just can't anymore."

"What do you mean you can't?"

"Oh Darnel, just leave it alone." She held onto the arm of the sofa and hoisted herself up.

"So you're leaving now?" he said incredulously.

She could tell that he really didn't believe her. "Yes."

"Lisa, I really don't understand what this is all about. I'm trying to do the right thing. I'm trying to be there for you. What else do you want from me?"

"That's it. I don't want anything from you. Yes, you are doing the right thing. You won't be penalized for it. I won't keep you from your child and that's a promise." She edged her way towards the front door. Darnel came up behind her and putting his arm over her shoulder, held his hand against the door to prevent her from leaving.

"What's the real reason?"

"I don't have to tell you—you already know."

"No I don't. Spell it out for me."

The tears welled up in her eyes, giving them a glossy look. She wiped the tears away before any could fall. "You'll never forgive me, Darnel. As much as I hate to admit it, you have every right not to. But I have to move on. I can't cling onto false hope. I can't hate me because you do."

"I never said I hated you."

"It doesn't matter. I love you and you know that. But I love this baby more. I have to do what's best for us. I don't want to win you back anymore. I'm all out of schemes and plans. I need you to love me in spite of what I've done. But you can't." Lisa placed her hand on his cheek. "But if I could take it back I would. If I could erase that look of disappointment off your face, I'd do it in a heartbeat.

"My mother once said: "If you love something set it free. If it comes back to you it's truly yours. If it doesn't it never was.

"At the time I thought that was the stupidest thing I'd ever heard. Me let go of something that I wanted. Never! Can you imagine?" Darnel smiled and shook his head.

Lisa couldn't fight back the tears any longer. She clenched her teeth, hoping it would help her regain some composure. Her teeth chattered and chills went through her head.

She leaned up and whispered in Darnel's ear. "I love you, but I'm setting you free."

Their faces brushed and she kissed him on his cheek, allowing her lips to linger for a moment.

He put his arms around her, but he didn't utter one word. She gently withdrew from his arms and exited gracefully.

17

During the next couple of weeks, Lisa felt very anxious. The countdown had begun. Nearly everyday Jason called to see if she had gone into labor. She spent some time with Mrs. Wilson until she left, promising to keep in touch. Mrs. Wilson asked Lisa to promise that no matter what happened between Lisa and Darnel, Lisa would tell her if Mike was this child's father. Lisa agreed. This was her only shot at a grandchild and Lisa wasn't going to deny her that.

In all this time Lisa hadn't spoken to Natasha. Not even once. As she was closing in on her due date, she wanted to put a lot of things in order. She thought that maybe her emotions had gotten the best of her. Maybe all those things she had suspected of Natasha weren't true. Lisa needed to know, so she called her mother and had her arrange for her two daughters to meet at her house.

When Tasha sauntered in, Lisa was already there sitting at the dining room table. Her mother led Tasha into the dining room by the hand. When Natasha first saw Lisa, she looked as if she wanted to retreat. But she pulled out the chair across from Lisa, put her purse on the table and sat down. Lisa looked over and gave her mama the look that everything would be fine. Her mother tiptoed out, closing the dining room door behind her.

Natasha looked across the table at Lisa and said, "I see you set the stage. You're also sitting where you're most comfortable. You must be prepared. So now that you've summoned me here, Big Sis, why don't you start talking."

"I'm not going to waste any time Tasha. I've been doing some thinking and perhaps I've been wrong about some things."

Natasha interrupted, "And what might that be?"

"The nature of your relationship with Darnel. It's very possible that I've overreacted to some innocent situations."

"Stop beating around the bush. Say what you want to say."

"I don't know what you're expecting me to say. You still haven't tried to explain what was going on."

"Nothing Lisa. Just like I've told you before. There was nothing going on between Darnel and me."

"Well, it sure didn't look like that from my angle."

Natasha jumped out of her seat shouting, "Are you here to start accusing me again? Because if you are, I can leave right now."

"Why are you acting so guilty, Tasha? I'm just asking a few simple questions."

"No, you're not. This is Natasha, Lisa. You think I haven't seen this stance before. The way you're sitting, the calm manner in which you are speaking. Those eyes. It's your trademark. The same one you practiced on me when you graduated from Law School. Am I on trial here?"

"Why, do you feel like you're on trial?"

"Oh Lisa, stop. I liked you better when you argued." Natasha circled around her chair. Then she sat down and she started fumbling through her purse for some gum. Lisa knew she was nervous, but wasn't sure if she wanted to know why. Natasha looked across the table at Lisa and said, "Are you sure you want to know, lawyer?"

Lisa took a deep breath and said, "Now is as good a time as any."

"Well, here goes. When you moved out of Darnel's house, he started calling me to talk. He couldn't understand what went wrong between the two of you. I didn't want to talk to him about you. So instead of talking to him, I offered to baby-sit Jason so that Darnel could have time to himself to think. Whenever I saw Darnel, I felt so bad for him. You were engaged, Lisa. This man thought you were going to be his wife. Then he found out that you had been sleeping with the guy at your office. I didn't understand it myself. I had no defense for you. What you were doing was wrong. I felt empathy for him. I couldn't fathom why on earth you would mess up something that was so good.

"Anyway, when I dropped Jason off, I would hang around and keep him company. He seemed so lonely and I really didn't have anything to do, so I stayed. I guess he didn't mind because I kept his mind off of you. Pretty soon he was inviting me to go places with him and Jason. So I went along. After talking with him for awhile, I felt he needed to get out and have some adult company. So I bought tickets for art exhibits, museums, movies even plays. Then I persuaded him to go. I told him that it would be good for him. We had some nice times. Actually, we enjoyed each other's company. I found out that we pretty much wanted the same things out of life, a family, kids then careers." She paused and took a deep breath.

"I thought I'd figured out why things hadn't worked between you two. It had to be because you weren't right for each other. I think I was infatuated with the idea that what I wanted was right in front of me. Darnel was preoccupied so he didn't have to think about you. I must admit—I was getting used to having a constant companion. The day you walked in on us there wasn't anything going on. I know I must have looked nervous, but it wasn't because of what you were thinking. I felt guilty because my good intentions weren't the same anymore. The line between friendship and more was becoming pretty cloudy to me. When you confronted me there was nothing going on.

"After you moved back in I thought things would be the same. To Darnel it was a friendship. That was all it ever was to him. I was there in his time of need. I don't know if you know this, but I went over to the house. Darnel apologized but he told me it wouldn't be a good idea for me to come around. He claimed it was because you were being irrational and that he was concerned about the welfare of the baby. I'm not saying he wasn't concerned about your child, Lisa, but I looked at him and it all kept coming back to you. You were more important to him. I realized then that he would never get over you. And it snapped me out of my delusion. So that brings us to now."

"Did you fall in love with him, Tasha?"

"No... No, I didn't. I fell in love with the idea of him. I know what love is and that wasn't it. You're the one who doesn't know what love is, that's why you threw it all away."

"Look, I don't want to argue with you about love. I feel I've been learning what it is and how important it is. I don't know what to say about your story. I know that I feel relieved. I know it may sound funny, but I don't know what I would have done if that story had ended differently."

"I've been wanting to tell you, but you've been a real bitch."

"I know." They sat there awhile not saying anything. They were both very stubborn women. Admitting they were wrong would never happen. "I guess I'll be going," Lisa said. She got up and walked down to where Tasha was sitting. She started to open the doors when she heard Tasha say, "I've missed you."

Choked up with tears, Lisa turned around and said, "Me too."

18

The day had finally come. Contractions! They had begun in the morning. Lisa didn't say anything to anyone. She had read enough books to know that since this was her first pregnancy, it was going to take awhile.

Lisa called her doctor to let her know. The doctor told her to come to the hospital when the contractions were five minutes apart and not before. Then she told her to relax. Lisa spent the rest of the day packing for the hospital.

Lisa called Tasha and told her what was going on. Natasha said she would go straight to the hospital after work. Lisa picked up the phone to call her mother, but she knew if she did her mother would be with her all day until Lisa went to the hospital. The contractions were enough pain—she didn't need any others.

For awhile Lisa really believed she was in control of the situation. Hey, this isn't so bad, she thought. The contractions were an hour a part and weren't that forceful. It felt like cramps. After awhile they were about forty-five minutes apart. She didn't know exactly when that had happened, she had been too busy doing other things. When they were around thirty minutes a part, the pain made her sit up and take notice.

Lisa called Darnel at his job. "Hi Darnel. I need you to pick up Jason from school now. Take him to your mother's house. After that come and get me and take me to the hospital."

"Is it time?" Darnel asked.

"Yes."

"How long have you been having contractions?"

"Since this morning."

"Why didn't you call me?"

"Calm down Darnel. Do what I said and then we can argue about this in the car." There was silence. "Darnel, did you hear me? Don't you start acting crazy on me."

"I'm fine, Lisa. I'm on my way." He hung up the phone.

About an hour later he pulled in the driveway. Lisa watched him through the window. He practically ran out of his truck. He knocked over one of Mama's potted plants on the porch. Opening the door, he ran to Lisa's bedroom yelling her name. Lisa called from the living room, letting him know that she was in there. He came up to her and hugged her. Stepping back, he looked her up and down. "Are you all right?"

"No, I'm not."

"What? What's wrong?"

"I'm in pain. What do you think? The contractions are fifteen minutes apart now. Did you pick up Jason?"

"Yes."

"Good. My bags are at the foot of the bed, will you go get them and put them in the car?"

He went to her bedroom tripping over himself the whole way. Lisa had to laugh. While he was getting himself ready, she called her mother and told her what was going on. Lisa argued with her for five minutes. Her mother kept insisting she wait for her, while Lisa kept telling her to meet her at the hospital. Finally, she got off the phone.

Lisa walked around the house making sure nothing was on, any water running or anything on the stove. When she walked into the living room, Darnel was standing there, waiting. She looked at him and smiled, "I'm ready."

As soon as Lisa arrived at the hospital, she was wheeled directly to the labor room. She had pre-registered and taken care of everything beforehand. She disrobed and was hooked up to the machine that was measuring her contractions. They took her blood. Her sugar levels were extremely high. The doctor ordered insulin for her IV immediately.

Her room looked to be in total chaos. Everyone was running in all directions. Through it all she saw Darnel's face which helped her remain calm. Her contractions were at a standstill and she had only dilated 7½ cm. Through all the breathing and contractions, her mother, Tasha, and Darnel decided to take shifts.

Lisa never knew the human body could take so much pain. During the whole time, she kept getting pricked for more blood samples. Her doctor was very worried about her sugar levels. She explained this to her and increased the insulin dosage.

After awhile she finally advanced to 8½ cm. Lisa was exhausted and so was everyone around her. She had sweated out her hair and looked a mess, but that didn't matter to her, she wanted this baby out. At around 9 cm, one of the nurses took blood again. She jumped when she read the numbers and left the room immediately. Lisa's doctor came in with Darnel behind her. Her mother was sitting in the chair. "Ms. Munroe, your blood levels are dangerously high. The insulin isn't helping and I'm afraid if they get any higher that you risk going into a diabetic coma."

"A coma?" Lisa asked.

"I think the best thing to do is to take the baby now by Cesarean section so that we can get your blood sugar levels under control."

"Is there any other way, Doctor?" Darnel said.

"I'm afraid not."

"Doctor, I'm already 9 cm. All I need is one more and I can deliver naturally. I don't want you to cut me," Lisa pleaded.

"Ms. Munroe, we're looking out for you now. The baby will be fine. We're trying to save *your* life."

"You said if my levels get any higher that I risk a coma. Give me an hour. I'm sure I'll be 10 cm by then."

"Ms. Munroe, I don't recommend that we wait."

"But I have time—don't I?"

"Yes, you have some."

"Please, just give me an hour."

Everyone in the room was silent. "Okay, Ms. Munroe. I'll give you one hour." On her way out the doctor ordered a blood test every twenty minutes or at 10cm, whichever came first.

Lisa's mother squeezed her hand and left the room. Darnel stayed.

"Lisa, are you sure you want to do this?"

"Yes, I want to have this baby naturally. Don't worry. I'm sure I'll dilate in time. Besides, if they cut me I'll never look good in a bikini again."

About thirty minutes later God answered her prayers. She finally reached 10cm. The doctor asked, "Are you ready Lisa? We're about to have a baby." Then they wheeled her to the delivery room.

"One, two, three push," is all she heard. Darnel was right there beside her, encouraging her. Lisa was crying she was in so much pain. At the same time she was happy. Things were progressing nicely or so she thought. She felt lightheaded and extremely tired.

"Come on Lisa; you have to push again."

"I can't," she cried. "I can't stay awake."

"Lisa, are you kidding?" Darnel said. "How can you be sleepy during a time like this?"

"Come on Lisa—one, two, three—push," the doctor yelled. Lisa pushed with all her might. All of a sudden they heard a beep that was loud and consistent. "Doctor, her blood sugar levels are through the roof!" cried one of the nurses.

Lisa looked over at Darnel in tears. "Darnel, if anything happens to me, I want you to raise this baby."

"Lisa. Sshh—don't talk like that."

"Darnel listen to me." She could barely control her crying at this point. "It doesn't matter whose baby this is? It's mine you know that. If something happens to me, this child won't have any parents."

"One, two, three push—"

"I know you love this baby, Darnel. Promise me you'll take care of it. Promise me!" she yelled.

"I promise," Darnel said. She could see a tear in the corner of his eye. She saw him lift his hand to wipe it away, but she had already seen it.

"One, two, three push—"

"I love you, Darnel. I know you still love me."

"One, two, three push—"

"Please say it. I wanna hear you say it."

"One, two, three push—"

"Listen! Somebody get me a piece of paper," Lisa cried. The nurse just looked at her.

"Do it!" the doctor yelled.

Lisa scribbled on a piece of paper that in the event of her death, she gave sole custody to the father, Darnel Harvin. Then she signed it.

"Here Darnel, sign it."

"Nurse will you please be the witness to this." The nurse signed it.

"Last one Lisa. Nice and hard—push!!!" and Lisa gave the hardest push she could.

"It's a girl!" the doctor exclaimed.

They took the baby over to the table. She had strong lungs—Lisa could hear her yelling.

She looked at Darnel she grabbed his hand with her hands. "I did it." She whispered. She squeezed his hand.

He bent over and kissed her. "I do love you Lisa," he said. Her heart was filled with so much joy.

"Go over and see her," she said. He let go of her hand and he went over to the baby. Lisa lay there smiling at him and then lost consciousness.

19

Lisa awoke in the hospital bed. Opening her eyes, the first person she saw was Darnel.

"It seems like I'm making this a habit," she said. Darnel ran out into the hallway and called a nurse. "What's the matter? Why are you getting so excited? I'm thirsty. Can I get some water? Why is my mouth so dry?" Darnel poured some water into a cup and held it to her mouth. Lisa looked down and saw all these monitors hooked up to her. She didn't understand why, because she knew she had already had the baby.

"You've been in a diabetic coma for a week."

"A week?" Lisa started panicking. "Where's my baby? Is she all right?"

"Calm down Lisa. She's right here." Lisa saw the baby in a bassinet at the foot of her bed.

"Oh, let me hold her." Lisa stretched her arms out towards her.

"Let's have the doctor check you out first."

The doctor came in and asked her some questions and explained what had happened. "It looks like you're going to be all right. I'll run a few tests to make sure. Welcome back, Lisa." The doctor smiled at Darnel, "I guess you were right. She's a fighter. You and the baby being here didn't hurt. I'm so happy for the both of you." Then she left the room.

"Bring her here, Darnel." He rolled the bassinet down to the side of her bed. He took her in his arms and sat down beside Lisa. He laid the baby in Lisa's arms. She was so beautiful. Her big beautiful brown eyes. All her little tiny parts. Her hands were so little and her fingers so tiny. Lisa put her finger in the baby's hand and she grasped on to it. It felt so right, so natural.

"I haven't named her yet," Darnel said. "I figured you would want to do that."

"So, what have you been calling her?"

"Little Lisa. She looks just like you."

"What about Hope?" The baby started puckering up her lips and smacking her gums. Then she let out a little cry? "What's wrong, boo boo?" Lisa cooed.

"She's probably hungry. Here let me get you a bottle." He went over to her bag and pulled out a bottle.

"Look at you. What are you Mr. Mom?"

"I've had no choice. She's been with me since she left the hospital. Your mom and my mom have been a big help."

Lisa gave Hope her bottle. Her first feeding with Hope. She couldn't stop staring at her. She didn't want to let her out of her sight.

After that she had to lie back down. It was enough exertion for one day. Lisa laid back and watched Darnel playing with Hope. She closed her eyes—*she had his heart. Yes, she has his heart.*

Epilogue

After Lisa left the hospital and came home, Darnel told her he didn't want a paternity test done. As far as he was concerned, Hope was his. He had fallen in love with her. Lisa insisted the test be taken because there were more people involved. He agreed, but he said he didn't want to know either way. He had already signed the birth certificate. He was very adamant about it. Lisa decided, however, that this was something she would do for him. It was in Hope's best interest anyway.

Darnel did eventually admit to Lisa that he was still in love with her and that he wanted things to work out between them. Lisa suggested they go for counseling together, to work through some of their problems. He agreed. Their first session was to be in two weeks.

Lisa finally received the results to the paternity test. Ninety-nine point ninety-nine percent, certainty that Darnel was Hope's biological father. She bought him a Father's Day card and put the test results in it. Lisa left the card in Hope's crib. The first thing Darnel did when he got home was to go to Hope. When he went into her bedroom, Lisa made sure she stayed in the living room. After a few minutes, she heard him let out a yell. He had screamed so loud that he woke the baby. Lisa went into the room to check on them and found Darnel holding Hope in his arms and crying. He shooed Lisa to get out and leave them alone—and she did.

One day Jason volunteered to keep an eye on the baby, as she lay asleep in her crib. Lisa somehow found herself in her old bedroom and decided to take a long hot bath. Meanwhile, Darnel returned from the grocery store. She heard him when he entered the bedroom. Pulling the stopper out of the tub, she grabbed for the towel she had placed neatly on the hamper. She looked at it for a second and then balled it up and stuffed it in the hamper.

Lisa walked out of the bathroom as if she thought nobody was there. She came face-to-face with Darnel. Her body was dripping wet and glistening from the bubble bath. He stood there in his dirty blue jeans with his shirt off. His chest said "kapow!" Lisa didn't say a word. She stood there letting him take it all in. He licked his lips and wiped his brow.

"I needed a towel," she said as her eyes willed him towards her. He darted out into the hall to the linen closet to retrieve a towel. He came up behind her and put the towel around her. "Lock the door," Lisa instructed. He marched over to the door like he was in a trance. Before he could turn around, she was on him like bees on honey. Darnel picked her up and threw her over his shoulder. He brought her over to the bed and laid her down. He took total control. It made him feel like he was in charge. If he only knew that's what she'd wanted him to do all along.

***

Darnel and Lisa took Hope on her first trip to the beach. Darnel walked with her along the water, while Jason chased the waves.

Even though Lisa has tried to amend some of her ways, sometimes she still found herself plotting and scheming to get the things she wanted. She didn't believe things just happened. She had to make them happen.

Her mother had said to her, "It was a big risk you took moving out on him. You should count your blessings that things turned out the way you wanted them to."

"Ma, I was serious. I was really ready to move on."

"You were about as serious as I am about posing for *Playboy*."

"Sometimes people need a little help in making up their minds, Lisa instructed her mother."

"Really? I'm glad you said that. Darnel had spoken to me some time ago about working things out with you. But I told him to go ahead and let you sweat it out."

Lisa's mouth was wide open. "What? I don't believe you."

"My poor delusional baby. Your naiveté is killing me. Your old mother and your old man set you up big time. But we did it for your own good. Sometimes people need help in changing their ways."

The sun was going down and it looked so beautiful as it shimmered across the water. For the first time in Lisa's life she felt at peace. She wasn't afraid of what tomorrow was going to bring.

About the Author

Anika Malone a native of New York has lived in Texas and South Carolina. She currently resides in North Carolina, where she is at work on her second novel.

Printed in the United States
2544